B Christmas Bake Off

Bella's Christmas Bake Off

Sue Watson

Bookouture

Published by Bookouture, an imprint of StoryFire Ltd.
23 Sussex Road, Ickenham, UB10 8PN
United Kingdom

www.bookouture.com

ISBN: 978-1-910751-61-9

ACKNOWLEDGEMENTS

Thank you to the wonderful team at Bookouture who never fail me and this time turned my Christmas cake batter into something extremely scrumptious. Christmas kisses to Oliver Rhodes, Kim Nash, Emily Ruston, Jade Craddock and the rest of the tasty team for baking until golden and adding all that yummy frosting!

To Nick and Eve Watson, thanks for putting up with my 'Christmasness' in July, and as always thanks to my lovely family and friends for their love, support and laughter.

And a special thank you to my readers, for buying my books, getting in touch and inspiring me in so many different and delicious ways. Happy Christmas!

Also by Sue Watson

Love, Lies and Lemon Cake
Snow Angels, Secrets and Christmas Cake
Summer Flings and Dancing Dreams
Fat Girls and Fairy Cakes
Younger, Thinner, Blonder

This book is dedicated to my lovely readers, the real women who may not be aged 21 and a size 10, but are funny, kind and beautiful... that's you!

Happy Christmas x

Chapter One

Naughty Custard and Severely Whipped Cream

I was icing the Christmas cake when he told me.

'Amy...I have to talk to you,' he said.

I lifted the palette knife to create a snowy effect on the soft, mallow frosting and stood back, then turned to him.

'What?' I was gazing at my beautiful frosty white cake. 'Silent Night' played on the iPod, and it was just three weeks before Christmas. I glanced up at Neil standing next to me, and the look in his eyes scared me so much I put down the palette knife.

'What is it? Are you ill...has something happened?'

He nodded, slowly, his eyes still cold, like they belonged to someone else.

'I was going to leave it until after Christmas to tell you, but I've...I can't go on like this. Amy, I'm sorry but it feels like a charade to go through the whole Christmas thing and...I've met someone.' He was standing in front of me now, making eye contact, ensuring the message was clear and there was no room for misunderstanding. My mind went blank. The pink tie I'd bought for him was loosened at his neck. He'd just come home from work. It was Friday evening. There were pork chops in the oven.

'Is this a joke?' There were no words for this. I'd sometimes imagined a scene where we parted, but it was usually the other way round and me telling him I was going. I wasn't ready for this, now – ever.

'Why?'

'Because I can't live a lie any longer, Amy,' he said, his speech obviously well prepared, learned by heart. I could see by his set jaw and steady gaze he was damn well going to say every word without interruption from me.

'You've been so busy with work, you've got your friends and your life and I feel like there's no room for me...' he started.

'Oh no, Neil. You sleeping with someone else is not *my* fault, so don't even try to pull that one,' I snapped, moving swiftly from shock to anger, aware I was spitting in his face – not pretty...or festive.

'I'm sorry, I'm not blaming you, but I just...I want to be with her. She loves me, she cares what happens to me, asks me about my day...I'm sorry, Amy...' He stood there, ashen-faced.

'So after twenty years you're just walking out on your marriage because some other woman asks if you've had a nice day?' I was becoming irrational, but who could blame me? 'Perhaps I should have made more like an American waitress and said 'have a nice day,' when I 'served' you your evening meal.'

The panic was rising in my chest, I couldn't deal with people leaving, the thought of being on my own scared me. Things hadn't been great for a long time between us, but he didn't have to go and throw it all away – not now, just weeks before Christmas. I glanced through the living room door at the Christmas tree, the lights twinkling, gifts from relatives and friends already underneath. This was a time for being together, for rekindling love and family, not abandoning it.

'I don't understand?' I asked, trying to calm down and not to bare my teeth like a wild animal. I didn't know how I felt about Neil, but I wasn't ready for this and I didn't want him storming off into the night and leaving me alone. I needed to keep everything on an even keel, especially myself. 'I know we've had our problems Neil, but all marriages have problems, we just have to work at them.'

'That's what I thought too, but...she's special.'

'Special? More "special" than the woman you married, who you've been with for over twenty years,' I snapped, losing any chance of staying calm at this.

'No...of course you're special too, but we both want different things, Amy.'

'Yeah, *you* want someone else.'

'It's not like that...I care about her.'

So this really was it? After several years of our relationship hanging by a thread, one of us had finally decided to do something to end it, but now it was finally here I felt sick. I was about to throw up, but swallowed hard to prevent it. Whatever I might think about him, I didn't want my husband's last moments with me to be infused with the sight and smell of me vomiting noisily in the kitchen.

'Who is she?' I heard myself croak.

'Someone at work, she works in the Legal department...you don't know her.'

'Well I do now, don't I?' I started. 'Because it looks like this woman who I "don't know" has been playing quite a big part in my life without me even realising ...'

He just stood there with his head down like I was reprimanding him. He reminded me of one of the teenagers I taught at school who'd been found smoking or downloading porn on their iPhone.

'Neil, the kids will be home from Uni in three weeks...and I made a cake...' I gestured towards the snow-topped, perfectly iced confection like it would make a difference to his planned departure. Three minutes ago this beautiful fruit cake had, along with the Christmas Tree, been the centre and beginning of my pre-Christmas world. We both stared at the cake as though it held the answers and if we stared for long enough all the bad things would go away. But they didn't, and when I looked back, the eyes staring out of my husband's face were a stranger's eyes.

'When are you going?' I asked, trying to bring myself round.

He shrugged, 'Tomorrow...?'

I suddenly couldn't bear another minute of this and as another wave of anger engulfed me, I called his bluff. 'Why wait? Go now,' I said.

'You think I should go *now*?' He looked almost relieved, which hurt and angered me even more.

'You can't wait to leave, can you?' I spat incredulously.

'No, no... I don't want to upset you...neither does Jayne; she's so upset and feels terrible about everything.'

That did it.

'Oh poor, poor Jayne is upset? Why didn't you say? You must go to her, how selfish I am thinking only of me when she's the one who's devastated...I feel awful for keeping you.'

He made an awkward move towards me and I picked up the palette knife in a threatening manner like I'd seen crazy people do in crime dramas on TV. In that moment, with the panic rising in my chest, I felt just as mad as those wild murdering types, slashing around with a cleaver. It was just as well my weapon of choice was only a round-edged, blunt decorating tool and not a big, sharp chef's knife, especially when I started waving it at him aggressively.

He edged back along the kitchen wall like the wimp he was, flinching as I punctuated my harmless but dramatic palette waving with swearing and ridiculous threats. I couldn't stop and the more he cowered, the more I flailed my 'weapon' around while starting on a detailed personality assassination. As therapeutic as this was, I had to stop because I was reaching volcanic levels and could feel a panic attack coming on. I stood back, put down the knife and leaned against the kitchen unit to get my breath back. Just as I put my head in my hands and he thought I wasn't looking, the little coward made a bid for freedom. He weaselled his way out of the kitchen and ran upstairs to pack his pyjamas and toothbrush, without even asking if I was okay.

'I could have died,' I yelled at him as I heard his tentative steps on the stair carpet before he put his head round the door like a rabbit in the headlights.

'I'm going to go now, because I think you need to calm down and me being here might just make things worse,' he said, like he was dealing with a petulant child.

Too late. I had a brown paper bag over my mouth (which I always kept at hand in the event of a panic attack) whilst continuing to ladle a thick layer of snowy frosting on the cake on auto-pilot like a woman possessed. In my state of shock all I heard was him mutter something about calling me 'tomorrow', and as he walked out of the front door I cracked, picked up the cake and blindly chased him down the hall. Halfway down the drive he turned back and I saw the fear in his eyes as he spotted my frosty confection coming straight for his head accompanied by my season's greetings; 'Happy bloody Christmas', I screeched along with other non-festive expletives I would rather not repeat. He ducked of course, but as the cake frisbeed past him and across the street the whole thing was witnessed by Alfie Mathews, the son of my neighbour, who also happened to be a pupil of mine. There was frosty icing everywhere, a large cake sliding down the garden wall, me standing in the doorway screaming like the madwoman in the attic ...and one of my pupils filming the whole spectacle on his mobile.

It was all very surreal and I was so distressed and disorientated I couldn't face tackling the film-maker so just staggered back indoors.

Once inside I slammed the door, sat down on a chair, and marvelled at how in less than thirty minutes my life had melted like snow in hot hands. Everything I thought I had, everything I'd thought I was, had gone in a whirlwind...along with the now smashed Christmas cake.

Eventually, I stirred and picked up the TV remote without moving from my seat in the kitchen, and turned on the TV.

'Ooh you have to have squidgy ones,' the voice purred from the screen on the wall. Neil had put it up there a couple of years ago because I liked to watch cookery shows in the kitchen, particularly Bella Bradley's shows, and the 'squidgy ones' to which she was now referring were chocolate brownies, which as always looked perfect – but then she had no need to throw them at anyone did she? I stared at the screen numbly. It seemed as though my life was collapsing, while Bella's was going from strength to strength. Each year her lovely home seemed to be glossier, more expensive, her Christmas cakes more ornate, her tree taller. Bella's eyes glittered from her fairy lit kitchen, colour matched in red and green with a hint of classy sparkle. The long dark hair, luscious red lips and happy marriage made her look at least ten years younger than she was and despite loving her show I couldn't help but sometimes feel a twinge of resentment. I wished my life had been as glamorous and successful as Bella's and felt the envy and regret even more keenly after what had just happened. I found vague comfort in watching Bella add mixed spice to a bowl, stirring vigorously, causing the reindeers on her tight red ski jumper to frolic across her full bosom. I wondered for the millionth time what it would be like to have Bella's Christmas, her marriage – her life.

What made the contrast in our very different lives so painful was that Bella Bradley used to be my best friend. We'd once shared everything, from secrets to perfume to clothes, we'd been best friends from our first day at school and watching her now on screen I found it hard to reconcile this well-groomed, accomplished woman with the crazy, funny friend I used to love. When we were kids Bella was the one who took risks while I stood on the sidelines watching in awe, and sometimes horror, while she got herself into the most horrific scrapes. Throughout her school days she'd been caught smoking, playing truant, swearing and writing obscene words on the gym wall – yet still she seemed to charm her way out of it all. I didn't have her charisma or her daring; I suppose that's why Bella's a TV star and I'm a maths teacher, I thought, absently watching her whisk up a batch of chocolate brownies with the kind of noises one would associate with an orgasm.

'Ooh that's very, very naughty,' she was saying, her eyes looking into the camera, a tight close-up of just her tongue licking chocolate-covered fingers I assumed were her own. Mind you, from the sounds she was making one had to wonder if her delicious husband was somewhere off camera reaching into her red-lipsticked mouth. Who knew what was going on behind that soon to be batch of warm bad boys?

Just thinking about Bella's husband reminded me of my own, or sudden lack of – and it made my stomach churn. I tried to shake the vision of Neil having sex with another woman, living another life in which I wasn't his wife or the mother of his children, but merely an obstacle to his happiness with her. Pacing around the house, I thought about the hushed telephone calls, the late nights, the sudden 'emergencies' when Neil was called into work suddenly at weekends. Were these all lies he told me so he could be with her? And deep down had I known? Had I become lazy and complacent, allowing it to happen, because I didn't love him anymore, but wasn't brave enough to make the break? I'll admit, over the years there'd been times when I'd doubted if Neil and I would make 'forever', but they were just blips weren't they? Didn't everyone have doubts that they'd married the right person? Of course they did – and they just kept their heads down and got on with it. After a while, life went back to what it was before, the daily grind of work and sleep peppered with disillusion and resentment – otherwise known as marriage. So having put up with and adapted to this predictable pattern for so long, I was surprised to find myself suddenly single. I wandered into the living room and stared at the Christmas tree I'd put up the previous week. It had been decorated with hope and anticipation for the season ahead. I'd hung each bauble imagining the four of us sitting round a glistening turkey on Christmas day lit by the glow of that tree. But looking at it now, days later, I felt nothing – just sad and disappointed.

It was an ancient white tree, and even the sparkly white fairy now looked less like a sparkly young girl and more like Miss Haversham, the ageing bride whose groom had left her on her wedding day.

I couldn't take it in, I looked at the sad fairy seeing myself reflected back - Neil had gone and my Christmas was over before it had begun. Then my eye caught the icy blue bauble we'd bought together on a trip to Paris one Christmas. Carefully plucking the bauble from the tree I held it, feeling the cool Christmas roundness in my palm. There was a raised hand-painted picture of a glittery, snow-covered Eiffel Tower, a lovely memory I hung every year and went straight back to the French Christmas market where we'd bought it. Holding the bauble, watching it sparkle, I was on the Avenue des Champs-Élysées, more than twenty years before, a cold wind was swinging the lights on the stall and heavy rain splashed our faces. Neil and I had been so young and in love back then we only saw each other in the twinkle of fairy lights in the rain. It was bustling with noise, festive music played and the air was heady with Christmas as we held hands and chose our special souvenir of our first holiday together. I was eighteen. Looking into the bauble now, watching the glitter change from white to pink to blue as I twirled it I felt sad for what we'd lost. Then I remembered with a jolt how later on that evening we'd argued about something trivial and Neil stormed out of the hotel. He came back very late and quite drunk and I cried all night while he slept soundly next to me. We barely spoke to each other all the next day, despite it being Christmas Day, and my dreams of Christmas in Paris floated off down the Seine. Funny how I'd forgotten about that, perhaps Neil's leaving had made me more cynical, more aware of what we were, and not what I'd wanted us to be? I should have known then we wouldn't last; if a couple fall out in the city of love on Christmas Eve then cupid's trying to tell them something. We were such different people, Neil and I, and in those early days I'd naively thought he would change, but he never did.

I thought of all the Christmas Eves since then that the kids and I had waited for him to come home. They always wanted to wait for Daddy, but he was usually 'caught up at the office,' and I was so busy making Christmas for them I didn't have the time or the energy to worry where he was. I did everything without him, not just Christmas, but days out, barbecues in the garden, even parents' evenings - it was usually just me and the kids. I lived like a single mum, with Neil working away, late at the office or on a golf course somewhere (though there were times I queried his 'night golf' sessions, which went on way too late for my liking). Suddenly, it dawned on me, perhaps he wasn't busy or golfing – perhaps he just didn't want to come home to me? While I was imagining pitch black golf courses and heavy late night meetings he was 'going home' to Jayne from the legal department. As my thoughts drifted back over my marriage to Neil, I realised I had stripped the Christmas tree until it was bare and everything was packed away. All trace of Christmas gone.

I was now alone, I had no husband and all I could think was 'How will I tell the kids?' My only consolation was that the twins were now both away at their respective universities and though the break-up of their parents' marriage would hurt, it wouldn't impact on their lives as it might have when they were younger. Resentment rose in my chest and I was glad Neil wasn't there with me because I had a whole block of kitchen knives and who knew what might have happened? Neil and I didn't have an idyllic marriage, we didn't ravish each other passionately every night of the week, life got in the way. Neil needed new friends, sparkly objects and flashing lights in his life – whereas I was happy with the status quo and a nice cup of tea.

I returned to the kitchen, my Christmas was over, but Bella was still on the TV creating a Christmas heaven in her home.

'People laugh when I put bananas in my trifle,' she was saying, making her eyes wide, her mouth forming a soft O. 'But I *implore* you, if you do nothing else this Christmas – *have a go with a big banana.*' This was breathed into the lens rather than actually spoken, and was pure cooking porn. 'Whisky soaked, damp with alcohol, crushed nuts, a scattering of sour cranberries to cut through that icky-stickiness and snowy peaks of cool, white, *severely* whipped cream. Oooh,' she was now dipping her finger in the cream, eyes closed, licking slowly, she was no doubt engaging more viewers than just the country's amateur chefs. Every straight male and gay woman in the UK must have been transfixed by Bella's culinary Christmas spectacle. I bit my lip, she was too much. Even Nigella would baulk at '*severely* whipped cream' to describe a bloody trifle.

'Bella's Christmas Bake Off' always started in early December and for years had prepared me and the rest of the country for the culinary season ahead. Bella basted beautiful, golden turkeys, cooked crispy roast potatoes, baked magnificent cakes and biscuits, causing power surges throughout the country as people turned on their ovens and baked. She would sprinkle lashings of glitter, special olive oils, the latest liqueurs and all in a sea of Christmas champagne bubbles.

Bella's style was calm, seductive, and gorgeous. Her very presence on screen made you feel everything was going to be okay and Christmas was on its way. She didn't just stop at delicious food either – her tables were pure art and her Christmas decorations always the prettiest, sparkliest, most beautiful. Bella Bradley had an enviable lifestyle and she kept viewers transfixed all year round, but her Christmases were always special. Her planning and eye for detail was meticulous, from colour-matched baubles to snowy landscapes of Christmas cupcakes and mince pies – and soggy bottoms were never on her menu.

So in an attempt to forget my own life and fill myself with something like Christmas cheer, I watched Bella now, as she poured the whipped cream on 'naughty' custard. Oh if it were only the custard in my life that was 'naughty,' I thought as she added edible pearls for decoration, fingering each one as she pushed them firmly into the cream. I sat in my little kitchen just waiting for the Christmas sparkle to land on me, the frisson of Christmas baking, the preparation, the anticipation that always came with the first 'Bella's Christmas Bake Off'. But this year I just couldn't get excited by her baking or her beautiful, twinkly home or her magnificent tree. She had everything – and I had nothing...which had always been the case, but now I didn't even have a husband anymore.

Bella's husband, Peter Bradley, or the Silver Fox, as Bella affectionately referred to him, was gorgeous. He was a foreign news correspondent who, when he wasn't making 'impromptu' appearances in Bella's busy kitchen during the show, could be seen on battlefronts across the globe. He'd wander into Bella's kitchen all five o'clock shadow and war-weary as she iced her voluptuous buns or titivated her tarts. He always looked quite out of place in this domestic idyll after doing a piece to camera in a war-torn city, but he was obviously happy to support his wife's career by just being there. Unlike my husband, he hadn't left her alone at Christmas for another woman – he'd stayed by her side, happy to brush the flour from her décolletage and stick his finger in her buttercream.

'The Silver Fox loves my plump, tasty breasts,' she announced while tearing at tender white turkey flesh and giving the camera a knowing look. Peter was there in all his war-torn glory, taking her proffered morsels with a twinkle in his pale blue eyes, a crinkly smile on his well worn features. He was so handsome, fit for his late forties, and no doubt, given his career, very strong, intelligent and brave. He was the perfect accessory to Bella, bringing just the right amount of rough masculine charm and good looks to her glossy girlishness. And as a delicious bonus, the Silver Fox wasn't afraid to show his feminine side judging by the previous year's Christmas special, when he'd flown in from Iraq to whisk cream in nothing but combats and a tight vest. I was transfixed - trust me, Christmas had come early!

I glanced back at the screen, Bella was now informing us that we had to rehearse for Christmas Eve. Rehearse? As if one Christmas stress-fest wasn't enough? She was wearing silk pyjamas and a girly grin which, given my current state, seemed to me like she was bordering on smug.

'So, imagine it's Christmas Eve – the turkey has soaked in something fabulous, and so have I, and now I've put my jim jams on,' she giggled, jiggling her breasts for no apparent reason – she did that a lot... even when she was making quiche. I noted with envy how her chocolate brown eyes matched the chocolate brown silk of her pyjamas and considered my own nightwear, a pair of frail pyjamas, once pale pink now edging towards grey after too many washes. If I needed any proof that her life was completely different to mine – it was all there in those ancient pyjamas.

'Me and the Silver Fox just love a pyjama party at Christmas,' she twinkled, a little wink and a sip from the crystal flute. 'But then, don't we all?'

'Speak for yourself,' I said, turning off the TV and finishing the last of a bottle of cava I'd found in the fridge. Oh yes, Bella Bradley had always been the lucky one, even when we were kids – but it didn't stop me loving her – she was my best friend. Then, when we were eighteen I did something stupid which affected her life so profoundly she left the area where we lived and I hadn't seen her since. I tried not to think how our friendship had been destroyed by what I'd done all those years ago. I still felt guilty about what had happened and longed for her forgiveness. Watching her on screen was the nearest I would ever get to her, and despite the odd twinge of envy I found it therapeutic to see her in a wonderful new life, knowing she was okay... even if I wasn't.

Chapter Two

Euphorically Single or
Desperate and Alone?

My state of shock at Neil leaving so cruelly and abruptly lasted for several days. During this time I discovered from various sources (a mutual friend and Neil himself) that Neil's new playmate was ten years younger than me and the proud owner of a pole attached to her ceiling for 'dancing.' Apparently this was situated by her bed, a vital part of her decor but something I'd omitted to buy when I last went to Ikea for bedroom furniture.

'I never knew what I was missing,' he announced the day after his departure when he popped in for clean pants and a fresh supply of haemorrhoid cream. I watched him throw it into his bag and wished I'd intercepted it beforehand and laced it with something spicy – or toxic.

'So what exactly were you missing with me?' I asked, not wanting to know.

'She makes me feel like a man in the bedroom.'

'Well you made *me* feel like a man in the bedroom,' I replied, without even turning to look at him. I was in bed sipping on the

Christmas sherry, where I'd been since he'd left. Alone in the marital bed I'd gone from feeling desperate and alone to euphorically single and back again, with intermittent pauses for a go on the brown paper bag. I could only contemplate one day at a time and my recovery wasn't aided by the fact that whenever I closed my eyes I saw a blonde woman gyrating on a pole and Neil on the edge of a bed clapping.

I went to work on the Monday after he'd left on the Friday and taught a double session of algebra to 10B while trying not to cry. A video of me screaming like a banshee and hurling cake at my husband was apparently up on You Tube (courtesy of Alfie my neighbour's son). I know this because they were playing it on their phones and I could hear myself in a tinny voice screaming 'Happy Christmas you fucking loser,' again and again. Consequently, this first lesson was something of a rollercoaster and after the class left I was found curled up in the stationery cupboard, dripping all over Year Ten notebooks and sobbing like a child with my brown paper bag. Tony Jones, the headmaster, discovered me, and assuming I'd been put there by the sociopathic gaggle that were otherwise known as 10B, called the police. Sylvia, my friend and vice principal, stepped in and after telling the head I was just 'tired', she tore into me.

'Jesus Christ, Amy, you are a dipstick,' she'd hissed in my face while ripping away the brown paper bag. Sylvia was also Head of English and had a way with words. 'I can't believe you came into work after what's happened. And climbing in the stationery cupboard? What's that about? Mr Jones had to go and have a lie down after finding you – he thought he was hallucinating – again,' she rolled her eyes, alluding to the poor headmaster's recent 'emotional challenges' which had caused him to take six months sick leave and develop a nasty twitch.

'You are a complete loon,' Sylvia was saying, holding out her hand to coax me from my stationary 'lair.'

I climbed out of the cupboard, thanking her for her sensitive comments.

'Neil's a dickhead and you're well rid,' she said as she helped me into the nearest chair.

'Yes he is,' I agreed. She'd often said this in the past and I'd defended him, but not anymore, I nodded energetically while wiping the tears from my face with a tissue. 'But Sylvia... it's the wasted years...all those wasted years.'

She went on to remind me that my marriage hadn't been a complete waste of my life and I had my lovely twins, Fiona and Jamie, who made it all worthwhile.

After Sylvia's counsel I managed to keep a lid on things at school for another twenty-four hours. Until the following day during an emotional assembly where John Lennon's 'Happy Xmas (War is Over),' was sung loudly and tunelessly by Year 8. Despite the student's unfortunate 'cover version', the song's poignancy remained, especially the line, 'And so this is Christmas, and what have you done?' I felt John Lennon was asking me this directly – accusingly almost – because as the years had passed and the Christmases had come and gone – I'd done very little. Thank you for reminding me, John. Every. Single. Year. Meanwhile this year he'd just about hammered the nail in the Christmas coffin for me.

I'd sobbed and dribbled throughout assembly, loudly – with no tissues – and had reached rock bottom by the time Sylvia took me in hand and led me to her office.

'Right madam,' she said firmly, pulling out a chair and putting the kettle on. 'I know it's early days and there are going to be a lot of tears, but you need something to take your mind off your sad, miserable life.'

As I said, she had a way with words did Sylvia – Head of English.

'I blame John Lennon...he does this to me every bloody Christmas,' I sobbed.

'Yes, well it's not his fault, God rest his soul – I'd direct your anger at the idiot who's walked out on you!'

'He betrayed me,' I cried, 'for a lap-dancing lawyer.'

'I don't think that's quite true. She might be a horrible human being, a tart and a home-wrecker – she might also be a lawyer, but I don't think she's an actual lap dancer.'

'She does lap-dancing kinds of things in the bedroom... with a pole.' Neil had reluctantly confirmed this himself (when pushed) on one of his return visits for clean socks and his Bear Grylls box set.

'I'm sure she does all kinds of things with the lights off – and on for that matter,' Sylvia nodded with pursed lips; 'but you don't need to dwell on all that now. It'll soon be Christmas and then the

New Year – it's all about fresh starts and new beginnings, and not about your husband's bedroom antics with apparatus and a wanton woman from the legal department.

'Anyway, I know just what you need,' she said brightly, handing me a mug of hot coffee which smelt vaguely alcoholic. 'Drink that. You and me are going out after work.'

'Oh no. You're not dragging me to some speed dating nightmare, Sylvia. It's one thing being rejected in the privacy of my own home by my own husband but it's another being publicly discarded at a table by a total stranger I don't even fancy.'

'No, not speed dating – not yet anyway. It's too soon for all that, you need to get Amy back before you even think about riding *that* horse.'

What Sylvia had in store for me couldn't have been further from speed dating. Later that evening as we pulled up outside St Swithin's homeless hostel, where she helped out as a volunteer, I realised that dating, fast or otherwise, wasn't on the agenda.

The hostel had just had its grant slashed and Sylvia had spent the past few months making the best of her time and talents to try and work miracles with what little budget that was left. I'd often baked bread and cakes for the hostel and given them to Sylvia at school, but I'd never actually visited before.

'I want you to meet some people,' she said, pulling on the handbrake. 'When I was going through hell with my divorce it was this lot that pulled me through – that and the knowledge that there's always someone worse off than you.'

Sylvia always said Christmas was extra special at St Swithin's, and with the small budget and donations from local businesses and the community – including our school – they always had a great time. But this year she explained that any donations were needed for basic rations and there was a big question mark hanging over their Christmas lunch, let alone any of the little extras.

Walking into St Swithin's I was immediately struck by the emptiness. I'd heard the expression no frills, but until I walked into that building I had no idea what it truly meant. Sylvia showed me the dining hall first, which seemed stark and unwelcoming with bare walls, no table cloths, just rickety tables where people sat in coats and big jumpers because it was so cold.

'Heating is a luxury, I'm afraid,' she sighed. 'Beatrice the manager has to keep it on a low setting even on days like this.'

It was freezing, almost as cold inside as it was outside, but I suppose at least they were sheltered from the elements in here.

Sylvia showed me round and one of the first people we met was Stanley, who used to be a train driver but whose love of whisky had taken him down the wrong track. He nodded and with a faraway look started to sing, 'And now, the end is near and so I face the final curtain...'

'He thinks he's Frank Sinatra,' Sylvia said. 'Spends all day singing, he takes requests, hosts his own "show" in the middle of the canteen during mealtimes...don't you, old blue eyes?' she said to him with an indulgent smile. He nodded and smiled then continued on with 'My Way'.

Sylvia told me the other residents weren't always impressed by Stanley's musical interludes – they had their own problems and would often tell him to be quiet while they ate. Listening to his rather rusty and racy rendition of 'Come Fly with Me', I could see why he didn't always go down well with the sponge and custard.

Next, Sylvia introduced me to Maisie, who wanted to tell me about her time in the ballet, apparently she'd once danced with Nureyev. She was shivering with cold when she reached out and held my hand saying, 'Daddy never let me marry Simon you know...' I asked her what had happened, but by then she'd drifted off. I wasn't sure what her story was, but like Stanley, who apparently once sang on the same stage as The Beatles, they all *had* a story. I didn't know why or how their stories had led them to this place, but it was clear to see they'd had tough lives, and if St Swithin's closed things were about to get even tougher for them.

Over a cup of tea in the kitchen, Sylvia introduced me to the hostel manager Beatrice. She nodded and handed me a tea towel to dry the plates as she made fresh bread and told me in her lilting accent of tales from 'my little rock', meaning her home, Jamaica. I heard all about her barefoot childhood, and judging by the look in her eyes she was back there as she kneaded the bread.

I suspected Beatrice, a former social worker, escaped into her Jamaican past because she was worried about the present and the lack of funds for St Swithin's which threatened not only the Christmas lunch that year – but closure.

'Perhaps we could ask people at the local allotment to donate vegetables? I'm sure the butcher in the town will help too...and not just at Christmas?' I suggested, the problem-solving maths teacher never far away.

She shook her head. 'We already ploughed that field. Folk don't have no money anymore. Local shops are closing down and the men on the allotments are selling their stuff or taking it home to their wives and mammies for meals and chutneys.'

Sylvia nodded in agreement; 'Everyone is short of money these days,' she sighed. 'The people who used to donate can't afford to any more, and the councils are slashing the budgets for places like this. You watch, there will be more and more homeless on the streets.'

I'd never met someone who was homeless before – I'd seen the odd person lying in shop doorways or sleeping on a bench in the park, but I'd never spoken to anyone in this situation. Meeting the residents of St Swithin's made me realise my own 'problems' were quite different. My husband leaving me was devastating – but not life threatening, yet for some of these people being without shelter on a cold winter night could kill them.

We walked together into a common area where Maisie and a few others sat on very shabby chairs watching an old TV propped up against the wall. One woman was a similar age to me; she didn't speak but Sylvia told me her husband had walked out on her, taking everything. 'She was left with what she stood up in,' Sylvia said discreetly, and I thought how I could easily be one of these people sitting here with nothing.

Everyone was glued to the TV as 'Bella's Christmas Bake Off' had just started, and the contrast between her environment and this one couldn't have been starker. Bella was standing in her beautiful, state-of-the-art kitchen gathering together the raw ingredients for Christmas cake and waxing lyrical, 'Ooh they are soft, plump and swollen, just how I like them,' she peered into the camera triumphantly clutching a handful of pale, bloated sultanas. Her mouth was quivering, eyelashes fluttering, and I stared at her, waiting for the Christmas hit. Around this time of year the programme had always made me fizz with Christmas anticipation, but here in this setting I suddenly felt uncomfortable about Bella's Christmas largesse. I was embarrassed by her organic bird, hand-reared beef and bloody oysters flown in from Galway that morning. Maisie and her friends were staring open-mouthed at the feast of expensive Christmas goodies laid before them in Bella's gleaming kitchen, her ingredients as unreachable to them as the moon.

'I always, always buy the best I can afford,' she was saying.

'Eeeeugh, so do ay,' said Stanley in a mock posh voice. Everyone laughed.

'Always buy what you can afford, Stanley dear,' said a woman laughing in between coughs.

'If I bought the best I could afford, that would still be nothing,' he roared. To these people, Bella's programmes were like something from another planet – where ingredients were like priceless jewels and everything she suggested was so impossible it was hilarious.

'And for a light Christmas Eve buffet lunch and those unexpected guests, I will now show you my amazing Fontana cheese and prosciutto ciabatta,' Bella was saying.

'Ooh what's she making now?' an elderly lady asked as she wandered into the room.

'Cheese and ham sarnie,' someone said. I had to laugh – because in spite of all the foreign words and expensive ingredients, that's exactly what Bella was making.

As she shone from the screen, her beautiful home glittering out like a star onto St Swithin's bare, shabby room with worn-out sofas, the difference was almost painful. These people were living with nothing, and here was a woman on the telly showing them the kind of Christmas they could never have. I'd always admired and envied Bella's home on TV, but now I realised the cost of her beautiful artisan kitchen gadgets alone could keep the shelter in food for a year.

❄ ❄ ❄

By 11 p.m. we'd finished washing and drying all the pots. I'd helped Beatrice make some bread and Sylvia and I had scrubbed the kitchen until it gleamed...well, the bits that weren't rusty and worn anyway. Putting on our coats to leave I said goodbye to Maisie and Stanley and waved to a group of older men sitting in the corner playing cards. When I'd arrived at the hostel earlier I'd been dreading going home to an empty, husbandless house, but climbing into Sylvia's warm car I was grateful to have a home to go to.

'I'm exhausted, but feel good for doing it,' I sighed as Sylvia drove me back through the icy roads.

'Yeah, it's cathartic,' she smiled, 'reminds you what Christmas is all about.'

Meeting these people had immediately made me see life on a much wider canvas. We are all born the same, we all embark on the same journey, but somewhere along the way some lives get derailed. It can happen to any of us, I thought as we passed the huge Christmas tree in the square. One minute you think you have everything planned out and your future is secure then wham, you're blindsided. I would never have dreamed I'd be spending Christmas without Neil this year, my future changed forever. With only my income I'd have to sell the house and though I wouldn't be homeless I'd have to live somewhere else and wouldn't be enjoying the future I'd envisaged.

That night changed me – it was simply tragic that these people had been dealt such bad cards. And in the depths of a freezing winter they didn't even have the basics most of us take for granted: warmth, food and shelter. My heart went out to them, especially at Christmas with no decorated tree, and no hearth to sit by, yet still they remained upbeat and Stanley seemed to have a song for everyone.

❄ ❄ ❄

Back home, I shivered with relief as I opened my front door and walked out of the icy cold and into warmth and sanctuary. I thought about how Maisie had shivered when she talked to me and immediately ran upstairs to rummage around my wardrobe. I gathered together a pile of old clothes, including a warm coat I'd had for ages but never liked, and felt bad when I realised I'd bought another winter coat in a more flattering style, which felt decadent now. There were also some very wearable, very warm jumpers that were actually quite nice, I just didn't need them and told myself I had enough. I also picked out a glitzy jumper covered in silver sequins, a gift from Neil the previous Christmas. It was glittery and fussy, and not me at all – which said it all about how much my husband knew me.

The Christmas before, Neil presented me with a bright pink woollen scarf and mittens covered in big woolly flowers – again, so not me. I found the horrific scarf at the back of my chest of drawers and wondered why he would give me such a thing. I wore dark colours, but he was always buying me bloody sparkly things in vivid shades...well, he'd now run off with a very sparkly thing, perhaps he'd get all his excitement from her. I had another unwelcome image of her sliding up and down that bedroom pole like a Vegas showgirl and tried to unsee it. I knew Neil well and after a while the novelty would wear off and it wouldn't matter what she did on that pole, he'd be distracted by something far wilder on The Discovery Channel.

I folded the winter coat carefully with the jumpers and scarf. I would give these to Maisie, she seemed so quiet, perhaps a little sparkle and colour was just what she needed. These were things I didn't need, they had simply accumulated at the back of my wardrobe, but for Maisie they would provide basic comfort, warmth and, who knew, even a little shimmer of hope?

The first thing I did after packing Maisie's parcel was put the kettle on and turn the TV on in the kitchen. As much as I was determined to move on with my life and leave Neil to his pole-dancing destiny, I wasn't yet used to the silence, and the TV filled the void. I saw Bella's face in a trailer for tomorrow's show, she was all over the TV and press this time of the year wearing her 'Queen of Christmas' crown and red silk apron and I couldn't help but think about the girl she'd been, my role in her destiny and hers in mine.

Although our lives had been dramatically torn apart when we were eighteen, and I hadn't seen her since, over the intervening years she'd remained the only link with my past. Mum and Dad were both dead and I rarely saw my two older sisters who'd both moved away as soon as they got the chance. Having Bella around (if only on TV) reminded me of when we used to cook together as kids in my mum's kitchen. Each year as soon as Bella's face came on that screen, I was taken straight back to that cosy kitchen of our childhood – before everything fell apart.

After sending Bella a Christmas card for years with no response, a few years before I'd decided to add something more personal – one of Mum's recipes. I had included various Christmas recipes each year since, from gingerbread to chocolate and cranberry brownies – Bella's favourite as a child. I saw these as a reminder of the good times we'd shared and hoped she'd feel the same. Just writing down those recipes reminded me of Mum in her kitchen – the soft, wobbly fold of flour into butter, the grit of sugar, the heady fragrance of chocolate, sweet vanilla and the warmth of ginger. But most of all the recipes brought back the sheer excitement of two little girls – best friends – waiting for Christmas. It was a time of carol singing and jingle all the way – life was all glitter and sparkle for those little girls back then...what a shame it fizzed away within a few short years.

I wrote the recipes and sent the cards as much for me as for Bella. The older we get the more we think about the past and I wanted to share my memories with the only person who had really known me apart from Mum.

Every year I'd added all my contact numbers, photos of the twins and snippets of my life – trying to reach out to my old friend. And every year I was disappointed not to receive a response. But Bella was now a big star and probably had someone else read her Christmas cards. I hoped Bella would eventually forgive me and naively thought that if we could just meet up again, we might be able to carry on where we'd left off at eighteen.

But Bella had obviously chosen to cut all ties with her past. I didn't blame her – but it still hurt. I just wanted to tell her that her secret was safe with me and I would always be her friend.

I turned the volume down on the TV, even in the programme trailers Bella's tinkling laughter grated on me this year. I just couldn't embrace her Christmas baking plans as I had before – because this year her perfect Christmas seemed more unattainable than ever – just like her.

❄ ❄ ❄

Neil and the kids used to laugh at me and my own 'Christmas tradition' of recording "Bella's Christmas Bake Off" to get in the mood from early December. They knew we'd been friends in another life but didn't really understand how Bella was the link to all the Christmases of my childhood, shared with my parents now no longer with us. Those memories of Christmas baking were so vivid for me still – Bella and I weighing out the almonds for marzipan, stealing mandarin oranges from the bowl and sharing their sweet, tangy fruit when Mum wasn't looking. 'I know what you two are up to,' she'd laugh, the spray of citrus permeating the air, and exposing our crime. Mandarin oranges were only ever around at Christmas when we were young and like everything else they were scarce in our house. But Mum never told me and Bella off for helping ourselves, and even now the sweet, citrusy hit of a juicy Mandarin orange says Christmas and Bella to me.

I was smiling to myself about this when the phone rang. It was Jamie, my son, telling me he'd been invited to his girlfriend's in Kent for Christmas, I told him he must go and though I was disappointed I tried to hide it, thinking it would just be a girly Christmas with Fiona and I.

Then the following day, Fiona called to say she'd been offered the chance of a lifetime to go on a research trip to the Arctic over Christmas with her boyfriend Hans. I pretended to be elated for her and urged her to grab the opportunity, avoiding any references to her father. When she said jokingly 'sorry to leave you on your own with Dad,' I just laughed.

'We'll have a late Christmas...our own special Christmas,' I said, desperately trying to cover up the sound of my scorched throat and my eyes threatening tears. I ended the phone call quickly saying my Christmas cake was burning and Fiona said she loved me and hung up. They had no idea their father had left, they never asked to speak to him when they called home which was telling - he'd never really been present in their lives. The only silver lining to the grey cloud of spending Christmas alone was I wouldn't have to tell the kids about our break up until after Christmas. I was determined not to say anything; I didn't want them to feel obligated to come home just because I was alone. I put the phone down after talking to Fiona amazed at how life can change in minutes – and I'd gone from a big family Christmas with kids, their partners and my husband to just me. Even Auntie Anne had declined my offer of escaping the old people's home and coming to mine for Christmas lunch. Mind you, she was under the impression I was Margaret Thatcher when I'd asked her, so I didn't blame her for saying no.

✱ ✱ ✱

A couple of days after my visit to St Swithin's with Sylvia I asked her if they might need help serving the lunch on Christmas Day, if indeed the budget was going to stretch to lunch.

'Need people to help? Do birds fly? We *always* need people,' she said.

'Then count me in,' I smiled and, to my surprise began to feel a little shimmer of festivity for the first time since Neil had left. I'd been dreading a Christmas alone, but this would mean I'd be helping people, I'd be with friends and I wouldn't have to think about Neil and *her* having sex on a bed of prickly tinsel. The people at the shelter had made me realise that despite my current problem of a disappearing husband, I was one of the lucky ones.

That evening I glanced back at the TV as Bella poured half a bottle of the finest brandy into her bowl of cake batter, I waited for tinselly anticipation to land like snowflakes all around me, but I felt nothing. Even when she produced what she described as 'a winter landscape of European cheeses', sprigged with holly and a frosty snow scene, I failed to get my fix.

'Ooh this is a juicy one,' she said, biting seductively at a maraschino cherry she'd earlier described as 'divinely kitsch'. She swallowed the cherry whole, giggled girlishly and raised a flute of champagne. 'Why have cava when Champagne is sooo much more bubbly? Cheers!' she said, taking a large sip of vintage Krug.

'I know, I know...it's a little indulgent,' she sighed, putting down the crystal flute and wafting her hand at the camera dismissively, 'but a girl needs something sparkly at Christmas.'

'A girl also needs a meal and a bloody coat to keep her warm,' I huffed, thinking of Maisie.

I opened the fridge and took out some cheese for a sandwich, making a mental note to do a food shop. It wasn't like me to leave the fridge empty, but as there was only me living here now why bother? Besides, there was only my income coming in now, but the mortgage and the bills would be pretty much the same, so I would have to be very careful with my budget. It took my breath away to realise that my life was just a couple of pay cheques away from Maisie's life.

I decided on a cheese sandwich and as I spread my home-made chutney on the cheddar realised what an impact the visit to the shelter had made on me.

Okay so I didn't have – money, a husband, a fulfilling career, a perfect body or the flexibility to wrap myself around a bedroom pole, but I had my health and warmth and a roof over my head – those people had nothing. And as Bella waxed lyrical about 'the finest ingredients' and 'little indulgences', and slugged back half a bottle of £500 champagne 'because it's Christmas', I began to feel angry. All the hurt and resentment, the disappointments of my own life and the reality of meeting such desperate people was whipping up inside me.

I wanted to turn off the TV but that little girl in me who loved Christmas and missed her mum wanted the sparkle, the promise of the season. So I continued to watch, trying to feel Christmassy while forcing down my cheese and pickle sandwich as Bella Bradley danced around the screen like a bloody Christmas fairy on acid.

In the same way that I watched 'Bella's Christmas Bake Off', my mum had watched TV chef Delia Smith prepare for Christmas in the late 80's. 'Delia Smith's Christmas' was a tradition in our family and usually repeated during December for years. I was about ten years old when we first watched it together and I recall Mum taking down notes by hand, working out timings and portions – it was all pre-Internet and in our case we had no video and no copies of the book so Mum's notes were all we had. I watched Bella from her kitchen at Dovecote, her beautiful Cotswold mansion, just as Mum and I had watched Delia from her lovely home in Norwich. I longed to drink in those drizzly shots of exquisite nibbles, glittering tables, and shiny baubles while imagining the succulence and seasoning of Bella's Christmas bird. But as hard as I tried I still couldn't gain any comfort from Bella this year and as she minced around her kitchen sprinkling one-hundred-year-old balsamic vinegar around like water – I wanted to reach into the screen and shake her. I wanted to tell her about Maisie and Stanley and how she couldn't comprehend a Christmas like theirs, nor could they imagine one like hers. I wanted to tell her she was in a bubble, a very expensive bubble filed with £600 hams and ludicrously priced champagne. But most of all I wanted to pour that champagne over her perfect shiny hair, because she had everything – and I had nothing.

I made a cup of tea and then immediately hated myself for being so self-pitying. It may not be the Christmas I'd planned, but I was damned if Neil and his lap-dancing pole-cavorting girlfriend were going to take that from me. I lit one of last year's cinnamon scented candles, put Michael Bublé's 'Christmas' on the iPod and as Bella twinkled on the TV I checked what was in the cupboards so I could do some baking too.

I had to work out my now very limited budget, so I sat down and (just like the maths teacher I am) did some workings out. Neil was keen to move on and I had realised quite quickly that so was I. The few times I'd had to speak with him over the phone he really annoyed me with his inflated ego and nervous sniff. I'd forgotten about his irritating habits and wondered if the pole queen had discovered the full portfolio of Neil's bragging, sniffing, clearing his throat in tricky situations or slurping. If not I guessed she'd soon be driven to distraction by his crass comments and disgusting ways with mucus. So in between his sniffs, throat-clearing and cocky remarks he and I had agreed we'd put the house on the market in the New Year, and until then would continue to share the mortgage repayments. After that, the house would be up for sale and I would have to find somewhere else to live, which was pretty daunting. Sylvia, (whose husband had also walked out on her a few years back) said to try and make the most of Christmas and not worry about stuff until it happened. I wanted to take her advice and as one of the most calming and comforting things for me was baking, I decided to start there. I shook my head in shame at the wanton waste of the Christmas cake I'd thrown at Neil, but told myself that throwing cake was cheaper than therapy.

Looking at my budget, I could still afford to make Christmas cakes for St Swithin's as I had done in previous years, and that's what I would do – for them and for me. Whatever was happening in my life, this was going to be the best Christmas St Swithin's had ever had. The food would be great, but I was also keen to make them feel at home so set about thinking up cheap ways of making that awful dining hall look warm and Christmassy.

When I wandered into Sylvia's office the following day and said not only would I turn up and serve on Christmas Day but I wanted to get involved with the shelter and had some ideas, she whooped. Locking the door and immediately abandoning her report on 'upholding the school's principles and policies with good practice and raised standards', she took out a notebook and pen.

'My only worry is I've left it too late to make proper Christmas cakes...' I said.

'But it's still a couple of weeks before Christmas Day, Amy, won't that be long enough?'

'Oh I can bake them in a few hours, it's just that Christmas cakes are usually made in the autumn. They need to mature, and during the two or three months before Christmas they have to be fed brandy on a weekly basis.'

'So do I, love, so do I,' she said, delving in her drawers. I was expecting her to emerge with a bottle of stashed brandy and was just about to warn of the dangers of secret drinking when she produced a completed silvery table runner with a flourish.

'You do the Christmas cakes and mince pies and I'll do the tables,' she said, with a big smile. She'd obviously given up on school work for the day and was flattening the table runner out along her desk, planning how she'd set the tables. 'Anyway, Amy – don't worry about brandy – some of the residents have been feeding on brandy for too long,' she laughed, 'and all it takes is one whiff of the barmaid's apron.'

'Okay, so we'll keep alcohol to a minimum. I don't suppose the budget can afford it anyway – which is why I've been delving around in my mind and trying to come up with ideas to dress the hall. Tin foil crackers on the tables ...and jam jars with tea lights in,' I suggested. 'I've got loads of tinsel I can bring from home too...'

'Ooh yes – let's try and bring a bit of glitter into the poor souls' lives,' she sighed.

'Shall we have a theme?' I asked. 'People like a theme at Christmas, even if it's just a colour or era.'

'How about a silver singles Christmas,' she giggled. 'You and I could dress in glitter and stick two fingers up to being married.'

'Mmm, the more I think about being married, the more I realise how unhappy I was. I still am, but that's about adjustment... it takes a while to get used to being on your own, but it's not the worst thing in the world. Being with someone you don't love...and don't even like, is worse than being alone. I think I fell out of love with Neil a long time ago...I just don't know anymore how I feel about him.'

'I do...but it's not repeatable within the walls of an educational establishment,' she sniffed.

I was keen to change the subject so I didn't have to think too hard about Neil and how many years he'd sucked from me, 'Bella Bradley's doing a "Dickensian" Christmas this year,' I said.

'Oh...Dickensian? Children with rickets, cramped living conditions, pollution and the white plague?'

I laughed, 'No. Red and green with oldy-worldy baubles.'

'Ah, *that* Dickensian Christmas,' she smiled.

Later that day I popped into the hostel to drop off the clothes I'd found in my wardrobe. Maisie was delighted with the warm coat and jumpers, but when I suggested another of the ladies try on a plum knitted dress and the cobalt blue jumper I'd found hard to part with, she turned her nose up.

'Ooh no, dear, it's not me – far too frumpy,' she said, pulling a face.

I hadn't taken it too much to heart until I offered the same dress and jumper to Pearl. She was an elderly lady wearing mostly layers of old coats and shabby cardigans who I imagined would be delighted with my cast-off knits, but she took great offence.

'Do I look like the kind of woman who'd wear something like that? I'm not one of them Amish people,' she snapped. I was a little embarrassed at being turned down, another slap in the face, but a reminder that being homeless doesn't mean you have to lose your style. And apparently Pearl had better taste than I did.

As the hostel budget was as tight as my own, I knew I would need to box clever with the baking and not be able to create the kind of extortionately priced Christmas confections Bella was conjuring up every day on TV. Growing up, my family had been poor and Mum's baking and cooking a highlight of our rather stark Christmases. Her recipes were brilliant, a talent borne out of having to develop her own recipes because she couldn't always afford the ingredients. She'd used beetroot in her chocolate cake and grated carrot in her Christmas cakes – making the most of the veg from Dad's allotment.

Until now I hadn't used veg in my baking despite it being quite fashionable, but without the money for all the usual ingredients, this year I would try it out. And who better to help me through this than my mum. So I took out her old box of recipes and started to leaf through all her notes and cuttings. I used Mum's recipes throughout the year but there was a special folder with Christmas scrawled across and one of Mum's doodles of a sprig of holly. Every

Christmas I'd take the folder out, just enjoying the way it made me feel close to her, like I was bringing her back into my life.

I smiled to myself thinking about how sumptuous our Christmas table used to look, with very little. One Christmas, Mum bought a small chicken instead of a turkey, but none of us realised because she made it look and taste so delicious. She'd added all the trimmings and served it golden and glistening with loads of fresh winter vegetables. I thought about this as I watched the TV, and wondered what Maisie and Stanley would make of Bella's lips quivering in anticipation behind a flaming pudding. Having been comforted by her 'plump fruits' for Christmas in previous years, I was now irritated by her flouncing around the kitchen smugly.

Wouldn't we all love to have the very best of everything? But then Bella had never had to worry about money, had she? As a child Bella and her family had lived in a big house and her parents both drove expensive cars and went out for posh meals. I remember a rare occasion when her mum took us for tea at a hotel. It was Christmas and as we pulled up outside the turreted building I could barely take in the enormous tree stacked with lights and topped with a huge star. Bella's mum was so glamorous, and I recall sitting at the table in church-like silence, glancing at her while discreetly fingering the thick, white napkin on my knee. She ordered herself a vodka martini and asked me what kind of tea I would like and as I wasn't used to such grandeur I innocently said 'hot', which made Bella smirk and her mother told her not to be so rude. Then she put her lipstick on and lit a cigarette at the table and I thought she was the one being rude, blowing smoke over our finger sandwiches.

Being with Bella's mum made me miss mine even more and when a little later she shook a cracker at me with one hand while holding her cigarette with another I wanted to cry. I wanted to pull a cracker with my mum, not this chilly ice queen with bright orange lips and smoke coming out of her nose like a Christmas dragon.

Bella's mother was dark-haired and voluptuous like Bella – but she was brittle too and as a child I could almost feel the chill around her. She couldn't have been more different from my own mother. My mum never wore make-up and was usually dressed in her flour-covered apron but she was always smiling – even though she didn't have much to smile about.

To make ends meet Mum regularly baked and cooked supper dishes for several women in the big houses on Leamington Row. Before she had kids, Mum had been a cook at the Barton-Pratt's home and Margaret Barton-Pratt – or Mrs BP as Mum called her – had recommended Mum to all her wealthy friends. Mum was reliable and cheap and at the same time she could master any recipe and provide wonderful dishes for dinner parties at half the price of the big catering company in town. The women would also call up and ask for simple suppers like fish pie, lasagnes, curries – and this of course would usually include an order for Mum's wonderful cakes and pies.

Dad used to say it was daylight robbery and Mum didn't charge enough. 'They can afford to pay a lot more, you're barely covering the cost of the ingredients,' he'd tell her. But Mum was kind – too kind, she adored working with food and was glad of the money. I realise now she was also flattered by the patronage of these women who always made a big fuss of her food. But looking back she wasn't really valued for her talent, they knew she was good but she was also useful, reliable and most importantly - cheap. They didn't see a human being, they saw a way to make themselves look good in front of their husbands and friends without spending any of their time or too much money. One December Mum worked for three days on a Christmas party and when the driver was sent to collect it he said they'd pay after Christmas. Mum was devastated, I remember her sitting in the kitchen sobbing, there were pots in the sink, flour all over the table...the detritus of all her work. Not only had they not paid her for the dishes she'd made, she'd borrowed money from my nan and a couple of friends for the ingredients. Dad had his arm round her, trying to comfort her saying it was all okay, but it wasn't, his wages barely covered the basics, the money she earned from the cooking was for presents.

'It's not just our Christmas, it's everyone else's,' she'd said, devastated that she'd put loved ones in such a situation at this time of year.

'I can't buy you that doll for Christmas,' she'd said to me later through her tears. 'And I'd left a deposit on our Annie's hairdryer and Gill's new dress.'

'It doesn't matter, Mum, we've got each other – "things" don't matter,' I'd said, echoing what she always said to me.

'Oh love, you're right,' she'd smiled, stroking my hair, 'but there's nothing harder than not being able to buy your own kids a Christmas present.'

I remembered telling her that one day I would be rich and famous and would buy her a big house.

'Other people will bake cakes for *you*, Mum,' I'd said.

'But I wouldn't want them to – I love being in the kitchen, darling,' she'd smiled.

I didn't understand then, but later I could see there was something calming and comforting about being in a kitchen warmed by an oven full of cakes and creating delicious food to share with the people you love.

Now I was in my own kitchen, going through Mum's Christmas recipes, remembering her like it was yesterday. I made a cup of tea and began leafing through the folder, each recipe a reminder of a taste, a moment – a time from the past.

Every now and then I'd look up from the recipes at the TV, to watch as Dovecote (always described in voiceover as 'Bella's beautiful home in The Cotswolds') was paraded all over the screen. Each year it seemed more stunning than the last – decked to the rafters, champagne on ice, gifts wrapped in colour co-ordinated paper and bows under the tree.

Christmas Eve drinks parties, girlie nights in with Christmassy cupcakes and cocktails and a backdrop of homemade pies, bread, and cakes were what 'Bella's Christmas Bake Off' was all about. Everything was smothered in icing sugar, and fairy lights – and the shiniest Christmas bauble on the screen was Bella.

Bella's personal life off screen seemed equally perfect and straight out of a glossy magazine. Except for one thing: she and her delicious husband had never had children and she never spoke about it in interviews, which intrigued me. I knew she'd always longed for children and even if that had changed I imagined she'd be keen to produce a set of perfect ones to match her interiors. She'd often invite 'friends' children' onto the set for the Christmas filming, saying 'it's not Christmas without children', as they ran around her kitchen dipping their fingers in bowls. Bella would scold the children affectionately, rolling her eyes to the camera, her long, luscious lashes brushing perfect cheeks. 'Kids!' she'd say, and it all felt so natural and real. For a woman with no children of her own she seemed relaxed in their company and positively revelled in their boisterousness. It made me sad to think she and Peter had never had any children of their own, and I often wondered why.

It was those moments, when she ruffled the children's hair and played impromptu hide and seek that won over the viewers and touched me too. Apart from her childlessness which was never discussed, Bella involved the media, her viewers and fans in every moment of her life. She often posted selfies with her perfectly risen soufflés her 'to die for' meringues which she titled 'Stiff Peaks.' She'd also put quite intimate photos of her or Peter – or both - on twitter. I remember one photo she posted was of the two of them in bed, his modesty covered only by a hand towel. Bella had also titled this 'stiff peaks,' and there wasn't a meringue in sight. Yes, Bella shared everything from post coital nibbles to supper plates eaten on the other side of the world on film stars' yachts. She had recently been described as 'The Kim Kardashian of Cake,' because of her constant selfies, tweets and her inability to hide anything from her fans – but I knew differently.

Nevertheless, it seemed to the rest of the world that she was a no-holds barred star who shared every intimate moment. Only recently, Bella had talked in some detail about the Silver Fox's vasectomy, which put paid to the infertility rumours and increased her TV ratings tenfold. It must have been an oversight on the director's part, but it wasn't an easy watch as she shared this revelation while slicing a large Italian sausage.

Bella was now leaning seductively on the bright red Aga, full lips, rounded breasts and rising bakes, telling me what to stuff my bird with. I could barely reconcile this glamorous, sophisticated woman with the girl I'd once known. From being little, we'd played together at school and travelled the bumpy journey through the love and lip gloss of our teens. We were inseparable, slightly competitive, but ultimately very close.

Thinking about the past again was bittersweet. I still felt so guilty about what happened between us.

Bella refused to talk to me after what I did. I'd called her at home but her mum was always curt and said she'd left the area but didn't know where she'd gone. The last time I called, she'd been very sharp, saying, 'look, I've no idea where she is – and I don't want to, I'm getting on with my life. My advice to you is to do the same.'

Then, when Bella had been gone about a year I received a postcard out of the blue. I was ecstatic to see her distinctive handwriting again. I was also pleased because the very act of getting in touch hopefully meant she'd forgiven me. 'Hi Ames,' it said, 'I'm in Watford now, I have a new boyfriend and he's gorgeous – he's asked me to marry him. It's going to be amazing!'

She'd put an address on the postcard and I immediately wrote back with my congratulations and offered to get the train and go and see her. But months went by, I heard nothing and it occurred to me that her postcard was merely a way of showing me that she was doing fine without me. Then a few months later another postcard with a pebbly beach landed on the doormat: 'Hi Ames, I'm living in Devon now, I met this lovely guy...he's gorgeous, got loads of money...' A year went by until: 'Dear Amy, I'm on holiday in Portofino with my new boyfriend David....' She wasn't trying to keep in touch, she was letting me know that despite what I'd done she'd survived and was having a wonderful life of money and glamour and had left me behind. One day, I opened a newspaper to see my old friend dressed up on the red carpet at some TV premiere. She was now apparently going out with a soap actor who played the bad-boy character in *Dalmation Road*. She looked wonderful and I hoped she'd finally found the happiness she'd been looking for. But just a week after she was on the front pages again, this time in tears with a black eye – it seemed playing the aggressive bad boy in a TV soap wasn't such a stretch for the actor in real life. I sent her a letter to her last known address, I thought she might need a friend, but I heard nothing. Perhaps she hadn't forgiven me after all?

It wasn't long after the doomed relationship with the soap actor that Bella finally seemed to have found what she was looking for in

Peter Bradley. She announced breathlessly on a TV talk show that the delicious foreign correspondent was her soul mate. A matter of months later they were married and the wedding was everywhere. She wore ecru lace and the ceremony took place in Venice, there were so many photos in the papers and magazines I felt like I'd been a guest. It was just as well, because I never received an invitation.

Marriage was obviously good for Bella, shortly after her nuptials, 'Bella's Bake Off' was launched and she was suddenly the woman we all wanted to be.

I sometimes wondered if she ever thought of me, her best friend, the girl who'd been her confidante through the tough years of growing up. In spite of what happened she'd risen like a phoenix – but I could still never forgive myself. I messed with her life and if she still hated me for it I couldn't blame her. Watching her on screen, her glorious Christmas displayed around her home while with mine was in tatters around my ankles, I wondered if it was karma.

Chapter Three

The Cook, the Thief,
the Cakes and the Mother

The following evening I flicked on the TV to see Bella again as she talked about the traditions of Christmas and reminded me of my own tradition of sending her a card and a recipe. This year didn't have to be any different, I never gave up easily and who knew, this might be the year that one of her lackeys decides to actually pass on the card to the woman herself. My annual 'Christmas card in vain' to Bella wasn't just about our tainted friendship and all the hurt we'd been through, it was about my mum too. It was about our shared memories of her – by writing out her recipes and sending them to the only other person who remembered her as I did I was keeping my mum's memory alive. The previous year I'd sent her mum's gingerbread recipe which was very special to both of us, but even that recipe hadn't prompted Bella to get in touch and I had to conclude Bella wasn't receiving my Christmas post.

If she'd opened that card and remembered the gingerbread houses she would have been straight on the phone demanding we get together...wouldn't she? Had I really been such a bad friend that she couldn't bear to see me ever again? We'd both said things in the heat of the moment, but surely she was ready to forgive me now?

More than thirty years after we'd first iced gingerbread in Mum's kitchen I was watching Bella ice a gingerbread house on screen. We were grown-ups now, but listening to her voice, her laugh and the way she screwed up her nose when she giggled told me the old Bella was in there somewhere under the make-up and the TV lights. Hearing her laugh I remembered the fun, the sheer innocence of our childhood friendship, bright pink and sweet like the icing on those gingerbread walls.

I sipped on my coffee allowing the sweet gingerbread taste to wash away the residue of sadness and regret still on my tongue after all these years.

✻ ✻ ✻

Of course Bella hadn't always been this raven-haired baking idol who tweeted daily about her latest recipes and instagrammed her table settings on the hour. As a young girl Bella wasn't particularly good at 'Home Economics' and I had to help her bake the lemon meringue pie for her final exams. But, like me, I think she enjoyed the comfort of baking, and together we'd often spend weekends making cakes and pastries at my house.

Bella would ask her mum for money and when other teenagers were buying drugs and drink, we'd buy jars of mincemeat and paper cases for Christmas fairy cakes. Then, entrepreneurial Bella had the idea to take our bakes into school to sell. She'd worked out how much to charge so we could make a profit and the money we made kept us in sweets and lip gloss throughout our time at school.

Bella didn't need the money, she just liked making it, whereas I was always the sensible one. By seventeen, Bella was becoming wild, she didn't want to bake cakes any more, she wanted to chase boys and smoke cigarettes. I didn't blow my money, I didn't smoke, I just stood by and watched in awe as she ran through life easily. Bella learned to charm her way out of trouble and get just what she wanted. Despite her wanton ways as she grew up, Bella was a kind friend, who often put me first. She went from a little girl with great toys to a teenager with great clothes and make-up – and she shared it all with me, her best friend.

Throughout my childhood Bella was always there – confident, funny, a bit selfish but you could forgive her everything, because when Bella was around, life was fun. I laughed at her jokes and I think I provided some kind of grounding. She loved spending time at our home with me and my mum – she was an only child and I had two sisters, but as they were both older than me their presence in the house was merely music from a bedroom stereo or a lingering waft of perfume. Bella envied me my sisters as much as I envied her only-child status. I wanted peace and quiet to do my homework but Annie and Gill filled the house with music and hairspray and I remember Bella saying, 'I just love all the noise at your house', which I thought was bonkers because sometimes I couldn't think straight because of the chaos.

Even now, watching her on TV and reading about her wonderful, glamorous life in magazines, I still felt our connection,
even if it was only one-sided. I sipped at my spicy coffee, which I
liked with gingerbread syrup this time of year and as I swallowed
the warm, fiery liquid a wave of Christmas nostalgia ran through
me and I was reminded again of Mum's gingerbread. The kitchen
would be filled with sweet, comforting warmth throughout December, and on gingerbread day – as we used to call it – Bella and
I would sit excitedly at the kitchen table waiting, just waiting, our
legs waggling up and down in anticipation of the gingerbread's
emergence from the oven.

'No touching until it's cool,' Mum would warn, '...or you'll
turn into gingerbread men!' And to avoid turning into gingerbread men, we'd lay off the sweet slabs and Mum would distract
us by asking us to select our icing colours while it cooled. Finally,
after what seemed like ages breathing in the tantalising scent of
warm, buttery gingerbread filling the tiny kitchen, Mum helped
us stick the walls together with icing 'glue'. Mum was always so
patient with Bella, who could be quite demanding and needy, constantly interrupting with questions or problems. Sometimes she'd
start crying and feigning 'tummy ache' if she wasn't receiving the
attention she so desperately craved. She didn't get much love from
her own parents and Mum was the adult she reached out to when
she was feeling vulnerable or sad. My mum was always able to
calm her down, and if she was ever frustrated with the demands of
this child, she never let it show.

Bella's parents were very different from mine, they were rarely home and when they were they'd argue terribly. Bella told me she would go to bed early with the TV on in her room to shut out their screaming. Mum had taught me to imagine myself in another person's shoes and said this particularly applied to Bella. I knew Mum did the same when Bella had one of her tantrums.

Within minutes Bella would be calmed and sweet, back to her old self and Mum would be there in the background, like nothing had happened. She'd just gently guide us through the wonderful process of mixing different coloured icing, turning the flat squares of gingerbread into brick walls, tiled roofs and little windows and doors. Sometimes as a special treat Mum would buy a quarter of boiled sweets and we'd melt them in the oven to use as stained-glass windows. Once melted, the vibrant pinks and yellows and greens of the fruity confections created the most beautiful glass-like jewels, which we carefully applied to the houses, tongues out, our faces contorted with concentration and flushed from the heat of the kitchen. I remember Bella once saying she wished she could stop time and stay in our kitchen for ever – I'd laughed at this, but a few years later I wished I could too.

❄ ❄ ❄

Of course Bella wasn't perfect, she was as flawed as the rest of us and no friendship is without its ups and downs. Bella stole my boyfriends, had temper tantrums, and her dramas always outdid mine because she played them to the hilt. There were times when I think she found my sensibleness quite tedious, 'Sensible is boring, Ames,' she'd say, and accuse me of being 'too straight'. Perhaps I was – even now – but then there wasn't room in Bella's life for anyone who might compete for the limelight, so in essence we were the perfect best friends.

On screen, Bella was bringing the tray of gingerbread out of the oven and I wanted to make some too. So I rummaged around and found Mum's recipe along with the one for leftover dough which made the most divine gingerbread truffles.

I found the truffle recipe at the back of the folder, it was written in long hand on paper stained with coffee and crusty with icing – a well-used recipe, I thought with a smile. I decided to make a gingerbread house and would take it to the hostel. But my real reason was pure selfishness – I hadn't made gingerbread for years and I wanted to smell that sweet hot gingerbread baking and conjure up that old feeling of pure childish joy for the season – I so desperately needed a Christmas baking fix.

I put flour and butter into a bowl with sugar, thinking how like old times it was, me and Bella making gingerbread together, even if we were in different worlds on separate sides of a screen.

I rewound the TV, I'd missed the beginning, but luckily always recorded Bella and was keen to see how she made her gingerbread. Looking at Mum's recipe I was surprised to see Bella used the exact ingredients and measurements, even the same method. I rewound the TV again – and to my amazement, Bella was even using the same wording: 'when you melt the golden syrup, butter and brown sugar in the pan, take a deep breath and be transported back to the

Christmases of childhood.' I'd written that in the Christmas card I'd sent to Bella along with the recipe.

So she had received some of my cards after all. I couldn't believe it – I'd sent those recipes as a private and personal reminder of our times together, a shared memory of Christmas, an olive branch even. I hadn't sent them for her to use on her bloody TV programme, word for word like they were her own. I stood in the kitchen mouth open, stunned, and when she then announced that she would be making gingerbread truffles with the leftovers I knew – she'd received every single Christmas card I'd sent over the years. I was shocked and hurt to think that not only had Bella ignored my cards, but she was passing my mother's recipes off as her own.

I gazed at the TV in shock as she continued to wax lyrical about her 'idyllic' childhood. 'Of course my own family Christmases as a child were spent around the kitchen table with my parents, and aunts and uncles and cousins,' I heard her say. 'This gingerbread and these truffles are just a flavour of my mother's Christmassy cooking. She was an amazing cook – the two of us would make a gingerbread house together on the big table in our kitchen every Christmas,' the camera moved in, her eyes sprung with tears. 'Don't even dream of touching it until it cools, Bella,' she'd say. 'If you do you'll turn into a gingerbread man!'

My heart lurched...this was like some weird culinary version of single white female...she was copying my mum's recipes and my lines...and adopting *my* childhood. That was bad enough, but at the same time she was erasing me out of it.

But now, I was shocked, unable to take this in and understand what was happening. She was shaking her head at her 'memories', stopping a moment for full dramatic impact to wipe away a tear. My shock was now turning into anger, as hot as the gingerbread and I could feel myself beginning to panic. 'The stained-glass windows from boiled sweets are featured in this year's Christmas book called "Christmas at my Mother's Table", and is the first part of a series of recipes from my mother's kitchen – available from all major outlets and online. I recently rediscovered Mum's recipes and though she hasn't been with us for a long time I want to bring her into the kitchen, and share her recipes with my friends...you,' she gestured to the camera, a salt tear, a golden syrup smile. She was looking straight at me and as I applied the brown paper bag to my mouth I glared straight back. Mum had always tried to help her, understand her and guide her - why was she doing this to someone who'd been so good to her?

'I want to share her kindness, her warmth and her wonderful, imaginative ways with food, starting with her Christmas recipes.' She lifted the book up again to the camera, the cover was a faded photo of herself as a child with her mother holding a Christmas cake. Both were smiling into the camera. I paused the TV to look more closely at the white icing, topped with fresh holly leaves – it was the Christmas cake my mother had baked for them all those years before! I felt the blood rise up through my body, the anger and injustice surging along with it. How dare she?

I pressed play on the TV again, my blood boiling as I watched her make Mum's white chocolate gingerbread truffles...and telling her viewers; 'I know white chocolate and ginger isn't a traditional combination – but try it, it's a revelation and I promise you won't be disappointed!' Again the exact same words I had written on the card.

I felt like I was in some made-for-TV movie – my stolen life flashing before me on the screen.

'So it's Christmas – just like Mum used to make...' she continued, with a little pause. 'I am so very excited, but forgive me for my tears, by using her recipes again after all these years, I feel like... she's back here with me, in the kitchen.' She took out a handkerchief and I wanted to throw something at the screen. The camera came in for a close-up then panned back to her face, tears now trickling shamelessly down that lying bitch's botoxed cheeks.

Your mother's table? Really? I thought, all hope of forgiveness dissipating into the spicy gingerbread air. I turned up the volume and listened closely to every single word she said, and whichever way I tried to work it out there were no grey areas here. Bella Bradley had stolen my dead mother's recipes – and not only was she passing them off as her own, she was selling the book!

Why would she do that?

All these years she'd been receiving my Christmas cards with recipes meant as a shared memory from me, a little aside about Mum, a moment from our childhood to smile about. She'd never acknowledged them, just stowed them away until she had enough to write a cookery book and Bella bloody Bradley was about to make a fortune passing the recipes off as her own. Over my cold, dead body.

'So in memory of my wonderful mother at Christmas,' she was saying, 'I'm inviting all you lovely Mums out there to call in, email, tweet and tell us what Christmas means to you. And wait for it…the best one will win a week of Christmas …with me! Yes it will be fabulous – I will show you how to cook the most delicious Christmas Dinner, how to set your table, and dress that tree – all in my own home. One lucky lady will win herself and her family a truly Bella Christmas! And that's not all – on Christmas Eve, when not a soul is stirring, I will come to your home and hold your hand and guide you through the best possible Christmas ever – just like my Mum used to for me.'

Right Bella Bradley – I thought – the gloves are off! I took the brown paper bag from my mouth and as she started on her 'No Nonsense Bloody Banana Trifle', I was on the phone.

Chapter Four

Desperate Housewives and Postal Pants

'I'd like to speak to Bella Bradley please,' I said, brusque and business-like.

I'm sorry you can't speak directly to Bella,' the voice sounded young, disinterested.

'But it's important.'

'Is it about the prize? If it's about the Bellatastic Christmas – then I can take your details and if you're very lucky you might get to speak to the queen herself.'

'No, I don't want a Bella-whatever Christmas, thank you. I'm an old friend and I need to speak with her immediately, it's a matter of the utmost importance,' I said. In my panic I'd morphed into high melodrama circa 1930's and had to stop myself saying 'post haste'.

'Sorry?' She seemed confused.

'I'm a friend...'

'You can't be,' she said.

'Why?'

'Because Bella doesn't have any friends,' she sniggered at this. 'Are you the woman who sent her pants in the post last week?'

'No I am not,' I snapped indignantly. 'Who am I speaking to?' I asked, desperately trying not to sound like the kind of woman who sends her pants to people on the telly.

'I'm Crimson, Bella Bradley's star researcher,' she said, and with that the phone went dead.

'Damn...damn,' I spat, redialling, thinking I may have to use some cunning to get past the charming Crimson. I waited as the phone clicked on and played 'The First Noel'. On an endless loop. For twenty-two minutes and thirty seconds.

'Hello Bella Bradley Show, are you calling about the prize?' It was the same monotoned disinterest I'd previously encountered. Crimson, again. Not perhaps the star researcher – the *only* researcher?

'I'm a huge Bella fan,' I gushed, changing my approach, trying to make my voice sound different so she wouldn't get wind of my shrewd Trojan Horse-style plan to speak to Bella. 'I watch her every Christmas and Christmas was my mother's favourite time of year and...I miss her. There's nothing I would love more than to have Bella provide a wonderful Christmas...just like my mum used to.' I tried not to get too upset saying this, but my throat tightened just thinking about Mum and what Bella had done.

'Are you deserving?' she asked, and I could almost hear a smirk in her voice.

'Yes...my husband's abandoned me for a pole dancer and I have no money to buy food or gifts for my children.' Hearing myself I thought, yes I'm just the type of vulnerable person these shows love to exploit. If only I could sing I'd be a perfect X Factor contestant with my heart rending back story. Mind you the lack of singing talent had never stopped anyone being on the X Factor up until now.

'Hubby's run off and left you and the kids penniless at Chrimbo! This is good,' Crimson said, with no hint of sympathy. 'Okay I'll need your deets.'

'My what?'

'Your details?' she said slowly, incredulously, like I was very deaf and very stupid. 'We're making a shortlist so Bella can choose which lucky "Mum" is going to have a "Bella Christmas",' her voice was heavy with sarcasm or boredom – or both. 'So we need to interview you live on the show.'

'Oh, I'm not sure...' Did I really want to go this far? It was beginning to feel a bit too real and I almost put down the phone.

'Don't get all excited, it's only been a few minutes since we announced the prize and we've already had loads of emails and tweets...and poison pen letters...heavy breathers, naked photos and death threats – so you've got fierce competition.'

I wasn't bothered about winning, I just wanted Bella to see my name and contact me – out of shame for stealing recipes if nothing else.

I took a breath and lied, 'I *am* excited – I can't help it, I just love Bella.'

'Yeah I bet you do,' she muttered. 'Anyway Bella wants the Mum that we choose to live somewhere that won't make her itch... so give me your name and address.'

I reluctantly gave her my details and she put me back on hold and another bloody round of 'The First Noel,' which by now it really wasn't, it must have been the twentieth at least.

'Hello Amy,' she eventually came back on the line. 'I'm just Googling your address to make sure you don't live somewhere undesirable.' Silence while she did her 'research'. I was tempted to give them the address of the hostel, after all there weren't many people more deserving than them - but I probably would have found myself cut off again.

'Your house looks okay and a quick Google of your name suggests you haven't murdered anyone, yet – mind you that could all change once you get to Dovecote.'

'Thank you,' I said through gritted teeth.

'When I said your house looks okay, that's *all* I meant. It's not like it's amazing or anything. We can't film anywhere really cool because Bella's fans would be scared shitless by anything more than a three-bed semi...but we can't film in a slum either. You tick the box though – it's somewhere in between, a sort of semi-slum.'

'I'm glowing with all these compliments...better not let them go to my head,' I said, forgetting the gushing girlishness for a moment.

'You don't sound too looney tunes so I'll put you on the long shortlist and you might, if you're *really* lucky, get a call from Bella, okay?' This all said in a hyper-sarcastic tone.

'Okay,' I nodded, knowing from her voice that the promise from a phone call from Bella was an empty promise they were making to everyone, just to give those pants-sending fans something to hold on to. I didn't stand a chance. My only hope was that Bella saw my name, which I hadn't changed when I got married because I liked being Amy Lane and it saved bother changing everything. This had all been so futile, who was I kidding? Bella and I now occupied two very different worlds and there was no way she'd reach out into the past to get in touch with me again.

I was about to put the phone down when Crimson said, 'Oh and...I meant to say, your Christmas will be paid for by the TV company and they pay a facility fee for filming in your house, from about £500 a day.'

'Oh... really?' I'd had absolutely no intention of really entering this ridiculous competition, I just wanted access to Bella, but this was suddenly very tempting – I might as well try and get something positive out of all this. A paid for Christmas lunch and a facility fee – I could think of some people who would be very grateful for that.

Crimson was still talking, '...I've put a tick by your name, not because I think you'll be any good, but because I'm bored of talking to desperate housewives and Googling suburbia. So wait on the line and when Bella comes to you, tell her everything you just told me about your mother blah blah and how you're really into her, she'll love that. Just be yourself and be all orgasmic and whiney about Bella and her baking.'

'Okay.' This was a little disturbing, I had clearly done the gushing 'crazed fan' a little too well and Crimson apparently found me suitably cringey. Neil's departure had definitely had an effect on my sanity.

'Yeah...oh and one more thing.'

'Yes?'

'It's live, so don't say fuck.'

'I have no intention of saying fu... the F-word,' I snapped indignantly, forgetting my crazed fan persona once again. I had no idea it was live, I assumed I would have to go through a battery of calls and it would be recorded later, but watching it unfold on the screen in front of me I could see Bella was taking calls. I hadn't thought this through, I'd just made that phone call in anger and I was about to be launched onto live TV. I rummaged around in my handbag, I might need a brown paper bag for this one.

Then the line went dead and 'The First Noel' started up again. I sat nervously waiting for a few minutes, working out what I would say after all this time – in front of millions of viewers. I had never envisaged my first real communication with Bella to be like this – live on air - but she'd given me no choice.

By the time she eventually came on the line I'd wound myself into a ball of stress – I was angry, hurt and so damned nervous I couldn't speak.

'Are you there...is that Amy?' she was saying. I could see her on screen, but it was hard to reconcile the two things. Bella Bradley the TV star was talking to me but showing no signs she knew who I was. I couldn't take it all in, I was very hot and bothered and providing a one-woman show of what I think is known in the business as 'dead air'.

'Oh dear...I think we have a technical hitch,' she was saying. 'I can't hear lovely little Amy...and her story's so sad,' she pulled her mouth downwards in a fake sad shape.

That made my hackles rise. She hadn't a clue who I was and was being so bloody patronising. She hadn't even bothered to check my surname, if she had she'd have known it was me. Then again, I was obviously so unimportant to her, would she even remember my married name?

'I would love a Bella Christmas,' I started. 'My mum always made Christmas special for me – and I'm particularly interested to talk to you about your new book, "Christmas at My Mother's Table".'

'Oh yes, my mother's wonderful recipes,' she sighed, brightening visibly at the unexpected joy of book promotion which would mean more sales and more money for her. Bella clearly didn't recognise my voice, but then after twenty years I supposed it had changed slightly.

'*MY* mother's wonderful recipes,' I snapped.

If she now realised it was me, she wasn't letting on, but I suddenly saw a flash of panic in Bella's beautifully made-up eyes. 'You must remember me, Bella, we used to be best friends,' I began, my voice fading, my mouth so dry I could barely get the words out.

On screen, I glimpsed Bella's perfect composure momentarily falter, but she gave a sickly sweet smile and regained herself, 'How lovely...an old friend...I'm delighted that you called.'

'Yes, I've been trying to get in touch for years,' I said.

'I...let me put you through to our switchboard, Amy. I am DESPERATE to meet up and chat about old times, but this line is for the competition. We've had so many calls and lots of Bella fans are waiting to have their chance to win a Bella Christmas,' she said, desperately trying to take control of the situation.

I knew I was about to be cut off, so I said simply, 'How could you, Bella? How could you steal my mum's recipes…'

❄ ❄ ❄

I looked up at the TV on the kitchen wall. I had been instantly disconnected and Bella was now taking another call. She was smiling but the tell-tale flushing of her mottled neck above those frolicking red reindeers told me she was rattled. It always gave her away as a child when she was flustered and it gave her away now despite all of the make-up and clever lighting. I had to give it to her though, apart from the flushed skin, there was no indication that she was shaken and as she ended the next call the show continued seamlessly. She peeled a banana like a porn star with a seductive smile playing across her lip-glossed mouth. And I was reminded of the girl behind the bike shed selling kisses for chewing gum.

'I NEED my five a day, during the festive season,' she added, cheekily, and I had a strong desire to plunge her head into some 'severely whipped' cream.

I couldn't take any more, so turned off the TV and threw away the dregs of my coffee. It was still early, but I just wanted to go to bed and cry myself to sleep. My husband had left me for a new life of exotic sex, and on top of this, I'd discovered my oldest friend, who hadn't acknowledged me for years, had stolen my own mother's recipes. Initially I'd been hurt and tearful about both betrayals, but now I was just angry and didn't feel I could trust anyone ever again.

I contemplated what to do next. There was no way I'd ever get to talk to Bella now, and even if I did, it wouldn't make any difference. The book was published and her theft would go unchallenged. I had to take my mind of this or I would drive myself mad with the injustice of it all and after that phone call St Swithin's wouldn't be in receipt of a £500 location fee or a 'Bella-bloody-tastic Christmas!' Meanwhile, I had promised to provide Christmas cakes for the hostel, which took my mind off the Bella situation and gave me a sense of purpose. I was going to give them the best cakes I could bake, better than any Bella cake with her plump fruits and exotic spices. I knew we couldn't go too strong on the alcohol given that some of the residents were a little too fond of the stuff, but my cake budget would stretch to a small bottle of brandy to 'feed' the cakes so they'd be moist and delicious. I popped out to the local Sainsbury's to buy the brandy and was just walking back with my miniature bottle when I saw Stanley, the Frank Sinatra guy from the shelter. He was sitting on a bench next to the town Christmas tree singing 'My Way' under the twinkly lights strung through the huge branches. He was happy enough with his backlist of Old Blue Eyes and his own miniature bottle of cheap brandy just like mine, and he waved me over.

'Amy, Amy, Amy... how are you?' he said, delighted to see me.

I went over to say hello and he patted the seat next to him so I sat down, and spotting that I was clutching a small bottle of brandy too he offered me his bottle to drink from.

'Cheers, love,' he was saying and pushing the bottle to my mouth.

I smiled, 'Oh no Stanley, thank you but I haven't joined you to have a drink. I'm on my way home, I bought this to put in my Christmas cakes,' I held my bottle up as I explained.

'For me?'

'No Stanley – it's for my cakes,' I said as he reached for it. He nodded, confused, and took the bottle out of my hand before embarking on a torch song medley from Frank's early career. I didn't quite know how to handle this, so gently pulled my bottle away from him, but he seemed to think it was a gift and as hard as I held it, the more he seemed to pull it back from me.

'No Stanley!' I said, firmly now. There was no point explaining again about the bloody cakes, he didn't understand or care – he merely saw kind Amy sitting next to him with a nice bottle of brandy.

He stood up and as we were both holding on to the bottle I moved with him, I wasn't letting go, I had no money for more brandy and was determined to keep this bottle and make the best bloody Christmas cakes ever. But Stanley was now singing loudly, and swinging the bottle back and forth, with me still clutching it, and being drunk he wasn't very co-ordinated. I couldn't believe I'd got myself into this ridiculous situation and decided to end it once and for all by pulling the bottle back with force. I heaved it towards me, but as he wasn't expecting this I caused poor Stanley to lose his balance. He fell to the floor as I shouted, 'Stanley. Oh Stanley, I'm sorry,' and got down on the pavement to try and pick him up. But it was a frosty night, the ground was slippery and within seconds we were both sliding around, falling over each other, clutching on to our respective bottles. Just at this moment, four lads from school appeared from behind the Christmas tree, and I was so relieved, they'd come to my rescue and get Stanley and I back on our feet.

'Lads, come over here,' I shouted, still flailing on the floor with Stanley spread eagled underneath me now singing 'Strangers in the Night.'

He knew every bloody word and he sang each one. Loudly.

'Lads, lads,' I called again from under the tree over Stanley's crooning.

'No thanks, we're alright miss,' one of them said and they all roared laughing.

'I need you to come and give us a hand,' I insisted, before landing on top of Stanley and seeing Josh Rawton – the little sod – film the whole scene. Great, that would no doubt be around the bloody school tomorrow along with the one of me hurling cake and abuse at my husband. This one would be new and different though – me pissed under the town Christmas tree straddling a homeless Frank Sinatra.

Once those little sods had got their shots and had a good laugh they were off leaving me and Stanley to fend for ourselves. Eventually I got Stanley back on the bench and handed him my bottle of brandy which he clearly needed more than my cakes did.

'You okay, Stanley?' I asked when he'd taken a glug.

'Keeps me warm, love,' he explained.

I nodded. The residents weren't permitted inside the shelter until 6 p.m. and so with nowhere else to go were forced to walk the streets all day. The cold was biting and I didn't blame him for finding what little comfort there was in a sip of brandy – what else did he have?

I sat a while with Stanley and after a few more numbers – with a rousing 'My Way' finale – I watched him stagger down the road, pissed and precarious on the ice. The town Christmas lights spelling out 'Happy Christmas' were swinging above him as the wind got up and spittles of rain hit my face and landed on the icy ground. I thought about Bella and my mum and the cosy Christmases we'd had round the kitchen table, with plenty of love and laughter. And I gazed at the Christmas tree and thought how life can change in an instant.

Chapter Five

A Hot Macchiato and a Hormonal SAS

It had been two days since my live call to Bella's show and as I wrestled with Pythagoras and 10B I wondered if speaking to me had had any impact on her life at all. Did she feel guilty for not returning my calls in the early days, never acknowledging my notes and Christmas cards? Had she realised the affect she'd had on me by writing that book filled with Mum's recipes and saying the work was all her own? Was she getting me back for what I'd done to her all those years ago? I was torn between wanting revenge and wanting to see her and to talk things through like we used to.

The following day was the final school day before we broke up for the Christmas holidays and I was getting ready to leave for work when I had a phone call from Crimson. I was surprised to hear from her and she was as mysterious and monotone as ever, 'We've now got the shortlist down to three 'Mums', and don't wet your pants, but you're on that list,' she sighed.

What?

'I have no intention of wetting...'

'Apparently Bella requested you personally,' she carried on talking over me. 'You must have convinced her you are a true life-long "Bella-ette",' she sniggered.

I was amazed. I'd assumed once Bella realised who I was and what I was accusing her of she'd have gone out of her way to keep me away from her precious programme. So why had she requested me? I didn't want to play her silly games and was about to tell Crimson that Bella could stick her Christmas, when I thought of poor old Stanley staggering through the town through a halo of Christmas lights.

'That's great news,' I said, playing along.

'So the winner will be announced during the show at 10.07 this morning,' she continued. 'You around?'

'Yes... I'll be on my mobile,' I said, wondering what the hell I was going to do with my 'challenging' Year Ten maths group who had already clocked off for Christmas in their heads.

'Okay you'll be called later...and by the way, it's live so don't say fu...'

'No, I won't say the F-word or wet myself – thank you,' I said and put down the phone, feeling mixed but knowing if by some miracle I won a Bella Christmas, she'd better be ready for an Amy Christmas too... because it wouldn't be the cosy day in my suburban semi slum they were all expecting.

❄ ❄ ❄

When I arrived in school, Crimson had already emailed asking if I could send a photo of myself so they could put it up on screen during the call. This was real, and if I was going to be on the phone on TV during school time I needed to let my colleagues know.

I went straight in to see Sylvia who was beside herself with excitement when I told her about the competition. I didn't go into too much detail, as far as Sylvia was concerned Bella Bradley was an old school friend I hadn't stayed in touch with – but she was very impressed.

'I'll look after your class and you can take the call in my office,' she said excitedly. 'It will be declared a student no-go and Bella Bradley HQ from 9.30am.'

This was a great relief as I didn't fancy having a difficult conversation with 10B shouting obscenities in the background. Some of the boys had recently taken to calling out varied and colourful words representing the male member and I doubted that would be allowed live on air. After several difficult sessions the previous week while trying to explain equations over a barrage of 'willy' words and associated sniggering, I'd decided if you can't beat them join them and harnessed their enthusiasm for the penis into a maths game.

'Okay – so if a willy is three quarters and a knob is fourteen, multiply this by a penis, which is one sixth – write down the equation and the answer,' I suddenly announced over the racket of a particularly difficult lesson.

I had been greeted with blissful silence, their faces were a picture, and their deep shock was soon replaced with uncharacteristic fervour for the subject, which as a teacher is all I ever wanted. This went on for the whole lesson until Mr Jones the head teacher popped in. I wasn't initially aware of his presence, but looking back I can see that opening a classroom door to hear a member of the maths department reeling off a list of words signifying male genitalia must have been a shock (bearing in mind our last encounter was him finding me in a stationery cupboard with a brown paper bag over my mouth). I turned to see him standing, rooted to the spot, staring at me as I looked straight back, causing much merriment in class. He made an enquiry as to the whereabouts of some textbooks and I smiled sweetly and answered his question like I hadn't just been multiplying three quarters of a willy by fourteen knobs for Year Ten. Consequently, the idea of Year Ten live and unleashed while I called in to a daytime Christmas cookery programme had made me even more nervous. So after the first lesson, where I'd blindly forged ahead with fractions, I popped outside into the freezing cold for a breath of iced air.

'Ooh they've all got it on them today haven't they?' Marie the French teacher hissed from her position by the back wall. She wasn't just a caffeine addict she also smoked about forty a day and could often be found sheltering round the back doors for a quick one. The psychology teacher said Marie had an addictive personality, but I reckoned I'd be mainlining more than coffee and fags if I had to teach a foreign language to Year Ten.

'Yes, I'm not in the mood for their antics, they're already swearing and switching off but there's still two long days left before we break up,' I sighed.

'I feel like getting flu and doing a sickie. Billy McBride in 10R has memorised every French swear word ever invented – I've just had to listen to an hour of French filth.'

'Hey, that's a romantic night in for some people,' I joked.

She sniggered. 'Yeah, I guess. But I feel violated and stressed... then there's bloody Christmas,' she dropped her cigarette to the ground and stepped it out with her shoe. 'Only a few shopping days left, Amy, have you done all yours?'

'Some,' I nodded. I hadn't, but I couldn't admit it even to myself – I'd been desperate to buy presents, but too scared to put any more on the credit card and was waiting for my salary to go in my account the following week. I planned to give the kids money and I'd already popped in with some talc for Auntie Ann in her retirement home. I always tried to get her visit out of the way early because it was usually stressful and surreal, and this year was no different. Once she'd excitedly ripped open the talc she began hurling it at me accusing me of being a terrorist and when I'd tried to take it off her she'd shrieked and pushed the panic button. I don't know the link between talc and terrorism but within seconds security arrived in the form of two burly men who manhandled me to the floor while Auntie Ann accused me of flying planes into buildings. It wasn't pretty, talc everywhere, Auntie Ann screaming and me lying there covered in white powder denying Islam while being straddled by two men.

'Yeah...I've still got lots of shopping to do, only given one present so far,' I said, marvelling at just how much Lily of the Valley talc was inside one tub. Suddenly the double doors whooshed open and an effervescent Sylvia appeared all breathless and excitable. I screamed. I always leaped at sudden noise or people appearing from nowhere but today this was heightened.

'Come on, Amy,' she said, flicking her bleached blonde fringe back off her face with a chunky, manicured hand. 'Time for your close-up.'

'What's this?' Marie asked.

'Nothing – just...something,' I muttered, wanting to keep the whole thing quiet. I didn't want everyone knowing what I was about to do just yet, I wasn't sure myself. It was one thing airing Bella's dirty linen to a million morning viewers, but I needed to keep it to myself until it happened – if Year Ten got hold of it they'd have put me all over YouTube...again. The internet has changed teaching as we know it, everything is out there now for the world to see and judge thanks to those little techno sods.

I'd been fuelled by anger when I'd called Bella's show, but now I was wondering how on earth I'd got myself into this. I didn't only have the issue of Mum's recipes to deal with, I'd started to think about that prize, and was putting myself under pressure thinking just how much I wanted to win for St Swithin's.

Sylvia opened her office, ushered me in and went off to set my class some work and keep them calm until my call was ended. After a few minutes alone I was just starting to relax when she suddenly appeared at the glass of the doorway, making me jump for a second time that morning.

'Oooh it's so exciting!' she said, putting down two paper cups of coffee and squeezing my arm while doing a little dance. I smiled gratefully, noticing she'd put fresh lipstick on 'for the telly' despite it only being a phone call. That she wasn't even involved in.

At exactly four minutes after ten the phone call was put through from reception on Sylvia's instructions. Judging by the two large cups of macchiato and the way Sylvia was nestling down into her seat, it seemed she was staying with me for the duration of the call. She clearly had no intention of slumming it with sex-obsessed Year Tens and missing out on this, but I dreaded to think what they were up to. I felt a twinge of guilt, then fear that in the absence of authority they may run rampant and take their current obsession with male genitalia to a new and dangerous level and storm the building like a hormonal SAS. Then, suddenly the phone rang, which caused me to leap about three feet in the air and Sylvia to do the same, covering us both with a gallon of hot macchiato.

'Christ!' I yelled down the phone.

'No...it's not Christ, it's Bella Bradley, but close enough...'

'Oh, hi...'

'Hi Amy. We aren't on air yet, this is a pre-call, I do a pre-call to warm up the callers.'

Silence.

If I ever needed a brown paper bag it was now – or a fully fledged panic attack would take me over and turn this situation into even more of a circus than it already was. I grabbed the brown paper bag I had waiting on the desk and breathed into it building up the carbon dioxide in my body and filling me with calm.

'Amy... are you still there?'

The sound of her smug voice overwhelmed me with fresh anger, replacing the calm and sweeping me up. 'So you can call me now, after all these years,' I said, knowing that my comment about the stolen recipes was the only reason she'd bothered to ring me. I saw Sylvia do a double-take from behind her macchiato mess, she wasn't expecting this, and if I hadn't been so angry I would have laughed.

'Look I've been meaning to get in touch with you for a while...I've just been...busy,' Bella said dismissively.

'Busy? For twenty years?' I spat.

'Yes.'

'Oh no you haven't.'

'Oh yes I have.'

'This isn't a bloody pantomime, Bella!' I snapped.

'Well you're trying to turn my show into a bloody pantomime, calling up live on air, pretending to be a fan and accusing me of all sorts.'

I felt tearful, and the only thing stopping me from crying was Sylvia's shocked face and red lips in an O shape, wondering what the hell was going on. Like the rest of the country she was in love with Bella and was completely taken aback by what she was hearing.

'Look, you and your family have always taken advantage of me and mine, and my poor mother was like a mother to you. What you're doing...it's just not fair, Bella.'

'Life's not fair, but if you continue to blackmail me about this, I will have to get lawyers involved.' Clearly there was going to be no attempt to build bridges or make amends.

'So will I,' I bluffed. 'My lawyer is reading through the recipes as I speak.' This was followed by silence on both sides, neither of us wanting to be the first to say something. I watched Sylvia watching me, her mouth open.

'So what do you want?' Bella said, almost in a whisper.

'I want to win a Bella-tastic Christmas...and I want you to acknowledge my mother's work,' I answered.

Silence again.

'All the years I've sent Christmas cards and letters asking if you forgave me and not once did you put me out of my misery. You couldn't even be bothered to answer me. You sent the odd postcard early on to show me how wonderful your life was but you couldn't just send a note to say, "It's okay, Amy, I forgive you." If you had I could have got on with my life and shaken off this terrible guilt. Well, now we are equal, because you've taken something from me,' I heard myself say.

'Okay, okay just calm down. I can't wave my wand and grant you a Bella Christmas like that – I'm not your fairy God Mother Amy. But if ... and only if, you were to win this prize, you would have to promise not to say a word to anyone about anything – and no little surprises live on air.'

'Okay,' I said after a few seconds, I wanted to make her wait, make her sweat.

'I'll see what I can do. My agent Felicity will email you a contract and we want your signature all over it,' she continued, just as Crimson had, ignoring what I was actually saying.

'Bella?'

'I need you to read the part of the contract that states there will be no more slanderous remarks on air. This includes any conversations with any third party regarding my past, present and future i.e. newspapers or, God help me, those witches at Gossip Bitch.'

'Okay, if you agree to what I want,' I said, sounding as cheesy as a criminal in a B movie. This was greeted by silence.

I thought she'd put the phone down and was about to swear profusely, assuming she'd gone, when I suddenly heard an intake of breath on the line.

'Now, when I come back to you we will be live on air. And all you need to say is you want for Christmas is a Bella Bakes Christmas, you are DESPERATE for Bella to pay a visit to your little kitchen in the provinces. Okay?'

'I wouldn't put it like that.'

'I would. And we don't have time to argue because I will be back on air in thirty seconds and we will come to you in less than a minute. We can both play hardball - so lots of Bella love and a salty sprinkle of gratitude should get you exactly what your sweet little heart desires.'

I just know she wanted to add 'bitch', but she had to restrain herself because I was calling the shots now.

'I want a special Christmas...' I started.

'Look, just say your lines, and keep schtum and I will be coming down your chimney with a bag of money, because that's clearly what you're after.'

'I don't...that's not...'

'Oh there's a swearing clause too – don't say f....'

'Yes, I fucking know,' I snapped.

It seemed everyone assumed I wanted money and was threatening to take my story about Bella's murky past and stolen recipes to the tabloids...and that I was compelled to say the F-word live on air.

The phone went dead for a few seconds then started playing 'The First Noel' again...and again.

I looked at Sylvia uncertainly.

'What?' she said. 'Do you need me to say anything on air?'

'No...thanks,' I smiled. I really didn't need to add an excitable Sylvia to the surreal conversation I was about to have in front of the nation with my former best friend.

Listening to 'The First Noel' as I waited on the line, the situation had made me think about the past and what might have been. Years after her death, my mum was being exploited by someone she'd cared for, and it broke my heart. I couldn't help but wish she'd had more self-belief and used her cooking talents for herself not for others.

I remember one New Year's Eve the Pilkingtons were returning from their holiday home in Switzerland and had asked my mum to provide and serve a buffet for forty people on their return. Mum worked tirelessly for a couple of days and I found her slumped on the bathroom floor when I came home from school. I was really scared, but she told me she was just tired. The next day her face was pale and I could tell she was in pain, but she wouldn't admit it to either me or the rest of the family. I saw her taking three paracetamol, and although she still didn't seem herself, by the evening of the buffet she seemed brighter. 'I'll be fine, I think it must have been something I ate,' she'd told me when I'd asked.

I was still worried about her as she was packing all the stuff in containers and waiting for the driver to come and get her and my sisters and the food. My sister was helping out as a waitress and I'd have given anything to go too but Mum said I was a bit young.

'Let her go with you,' Dad said from his chair. He was worried about Mum too and I think he wanted another family member there looking after her. It was testament to how weakened she felt that she gave in and agreed.

I was delighted, I felt so grown-up, and when we arrived I was excited and surprised to see Bella and her mum and dad were there as guests. I felt so proud to be a waitress I waited until I was wearing my pinafore and carrying a tray of canapés before I went over to say hello.

Bella screamed for joy when she saw me, 'Ames...look at you – how fabby!' she squealed, hugging me and almost knocking the tray out of my hands. Her father was always very formal and muttered, 'Hello Amy,' but her mother just smiled coldly in my general direction and turned away. I didn't understand her reaction, she'd never been warm and welcoming like my mum, but she knew me well and we'd chatted when she came to collect Bella from my house. Bella seemed oblivious to this coolness and was asking if she could help out too. 'I want to wear an apron like Ames...please can I be a waitress too?'

Her mother looked from Bella to me and back again, and staring directly at me said, 'No, Bella – you're better than that.'

I was devastated, my throat closed up and I spent the rest of the evening quietly serving. Bella barely spoke to me and when Mum asked if I was okay I didn't have the heart or the vocabulary to explain what had happened and how it made me feel. But that night I learned a valuable life lesson: we're not all the same, and friendship doesn't always cross boundaries as it should. Sadly I didn't see this for what it was at the time – a couple of judgemental snobs who felt I was good enough for their daughter when they were too busy, but when it came down to it I was socially inferior. They loved my mum when she could provide the fancy canapés they could show off to their friends, but none of them even came to see her when she became ill.

Now I felt like I'd let her down further by sending those recipes only for her to be exploited again. I felt foolish and was determined to make damn sure I got what I wanted from Bella by fair means or foul, if only to avenge my mum and give St Swithin's a Christmas they'd never forget.

As I'd grown up and become a mum myself I'd realised how hard life and death had been for her, but she kept smiling. Mum never had anything, she struggled most of her life and no one ever really acknowledged everything she did. We all loved her but perhaps took her for granted. I'd spent years feeling guilty about Mum and how I'd never been able to do anything for her, improve her life, take away her pain. And now this final insult from Bella had brought it all to the surface. I had to see her and make her realise what she'd done to me – and to my mum's memory.

Chapter Six

Let them Eat Cake

While I was waiting to be put through to Bella, Sylvia had managed to pilfer a flat-screen TV from the headmaster's office so we could watch the show when the call came through. She'd asked Mr Robinson, the caretaker, to come and set it up, but there was no sign of him and time had run out so she was now grappling with it. I was just about to get up and give her a hand when 'The First Noel' stopped abruptly (thankfully) and a rather shrill voice said, 'Hello is that Amy? Little Amy Lane?' It was her. Bella Bradley... this time in TV personality mode, all posh speak and girly giggles.

I could barely talk, so quickly breathed into the paper bag for a few seconds. Yes I was nervous, I was live on air, but I was also distracted by the circus going on around me. Sylvia was trying to get the TV to work by twiddling with the connections, and in order to reach them at the back she'd had to virtually mount it. Sylvia was short and quite round and was now having problems fitting herself around the huge TV. Then just at the point where she was virtually on top of it with one leg wrapped round, Paul Watkins from 10B appeared through the window in the office door. He was videoing the whole spectacle. I couldn't leave the phone to stop him, so waved my paper bag frantically and shouted for him to STOP THAT NOW!' which alarmed Sylvia who thought I was addressing her, and almost lost her footing. She was now straddling the TV while I kept shouting and waving – and Paul continued shooting.

'That'll be on YouTube in ten minutes,' I said, as he eventually put down his phone, laughing. I communicated one of my 'furious' looks at him.

'You Tube?' the voice said, followed by tinkling fake laughter. 'I think we have a crossed line.'

'Hi yes...no, it's all fine, sorry this is Amy,' I finally said, trying to calm myself while shaking my fist at the sniggering teen.

'It's lovely to speak with you little Amy – now tell us all about yourself.'

I was half-listening, I could barely concentrate with Paul still standing there. And if he got his phone out again and filmed me, he could really drop me in it with the headmaster. I hadn't planned to advertise the fact that I was skipping class to be on the telly.

Unable to extricate herself from the TV set up, Sylvia was also shouting and waving at Paul to stop. But what we were doing in reality was providing pure comedy gold for his little video. This was a Christmas gift to Paul Watkins.

'Don't play that game with me...' I yelled, as Paul lifted his phone to continue filming.

'Oh dear...I'm not playing any games...is that little Amy?' said the voice on the other end.

'Yes...hello, Bella, I'm so sorry. Yes it's Amy,' I said, waving my fist at a departing Paul while Sylvia slid slowly down the front of the screen, her feet desperately waggling until they reached the ground.

'Yes...so, lovely Amy, tell me what a Bella Christmas would mean to you?' I wondered what she was thinking, she seemed so bright and breezy, like we hadn't just had a hissed conversation about blackmail. I looked at the screen, which Sylvia had miraculously brought to life, and noticed the red mottle slowly creeping up Bella's neck.

I swallowed hard, 'My husband has gone,' I said, through dry lips. 'And this is the first time my kids will be away...and...'

'Fabulous!' she said, clasping her hands together. It was clear she wanted to keep this short and sweet in case I suddenly blurted anything out.

'So you want a great big bird and all the Bella trimmings?' she was saying, and looking into the camera, winking.

'Yes...and it would be good to see you too. We have stuff to talk about,' I added, giving her the message that I wanted more than just a stuffed 'Bella' bird and a masterclass in goose fat.

Silence.

'Ha, you're obviously desperate for help, you NEED a Bella Christmas and...' she paused for dramatic effect, 'I am DEEEElighted to inform you that you are the winner, lovely Amy Lane!' the voice chorused down the phone.

'Thank you,' I was saying while nodding at Sylvia who did a little dance.

'You deserve it, lovely Amy. Your husband's abandoned you for a topless dancer and your kiddies are going hungry, goodness you must be exhausted, not to mention worried to death about Christmas.'

'Well, he didn't...it's not quite...'

'I can only imagine the hardship, the heartache...your little ones' faces when they come downstairs to an empty fireplace... where Santa *hasn't* been.' Her lips were quivering, the camera was closing in, she was milking this for all it was worth.

I refused to be patronised and exploited by her, I wasn't 'poor little Amy', I was the one holding all the cards here for once in my life. 'My children are adults,' I said. 'They won't be wondering where Santa is...'

'Oh...yes, but whatever age our children are, they still expect a visit from the man in red,' she said, clearly shaken by my refusal to join in.

'I think at the age of twenty, they may be a little bit disturbed at the sight of an old man dressed in red creeping through their house,' I responded, now cool as a cucumber, but still clutching the paper bag, just in case a panic attack overwhelmed me at the wrong moment.

She laughed that false laugh again and I wanted to smash the phone. I felt strangely offended that she'd use this laugh on me – after all these years she was using her TV voice and only speaking to me because she was scared I might tell.

'I'm delighted to have won – but I don't want the prize,' I suddenly heard myself say.

Sylvia had just taken delivery of two more coffees and having taken a huge mouthful spat it everywhere. She was destined not to get any coffee that day.

'Don't?' was all Bella said on the other end of the phone, I looked up to see her large face on screen, lips still quivering, eyes now darting around. Even I knew this would make good TV.

'Yes...' I cleared my throat. 'I was inspired by you,' I started, before going in for the kill, 'I read once in an interview that you said you spend most Christmas Days at a homeless hostel near where you live.'

She nodded, uncertainly, clearly worried where this was going.

'The thing is, I recently started to volunteer in my spare time at a local homeless shelter too – sadly there have been massive cuts made this year...'

She put her hand to her mouth in mock horror and I almost laughed.

'...and there won't be any money for Christmas dinner...'

'Oh, aren't you lovely?' she gushed all over my words, mouth smiling, eyes dead, her voice filling the air with such sticky-toffee sweetness it made my jaw ache. 'What a wonderful human being you are, Amy, fancy giving up your own time to help the homeless when you're almost homeless yourself.'

'No,' I said firmly, 'I don't have much, but I have enough. It's crazy to say I'm almost homeless, I'm a teacher, I have a roof over my head, I've had a tough time but I'm not destitute. Me and my kids will eat at Christmas, my mum taught me how to make a wonderful Christmas dinner on a shoestring, she was a wonderful cook,' I added pointedly. 'Therefore I would like to donate my prize to the St Swithin's Shelter for the homeless...where I would like you to come and spend some time cooking Christmas dinner with us all.'

The shock on her face was pure joy to see. 'No, no, no,' she blurted, too quickly, 'we want this Christmas to be all about you. I want to give YOU a Bella Christmas,' the camera closed in on her face, a study in horror.

'But Bella, these people have nothing, and nothing to look forward to except Christmas dinner at the shelter...'

'NO,' she almost shouted.

'Okay...it's your call, you can make that happen. Or not.'

She looked like she was about to collapse. Someone was obviously giving her instructions in her ear and she huffed and puffed. 'A percentage of the proceeds from Bella's Books is always donated to deserving charities at this time of year,' she suddenly piped up, her composure coming back as if she'd been given the lifeline she needed to get out of this.

'Yes, but having you there, helping them cook and give them back some dignity will mean so much more than a cheque in the post. We can show the country their plight at Christmas...well *you* can Bella...surely this isn't asking too much of a woman who gives so much.'

'No, I'm sorry ...'

'Not only could you provide one hundred homeless people with Christmas dinner, but if you bring your cameras, with your celebrity we can draw attention to the problem. You can give them the Christmas gift of a future,' I said, completely over-dramatising.

I heard voices in the background, saw her anxiously shaking her head on screen. She was listening to instructions in her ear again.

'Look, Amy,' she started, her voice as steely as her kitchen knives. 'If you *insist* on doing something for the...*homeless,*' she said through gritted teeth, 'then let me send them some of my Bella's Bakes? They are now available online,' she added brightly, giving out the website address without missing a chance to plug the merchandise.

'So what are you saying...let them eat cake – Christmas cake perhaps?' I asked, knowing this comment wouldn't be lost on the public, or any bloggers and journalists watching.

'No...no...' she stared at the screen, panic rising in her eyes, lips twisting into a grimace. She'd never encountered conflict or questioning on her cosy cookery programme, she'd only ever been feted by fans, and faced with me she was lost.

'I don't want to seem ungrateful,' I went on, 'but anyone can cook a family lunch, and Christmas lunch for under ten people is like a Sunday lunch with knobs on. But Bella, this lunch could involve up to a hundred people – maybe more, all hungry, all poor, all probably cold – and *all* deserving.'

'Oh no... oh, hang on, my producer's telling me...oh fuck!' she said, giving an audible gasp, as did Sylvia.

'It's live, please don't say "fu..."' I started.

'Oh God, stop... no. Oh yes, yes,' she cried, looking almost tearful.

'Wonderful,' I said. 'So that's a yes. Thank you, Bella, I'm so looking forward to this...' But I'd already been cut off, and when I looked at the screen Bella was now talking about 'swollen fruits' in her Christmas pudding like she hadn't just said the F-word live on air.

I put down the phone, feeling slightly uncomfortable about what I'd just done. It wasn't in my nature to be so forceful, so assertive, but anger was driving me – I just kept thinking about my mum and the people of St Swithin's. I'd also thought about the Neils and Bellas of the world, who'd hurt me and left me behind without even looking back, and felt justified. I was determined to turn the tables for once and make some of my own demands on behalf of me and my mum, who'd always been a doormat for the likes of Bella's family.

'You bloody dark horse,' Sylvia said, hugging me like I'd just run a marathon (I felt like I had). 'I don't know what that was all about, I bloody love you right now. Beatrice is going to have a heart attack when she finds out and the residents are going to think they've won the lottery. I don't believe it.' And after mauling me into another bear hug she preceded to jump around the postage-stamp size office like a woman possessed. Fortunately Paul Watkins wasn't around to film this - or the moment the TV fell off the wall.

Later that day I received a call from Crimson. 'Lucky girl,' she started, sarcasm dripping down the phone. 'A car will pick you up at your home tomorrow morning at 7 a.m. and bring you to Dovecote – it's only about twenty miles, so you should be here by

7.30. It will take a couple of days to film, so bring something to wear. Bella's looking forward to a big old catch-up.'

I bet she is, I thought, and so am I. 'That's good, because there's a lot to talk about,' I said, and put down the phone. I immediately texted Sylvia to confirm it was all happening, then I texted the kids, who said 'Go Mum!' (Jamie) and 'OMG that's fantastic! What are you going to wear?' (Fiona). I hadn't even had chance to think about clothes – perhaps it was time to treat myself to a couple of TV outfits after work?

I wandered around the local retail park that evening, fighting with frenzied Christmas shoppers just to find something to wear. I wanted something understated but colourful for my TV debut, but it wasn't easy amid the mass consumer panic. I couldn't concentrate on shopping, I just kept wondering how Bella would greet me after all these years. What would the dynamic be? If the phone call was anything to go by I reckoned she might push my face in one of her 'naughty' custard tarts! Whatever happened, I couldn't wait to see Bella Bradley unplugged, in her own home without cameras and make-up. Perhaps under all that slap and botox I'd be able to dig deeper. Who knows, I might find my old friend in there somewhere?

Chapter Seven

Baubles, Bangles and Baileys

That evening after I'd eaten supper I looked outside the kitchen window and through the darkness was a light sprinkling of snow. I held my mug of tea and wondered what the next few days would bring.

I was still looking out onto our tiny lawn when Fiona called my mobile; 'I rang because I'm really excited for you, but I'm worried too, Mum. I hope you get there safely in the morning, before the snow sets in,' she'd said.

'A professional driver's taking me, I'll be fine.'

'Has the snow made you sad, Mum?' she asked, which was probably the real reason for her call.

'Yes, I'm a bit sad, sweetie, but I'm fine.' The snow always made me sad, because it reminded me of the worst day of my life.

I'd been fifteen when my auntie had woken me on a cold, December morning to tell me it was snowing... and that my mum had died. I'd never imagined this in my worst nightmares, despite Mum being ill for some time, and at first I refused to believe it.

'No, not before Christmas, she wouldn't,' I kept saying, refusing to let any more information in. It was Mum's favourite time of year, and despite it always being about hard work and financial worry, she'd be as excited as us kids on Christmas day.

My life changed forever the day Mum died and our home was never the same again. It seemed to hold onto the cold of that desolate wintry December morning and I felt as though I would never be warm again.

I thought about that first Christmas without Mum later as I watched a recording of Bella decorating her own tree at Dovecote. She was about to make us all feel very unworthy as she stood by the huge piney fronds threatening to 'glitter every single one,' later in the show.

I was settling down to watch when Sylvia popped round with a bottle of Baileys and some jewellery she'd offered to lend me. She said the prospect of seeing one of her necklaces on TV was just 'orgasmic'... a very Bella word.

'You've been watching too much Bella already,' I smiled offering her a seat at the kitchen table.

'Yes, I love her – and I always have to watch 'Bella's Christmas Bake Off' with a Baileys at Christmas,' she said, plonking the bottle on the table and emptying out a million years' of baubles and bangles.

I took two small glasses out of the cupboard and turned the volume down on the TV.

'You practising your Christmas with Bella?' Sylvia asked, pointing to the TV.

'Yeah,' I smiled, 'like I need to glitter every branch of my Christmas tree – I ripped it down when Neil left.'

'Ah really? He's ended your marriage, don't let him take Christmas from you too, love,' she sighed.

'You're right, but I don't have the energy to reclaim Christmas tonight,' I said.

'Oh forget about him, just look forward to tomorrow when you're stood with Bella Bradley telling us how to create Christmas Charlotte Russe,' she laughed, squeezing my arm excitedly. My stomach dipped, I was so nervous, I knocked back the Baileys in one – it was warming and creamy and delicious and tasted of Christmas.

I'd drunk Baileys last Christmas with Neil – now just thinking about him sucked away all my Christmas spirit. He had rung me earlier and I'd told him all about my trip to Dovecote and that I'd be on Bella's programme.

'You?' he said, like he didn't believe it.

'Yes, why are you saying it like that?'

'Well, you're... you're no Bella Bradley are you, I mean she's gorgeous?'

That stung. 'I'm not trying to be her – and it has nothing to do with looks, I've just won the prize to cook with her and then she's coming to cook for the hostel on Christmas Day.'

'When is it being filmed – at the hostel?'

'Christmas Day... I just told you.' He never listened.

'Oh... it's just that I thought I'd come home for Christmas Dinner and see the kids and...'

'Well they aren't here – and neither am I.'

'But what will I do?' he said in all seriousness.

'I don't know, Neil. Maybe you could help Jayne grease her pole?'

I slammed the phone down, too enraged to talk.

'I'm worried what I'll look like on TV,' I said to Sylvia as we pored over her 'statement jewellery' and shared the Baileys. 'Neil said Bella's gorgeous and it made me think about how I...'

'Stop that right now,' she said, wagging her finger at me.

'You're an attractive woman, Amy, and don't worry, you can hold your own against Bella Bradley anytime. What would Neil know – he lost his taste in women the day he left you.'

I glanced up at the TV screen, the Silver Fox was now massaging oil into Bella's baking tins; it was quite distracting. At least Bella had finally found her Mr Right – but then she always landed on her feet.

'Neil is a dickhead – if you want to know, I never liked him,' Sylvia was saying as she poured us both another couple of drinks. I'd told her 'no thanks' after the last one, but Sylvia was on a roll. Was this the second or third glass? – I wasn't sure but I had a very early start and could hardly turn up on national TV half-baked. Generation YouTube already had me down as a homeless drunk.

Sylvia had been through a nasty divorce herself, but always stayed cheerful, helped others, and when it wasn't the homeless or some kid at school she'd identified as neglected, she was helping me. Just thinking about all the support and kindness she'd given me recently made me reach out and hug her.

'What's that for?' she said, hugging me back.

'Thanks for helping me through all this - I'm so grateful to have you in my life,' I said. After everything that had happened with Bella I had been wary of making friends, becoming too close. But since meeting her several years before, Sylvia had restored my faith in friendship, she was uncomplicated and selfless and I loved her for it.

She was half watching Bella on TV and smiling. 'Funny to think you'll be there tomorrow, actually at Dovecote... in her gorgeous kitchen. Everyone at school's recording it, I can't wait.'

'Yeah... it's exciting,' I said. 'Nerve-wracking, but exciting.'

'Look at her, she won't be rushing round Debenhams at ten to five on Christmas Eve, will she? I bet she has everything delivered and wrapped and she just "does" Christmas,' Sylvia sighed as she gazed longingly at Bella on screen.

We both sat watching Bella 'sparkle' a tree branch, lost in our own thoughts.

'Bloody hell, I wish I had the time to add glitter to individual branches,' Sylvia laughed.

I nodded; 'Christmas is stressful enough without having to do that. While she's glittering fronds, the rest of us are cleaning the house, out shopping and worrying if we've got enough money for everything.'

'And drinking Baileys,' she laughed, holding up her glass before becoming more serious. 'Amy, don't let Bella's life get to you while you're there,' she said. 'Money, beauty, a handsome husband, a mansion and a successful TV career isn't everything.'

We both laughed and she poured us another Baileys... though I couldn't remember finishing the last one.

Chapter Eight

Bella on Broadway

The following morning I woke and for a few seconds my mind was blank. Then I remembered what was happening that day and I almost threw up with nerves and a slight hangover. I looked around my room at the dated floral wallpaper, the old bedside tables Neil and I had bought together years ago – and thought perhaps it might be time for me to move house after all.

At the age of forty I'd be starting a new life on my own, which was scary, but exciting too. Why couldn't I have just a little bit of happiness, like Bella? Why did my life always have to be dull? I put on my old dressing gown, absently thinking that too needed to be replaced.

I'd bought a lovely below the knee brown skirt, an autumnal blouse and a long cardigan for the first day's filming. I'd spent money I didn't have but I was going on national TV and I'd worry about that when my credit card payment arrived in January.

I dressed quickly, made a cup of tea and breakfasted on Christmas cake. Tasting the moist fruitcake and nutty, buttery marzipan made me feel quite Christmassy, but the house showed no sign of the season. I thought about the decked halls and holly boughs that would greet me at Dovecote and what Sylvia had said the previous evening about not letting Neil take away my Christmas. I checked my watch; the driver was due in half an hour and I was ready, so I quickly ran upstairs and dragged out the Christmas tree I'd taken down days earlier. I grabbed a bag of baubles and put the tree back up in the living room, adding a few ornaments, but this time leaving any 'Neil related' ones in the bag. Then I poured myself a glass of sherry – yes it was early, but I needed it for my nerves – and it was almost Christmas. Sitting by the tree drinking the sherry renewed my faith in the season, and that morning as the snowflakes drifted slowly past the window I felt a little bit excited about Christmas. This was going to be a very different Christmas than the one I'd been expecting – and perhaps that wasn't such a bad thing after all?

❄ ❄ ❄

The car collected me as arranged with a lovely driver called Frank and we set off to travel the twenty-odd miles to Bella's country retreat in the Cotswolds. I knew from the glossy photos and breathless descriptions I'd read in magazines that Bella lived just outside Broadway, described as 'The jewel of the Cotswolds, a little village nestling beneath the Worcestershire hills'. I sometimes took the kids for daytrips in the summer when they were little, and just coming back here where nothing had changed made me feel safe. I loved the cosiness of the past and could feel my nerves calming slightly as we drove down the country roads we'd travelled as a young family.

I missed those days with the kids – being parents to twins had been total madness – everything happening at once – and in double doses. From first steps to first schooldays to first loves – to university, everything was in twos. Since their birth our lives had been transformed from calm to chaos and only in the past year when they both went off to uni had the calm descended again. Funny how you can get to love chaos though – I'd once complained of the noise of loud music and constant arguing, but now I had a whole house to read a book in and it felt empty. Be careful what you wish for, I thought, feeling as if everyone had gone to a great party and left me behind. Perhaps now, with Neil gone, it was time to find my own party?

I wound down the window and despite the freezing cold took huge gulps of country air, calming my nerves and filling my lungs with a tingly chill. The child in me was excited to see the snow really begin to come down – it made me sad because of Mum, but at the same time she loved this time of year and I had to stop seeing snow as a reminder of something bad. I smiled thinking of mum's joy when she'd look out of the window and shout, 'It's snowing, kids!' Neil's leaving meant there were going to be great changes ahead for me – but in order to make the most of my future I had to allow myself to enjoy any drop of snow or happiness that came my way. I was determined to try and shake free the guilt and sadness of the past – at least for Christmas.

I gazed out of the open car window at huge, twirling snowdrops now falling heavily from the whitest skies, slowly turning the golden Cotswold stone to sparkly white. The buildings were a lovely cliché of a Christmas shortbread tin – the kind you can never throw away even when it's empty. It was like a film set of Dickensian England, with tumbledown tea rooms and gift shops selling stuff you will never need but can't resist buying just because you're there. I spotted a lovely deli and imagined Bella shopping there for artisan breads and Italian olives, before popping into the gorgeous little tea rooms for hot Earl Grey and designer scones. We swept past the fabulously expensive interiors shop at the end of the high street and I just knew Bella would have an account there. It housed some of the most beautiful but expensive stuff I'd ever seen – a cushion cost as much as one of our sofas – I bet those cushions were scattered everywhere at Dovecote. Oh yes, this place was unreal, beautiful, and from what I'd seen of her on the telly over the years it was very, very Bella.

'Looks like this snow's going to stick,' Frank the driver predicted from his front seat and I nodded. I wasn't sure what to say, how to address him – I'd never been chauffeur-driven before and I felt quite uncomfortable. I suppose it was something Bella was used to, she must be driven everywhere. There you go again, I thought – I had to move on, stop comparing our lives and just enjoy the ride – literally. It was nice being able to sit back and enjoy the scenery.

'Some of these buildings date back to the sixteenth century and even earlier,' the driver said, coming over all tour guide-ish.

'Gosh,' I responded, 'I feel like we're back there – it's so different, like driving into the past...' which was just what I was doing by going to see Bella.

Bella's family might have had money, but her parents were always at work in their business and they had little time for their only child. One year when we were both ten, her mother asked if Bella could stay with us for Christmas. I'd overheard Mum telling my nan in a slightly angry voice that it was because they wanted to go somewhere warm for a holiday and didn't want 'the hassle' of a child. As we'd never had a holiday apart from the odd day out at Weston, I thought of warm places as ovens and fires and in my childlike way thought they wanted to leave Bella with my mum for Christmas because it would be safer and happier than this furnace-like holiday location. But Mum said to Nan she was shocked any parent could leave their child at Christmas and told me to pretend to Bella it was me who asked if she could stay with us to spare her feelings.

'But Mum, that's not true,' I'd said, frowning and confused at the mixed messages adults sometimes gave us. 'You said I mustn't tell lies.'

'There are some lies that you can tell,' she'd explained, stroking my hair, 'and this is a good lie because it will stop Bella from being upset. This is our secret Amy – and you must never tell anyone a secret.'

When Mum 'broke it' to Bella that she wouldn't be having Christmas in her own home we both waited for the tears, but after a moment to process the information, Bella was delighted. She was needy, attention-seeking and lonely – and in the absence of her own family around the kitchen table, she had mine. This is just one of the many reasons why I was finding her theft of Mum's recipes so hard to take. How could she take my mother's kindness and use it for profit? I didn't understand how she could do this to someone who'd done so much for her, but I was determined that one way or another spoiled brat Bella was going to pay for this.

❄ ❄ ❄

Sweeping past the high street on the way to Dovecote, we were suddenly surrounded by fields. They were patchy now, but soon a blanket of white would cover them completely, the driver was right, this snow was sticking, and ten minutes later when we pulled in to Bella's sweeping drive, her enormous Cotswold-stone home was virtually white.

It looked just like the cover of a Christmas 'House Beautiful'. She couldn't have planned it better for her TV show, the snowy exterior, lights twinkling in the bay, trees on either side of the huge double doors, and a golden glow coming from inside the kitchen. As we drove around the side, we were greeted with a bustling scene of TV vans parking up, cameras and crew being unloaded and even a small marquee being erected on the acres of lawn. I took everything in, eager for my first glimpse inside Bella's world.

'What's that?' I asked the driver, pointing to the large white tent almost disappearing in the snow.

'Canteen, for the crew to eat...the food truck's round the back, out of shot.'

'Oh...I would have thought as it's a cookery show the crew would eat what's cooked in the kitchen.'

'Ha ha, oh no, love. It doesn't work like that...besides, I'm not sure I'd want Bella's cooking!'

I thought that was perhaps a bit rude, she wasn't a great cook when I'd known her, but she seemed very competent and creative on screen - when she was using her own recipes. The world of TV was a mystery to me so I didn't ask any more. I supposed Bella was busy cooking for the cameras and didn't have time to make meals for the TV crew while she was filming. I didn't blame her either, there were too many mouths to feed – as the TV crew congregated on the front lawn I was amazed to see just how many people were involved in the making of one programme.

I almost felt my legs give way as I climbed out of the car, it all felt so unreal, I was here at Dovecote and finally about to meet Bella after all these years. As I waited for the driver to unload my bags I was suddenly accosted by a rather anxious woman who introduced herself as Felicity, Bella's agent. 'Dahling,' she squealed, bundling me into the house before I could even say hello.

'Hi Felicity...' I started.

'Call me Fliss, it saves time,' she said brusquely, running her hands through her short blonde hair, her face beautifully made up but not concealing the stress around her eyes. As she ushered me in, I was able to take in her bright pink outfit with matching kitten heels, which seemed quite out of balance for her short, wide stature.

Standing in that huge hallway with stone floor and an impossibly high ceiling, I had to stop and stare. I'd seen it many times on the TV, but here, now, I couldn't believe I was actually standing there. 'Wow, it's so beautiful,' I gasped.

'It's not a bad old bothy, is it?' Fliss sighed, looking around. 'It's swallowed up half my life and all of Bella's – this kind of real estate comes at a high price, my dear,' she looked at me then looked away quickly.

'Now, we want you to enjoy your stay', she said, suddenly moving on, with one foot on the stairs. 'Whatever you may think, and for whatever reason you're really here, we want you to enjoy this whole Christmas experience. But I beg you, please keep anything you may see or hear to yourself.'

'Like what?' I asked puzzled, but before she could answer I heard Bella's voice.

'Do you like my home then?'

I looked up to the top of the huge staircase where the voice was coming from and nodded.

'It's lovely... hello Bella.'

She was standing at the top of the stairs peering through the weight of holly boughs and mistletoe. I saw the arm of a red cashmere robe and below were slippers shaped like elephants (I'd seen them online, they cost as much as last year's family holiday). Eventually she peered round the boughs of holly and our eyes met for the first time in over twenty years.

'It's you, Amy... it is you, after all these years.' Her arms were out to welcome me, but the rest of her body language was saying something quite different. Her smile wasn't reaching her eyes and she wasn't moving towards me – the message was clear – she wasn't coming downstairs to me, I had to go upstairs to Bella.

There was an awkward silence where I didn't move and we just looked at each other. It felt less like two old friends and more like a stand-off in a western. What did I expect? She was being forced to entertain me here in her beautiful home and she simply didn't want me around. I was the past, her past – and I knew too much. This was purely about her 'playing nicely' to keep me quiet and keep her secrets and lies concealed from her adoring public, including her staff and the TV crew. It must have been a strange situation for Bella, who'd never done anything she didn't want to do in her life. As a kid her parents had spoiled her with money and 'things' to compensate for their absence and now she was indulged by everyone around her because of her fame. It must have been quite a shock having me suddenly reappear like the ghost of Christmas past.

I was still looking up the stairs and she was still looking down. It might have stayed that way for hours, but she suddenly seemed to remember why I was there – and put on her TV Bella mask.

'Let me show you your room, Amy,' she said, her face lit with false brightness. 'You're in the Mary Berry room, follow me.' She headed off down the landing and I was clearly expected to follow – one nil to Bella.

Fliss galloped behind Bella up the thickly carpeted stairway on those poor kitten heels, no doubt keen to keep her PR eye on proceedings, while I went to grab my bags, but a young man appeared at my side and took them. Bella had staff! There were various people milling around who looked like they belonged here, a woman was polishing mirrors, another was running upstairs with a breakfast tray, no doubt for Bella. Wow, I thought – I have to carry my own bags and make my own breakfast – how far she's come.

'Come on Amy, we've got a programme to make my love,' Bella was now calling me from the top of the stairs.

I nodded and took my time, I didn't rush - Bella may be calling the shots, but I didn't have to dance to her tune.

'All the bedrooms are named after famous TV chefs. The Jamie Oliver is a butch, rough-and-ready rustic style, Martha Stewart is clean and fresh – nice plaids and contrasting New England shades...' Bella was saying.

'But no bars on the windows!' Fliss added, roaring with laughter as she staggered up the final step.

Bella was standing in the doorway of 'The Delia Smith', and as we reached her she smiled at me and I almost glimpsed the old Bella. 'The Delia's all about team colours, yellow and green and bloody footballs everywhere, I can't stand it – but Delia would love it,' she winked. I smiled, bemused by her apparent friendliness, was she thawing so soon? I hoped so – perhaps it was a sign she would concede to my 'demands' and not just her way of charming me so I gave up and went home.

'I love Jamie and Nigella and Mary,' she sighed, drifting back into TV Bella voice, 'and I live in hope that one magical night they will all come to stay in their own rooms at the same time – imagine.'

'That would be good,' I said.

'Good?' Fliss interrupted. 'Dahling, it would be a PR feat of epic proportions – imagine the ten-page spread in Hello for that one? No...no, scratch that, it would be a PULL-OUT, or a souvenir special at least...oh be still my beating heart. Dahling, it's the kind of spread an agent like me dreams of.'

Fliss was such a drama queen you couldn't ignore her – but Bella was obviously used to this high-octane performance, she just rolled her eyes and carried on down the hall. I simply followed, feeling the soft carpet beneath and drinking in the panelled walls, the beautiful artwork and the clever lighting, illuminating the beautiful bits while hiding any flaws. As much as I hated decadence I was fascinated by Bella's world– and the sheer luxury of being able to devote empty rooms to named culinary celebrities was amazing to me. Especially now I'd have to downsize when I sold the house.

'You'll love The Mary Berry,' Bella was saying. 'It's safe and secure, and sleeping in there is like being wrapped in a mother's arms...don't worry, I don't mean *my* mother's arms,' she giggled. 'I wouldn't do that to anyone – not even my worst enemy,' she said, holding my stare a little too long. I looked away awkwardly, her mother's coldness was obviously still an issue in Bella's life. She hadn't been lucky like me – I suppose the parents we're born to is all down to luck and poor Bella got the short straw on that one. 'Nigella's lovely,' she said, quickly moving on, anything remotely distasteful was quickly disposed of in Bella's world. She was gesturing towards a black painted door on the other side of the hall: 'Scarlet velvet walls, black silk, huge pendulous chandelier...but the whole concept's a bit tramp-camp for my tastes,' she added, turning up her nose.

By now we'd arrived at yet another huge landing bedecked with Christmas arrangements, a large wooden banister decorated in green garlands and framed pictures of Dickens' book titles decorated the walls.

'I'm doing Dickens this year,' Bella gestured towards the pictures.

'Yes, I read about your Dickensian Christmas in The Radio Times,' I smiled. The smell of pine was spiky and strong, laced with oranges and cloves, it was so Christmassy and despite everything I couldn't help but feel a slight shiver of anticipation. 'It's very festive,' I remarked as she ushered me along the corridor to The Mary Berry Room.

She asked Fliss to arrange some coffee and when she'd gone Bella opened the door. 'Sometimes I just have to get Fliss out of my face,' she sighed, dropping her TV persona temporarily, for which I was very grateful.

'Yes, I can see she is quite a face full,' I smiled.

'So, here you are, the Mary Berry Room,' she said, waving me in.

Walking into the room, I was suddenly so rapt by the interior I almost forgot why I was there. The walls were pale buttermilk, and I don't think I'd ever seen a bed quite so huge – circular, like a ginormous wedding cake, piled with enormous cream cushions dotted with rosebuds. The carpet was thick and expensive and there was a huge portrait of Mary Berry over the fireplace, looking like European royalty in a tiara and off-the-shoulder gown. A large bookcase lining the wall was stuffed with Mary Berry cookery books, and on the bedside table Mary's autobiography lay by a signed, framed photo of the veteran kitchen goddess in pastel cardigan and pearls. It really was the most elegant style and I couldn't help thinking that Mary Berry would have very much approved.

'Ames...' Bella said, bringing me back into the here and now.

I looked at her and detected panic in her eyes, pleading in her voice as she spoke, 'I can't say too much out there, in front of everyone, but I was surprised when you called. I did want to see you, after everything happened, you disappeared and...I couldn't trust anyone ever again after what you did...'

'I know, but I couldn't find you.'

'I sent you some postcards years ago, did you get them?'

'Yes, I wrote back, but you kept moving...'

'I had to Amy...'

I was about to respond, but just at that point a man popped his head round the door.

'Ladies,' he said.

'Oh...hi Tim. Amy, this is tiny Tim, the director, he's short with an attitude but he gets there in the end,' Bella laughed, consummately covering her frustration at his ill-timed arrival. I was irritated too – I was just getting somewhere with Bella and maybe we could have cleared the air a little – our conversation was awkward and stilted and I doubted we'd resolve anything if it stayed that way.

Tim looked quite put out at Bella's 'Tiny Tim' reference, but I suspect he was a little scared of Bella who was after all the presenter and queen of Christmas.

He held out his hand. 'And you're our "real person", as opposed to all the fakes around here,' he said, looking at Bella, who smirked and turned away.

'Yes – I'm real. I'm Amy – I won the prize.'

'Mmmm and *what* a prize,' he said. I wasn't sure if he was being sincere or sarcastic. 'I must tell you... Amy?'

I nodded.

'I don't normally do these gigs... I'm usually treading the boards, I'm a born thespian...'

'A born what?' Bella was teasing him, gently but with edge, she'd always had a wicked sense of humour.

'Theatre to you,' he snapped back. 'Sorry Amy, but Bella only understands TV baking,' he winked at her but I could tell he meant it.

'Amy, I've just spent the last two weeks in Eastern Europe serving some salty Shakespeare,' he smiled as Bella headed off down the hallway back to the stairs. Any inroads that had been made had been undone by Tim's arrival and the way he was now monopolising me. Bella couldn't seem to get away fast enough.

'I'm good with a camera, but I'm better with a proscenium arch...' he was saying, as we followed Bella in hot pursuit, 'give me the smell of the greasepaint every time.' I tried to look impressed. I didn't want to know about this stranger, I wanted to see Bella, talk to her properly after all this time, but Tim was in my face and now Fliss had reappeared with a cameraman.

Standing on the bottom stair and leaning against the wall, barring my escape, Tim was determined to tell me all about himself.

Warming to his theme, his eyes meeting mine, his hands were in an over-the-top wringing gesture; 'It's all about performance, Amy.'

Bella appeared again having swept through the kitchen on her way to make-up. 'The nearest thing you'll get to "a performance" is Widow Twanky and a six-week stint in Cinderella in Margate,' she laughed.

He was hissing, she was spitting, but it was all in good humour – Tim seemed to enjoy being teased by Queen Bella.

'I'm about to take Amy into the sitting room and give her a quick debrief about how everything works,' Fliss said, giving me a sideways look. I imagined she wanted to read me the riot act about what I could and couldn't say and do. Yes, I'd no doubt given them all the impression I was on the verge of singing like a canary to the tabloids – but in my heart I could never do anything like that. Nevertheless, Bella and Fliss obviously didn't trust me – which was fair enough, I didn't trust anyone myself these days.

'Amy and I have lots to catch up on...you can't take her away from me,' Bella said, like a little girl whose favourite toy was about to be snatched.

'Yeah, but before you get your baubles in a twist we need to talk about what exactly you two are catching up on.'

'Fliss, please, Amy's only just arrived, she doesn't want to find herself in the middle of a "domestic", we have standards.'

'I may be a PR genius but there are some things even I can't cover up with Pan Stik and a double-page spread in Woman and Home,' Fliss snapped back. 'I need to be the first one to talk to Amy – she needs to know the score...'

'There is no score!' Bella said, with a familiar sulky look. 'I know the script because you've told me a million times. As far as the crew are concerned she's an old friend, to you and I she's an old friend who's threatening to blackmail me if I don't go to some filthy hovel and spend Christmas Day making slop. But to our viewers she's lovely Amy, who won the prize of a big, Bella Christmas,' She said, turning on the TV cheer as if already on camera.

I started to protest, but couldn't get a word in.

'Yes – and all I need YOU to remember,' Fliss said, pointing at me, 'is that what happens in Dovecote stays in Dovecote... or the homeless starve.'

'Charming,' I said, thinking how like a pantomime villain she was – but before I could add anything, Fliss was off again.

'I don't need any of this. I could be in Aspen this Christmas, but instead I'm stuck here trying to make a silk purse out of the proverbial sow's ear,' Fliss was saying. 'As if I don't have enough to do, it's looking like a great big "happy damage limitation Christmas" for me while I untangle your twisted youth – which just popped up like the Ghost of Christmas Past,' she said, gesturing towards me. I'd been called some things but 'Ghost of Christmas past' was a new one.

'Oh, take no notice of grumpy old Fliss,' Bella smiled her charming smile. 'You and me have lots to talk about Amy, so come through,' she said, coldly, steering me out of the hall and into the elegant sitting room.

I heard Felicity's voice grumbling and fading as we entered the room, which was cosy and 'antiquey' with duck-egg blue velvet sofas, enormous lamps and a huge hearth with a crackling log fire. Bella gently guided me to an armchair near the fire, the blast of heat was welcome after standing in the rather chilly hall, and as she took a seat opposite me she asked if 'anybody anywhere' was bringing her the coffee she'd asked for.

'You have a lovely home,' I started, feeling awkward, like I was talking to a complete stranger.

'It *should* be lovely, it cost me a bloody fortune to buy, and even more to maintain, and it's all real, no fake antiques at Dovecote,' she said, gesturing to an old clock on the mantle.

'Lovely,' was all I could say. There was something about her demeanour, brittle and cold like her mother, the old Bella who'd appeared briefly upstairs, the one I'd known since childhood, wasn't in the room.

I was upset, I'd only come to Dovecote for St Swithin's and my mother – but meeting Bella again I realised that deep down I'd naively hoped it would be like old times. I suppose I'd hoped that when we finally met at Dovecote we'd just collapse into giggles immediately reverting to our younger selves, slipping back into that easy friendship of our youth. Perhaps that's what I was looking for... my youth? I longed to see the real Bella, my old friend who I used to laugh with, the girl who was honest and open and hilarious. Yes, the old Bella had the potential to be annoying and a bit of a show-off sometimes, but this new TV Bella was an annoying show-off *all* the time. She pulled her robe around her, 'I have to say, Amy, I didn't expect to ever see you again,' she started.

'I'm sorry, I don't want you to feel I can't be trusted.'

'But you can't be trusted,' she said, looking incredulously at me.

'Yes I can, Bella. Look, I know I came on a bit heavy about the recipes, but they're important to me... and you took them.'

She stared at me through glassy eyes, but before she could answer the door of the sitting room swung open and a young girl dressed in rather dark clothing trudged in carrying a tray of coffee. She was what my kids would call 'a Goth' – her hair was dyed jet black and backcombed up, her eyes painted with thick, black eyeliner and her lips dark. I was surprised Bella had employed someone who looked like this, but perhaps this girl was good at her job?

'Put it down there, Crimson darling, we'll pour our own,' Bella said, crossing her long legs and leaning forward.

'Oh, Crimson?' I said. 'You're the researcher I spoke to on the phone..?'

'Yes... that's right,' the girl answered slowly like I was a child.

Bella ignored her and picked up the coffee pot. 'Mother?' she was smiling at me with an enquiring look on her face.

'Yours or mine?' I said. 'Where shall we start?' I was relieved and surprised she wanted to get down to the elephants in the room so quickly.

'Oh...no, I meant the coffee. Shall I be mother and pour it for you?' she said, like I was a complete idiot. I flushed and Crimson left the room sniggering.

'Yes... you pour for me, thank you,' I said, feeling stupid and trying not to sound tense... which was making me tense and stupid. I pulled my handbag towards me and discreetly checked to make sure I had a brown paper bag while hoping to God I wouldn't need it. Imagine the scene, me and Bella meeting in her beautiful sitting room after all these years with so much to say, her sitting there all manicured and glossy and me dribbling into a brown paper bag.

This wasn't how I'd imagined our first meeting. I'd hoped we could thrash out the past and get on with the present, but I suppose my hostel demands, accusations of theft and veiled threats of public exposure had put paid to that. Besides, Bella's world was all so stage-managed now, the messy stuff of our youth, our mothers, stolen recipes and the homeless was probably deemed unmentionable in a room like this. Sitting here in her expensive world of privilege, I doubted Bella and I could ever pick up where we left off and be friends again. Just looking around at the antiques, the huge sash windows, the high ceilings and the Farrow and Ball wall shades was confirmation – if I needed any – that we now lived in very different worlds.

Bella poured black coffee into china cups from the ornate silver coffee pot, holding it high in her elegant hand, steam rising, a spectacular diamond glinting from her ring finger. As she handed me a cup and saucer, her perfect, scarlet nails touched my own unvarnished bitten ones and we both pulled away quickly.

Like mirror images we took a sip of coffee and our eyes met briefly, then we continued to sip in sync and silence. The warmth of the fire was welcome and calming and I sat back among the cushions, the aroma of the rich brew filling my nostrils. Carols played in the background and a beautiful twinkly branch glittered over the mantelpiece, sending shards of light around the room.

'It took you hours, didn't it?' I said, thinking about how Sylvia and I had watched Bella laboriously glittering each branch on TV the previous night.

'No... it took Crimson hours,' she laughed. 'I couldn't be bothered glittering every bloody twig, life's too short.'

'Yes, life is short,' I said, 'so why throw away a friendship? Why do you still, after all these years, refuse to forgive me?' I heard my words land in the steamy coffee silence.

'Oh Amy, it's too complicated... you don't understand.'

'I don't understand why you have cut me off and ignored my Christmas cards for years,' I said.

She looked down, played with the tiny silver spoon on the saucer.

'You ruined my life when I was a teenager,' she started, 'but I'll be damned if you'll do the same now.'

I was shocked, she wasn't looking at me, just stirring her coffee slowly. The words were strong enough to convey her hatred. It had been easy to talk on the telephone and almost satisfying to watch her squirm on live TV, but this was different. We were alone in her home – face to face – and I suddenly saw what she saw. I had caused all that trouble in her past and now I was back to cause more trouble. What sort of person had I become? Neil's departure had scarred me, and Bella's betrayal of my mother had hurt me and perhaps hardened me too? It occurred to me that I was now taking all that pain and upset and loading it onto Bella.

'I'm not a bad person, Bella. I never meant to hurt you,' I said, a catch in the back of my throat. I feared she may not have forgiven me, but to say I'd 'ruined' her life really stung. 'And me being here now is all so mixed up – I'm going through a tough time and I'm angry because you've taken something that belonged to me and... you've made me suffer all these years.'

'I made *you* suffer? That's funny.'

'You know I meant no harm, Bella. I thought I was helping you...'

'Helping? Is that what you called it? Is that what you're doing now?'

'No... I'm sorry about what happened... before, and I don't blame you for believing I "ruined" everything. But I didn't do it with malice, and if you want to talk about "ruining lives" what you're doing now, refusing to forgive me for what happened years ago, has ruined mine. I worried about you, I couldn't sleep...'

'Neither could I,' she snapped. 'I'm glad you know how that feels.'

'So this is your revenge for what I did – using Mum's recipes?' She didn't answer.

'Bella, it's malicious – it's... it's theft.'

'Theft is a very strong word. If you mean that each year you sent me some Christmas recipes in a card and now I've adapted them for a book... then that's different.'

'It's not, you're claiming them as your own.'

'Did you claim copyright? Do you have lawyers involved? Is there anywhere on those cards or those scrawled pieces of paper that say "please Bella don't put these in a book"?'

I was shocked at her vindictiveness, the way she was looking at me like I was a bad smell under her nose.

'I don't know what kind of world you live in Bella – oh hang on, I think you just gave me a clue. And in answer to your ludicrous question, no, I didn't think I needed to protect bloody copyright because they were notes to a friend... they were meant just for you and no-one else.'

'Like when I told you not to tell anyone – that was meant just for you.'

She had me there.

'Well yes, I understand that you might feel I... betrayed you, I told your secret – but I didn't put it in a bloody book, did I?'

'You might as well have done.'

'I'm sorry, I'm so, so, so sorry. I don't know what else I can say. I can't change what I did and what happened as a result of that – but trust me I've lived with the guilt ever since. If you publish these recipes you will live with the guilt too. I know you loved my mother, she was there when your own mother wasn't – and you are taking something precious from me, but mostly from her.'

'Don't be so nasty, I'm honouring you and your poor mother by putting her recipes in my cookery book. Now, everyone can share them....'

'I doubt you'll share any of the royalties though,' I spat.

'Oh, it's about money, is it?' She put down her cup and saucer, sat back and glared at me. 'Why didn't you say? So how much do you want?'

'I... no. I don't want anything. You've got this all wrong...'

'When I really needed you, when I was lost and alone, you – my best friend – were nowhere to be seen. Then twenty two years later, when you've got no money and your husband's left you for a stripper, you call me up. You threaten to reveal my teenage past, accuse me of stealing something *you* sent to me, and blackmail me into filming in a homeless shelter on Christmas Day. Now you're complaining that I'm not sharing my royalties with you.'

'No, it's not like that. I'm not interested in your money, I don't want anything for me... it's about Mum and the shelter. I can see I've been clumsy and made myself look bad, but honestly, everything I've done has been done in kindness...'

'Oh stop being so damned pious. I don't want to hear about you, your mother's bloody recipes or some awful stint on Christmas Day with filthy homeless people,' she said, sounding just like she did when she was a kid.

We both sat in silence, I was shaking with rage and anger and hurt and Bella looked shaken too. After a few minutes she started to speak.

'Look... Ames, about the homeless... thingy,' she said, her tone suddenly quite different, she was trying to cajole me now.

'What about it?'

'Well it's like this,' she said slowly and calmly like she was trying to make a violent, insane person see her point of view. 'No one wants to turn on their TV to watch homeless people drooling over their turkey on Christmas Day. It's enough to put viewers off their sprouts. My audience want perfect families, biblical epics and beautiful cookery shows, they don't want this... this homeless... rubbish. It will be a disaster. And the real tragedy in all this... is that your little shelter wouldn't get any coverage because the viewers would be turning off in their droves.'

'Don't patronise me, Bella.'

'I wasn't.'

'You were – and in my humble opinion, as a viewer – I can tell you they wouldn't turn off.'

I watched her play with her beautiful nails, and realised that she was still a spoilt little kid putting herself first.

'Well, you've given me no choice in the matter, with your threats to run to the papers with some made-up stories. As I said before, once more you've come into my life and wrecked it.'

'No I haven't... I still care about you, I don't want to hurt you or wreck anything... but it seems you're going all out to hurt me. I miss the old Bella,' I said, trying to reach her.

'Well, the old Bella's gone now,' she said sadly into the silence. 'We seem to have no other option here. So, if it will stop your whining, I'll do it. But trust me, no one will watch it – my viewers want me in my perfect kitchen serving a big Bella Christmas to nice employed people in their own homes with their own teeth...'

'Oh what a lovely world you must live in, Bella,' I sighed. 'You have the luxury of being able to ignore everything that isn't pretty to look at.'

'Yes, you're right, I do. Reality can be a bitch and I hate looking at it – talking of which you aren't wearing that, are you?'

'Yes...why?' I said, looking down at my lovely new autumnal blouse while pulling my new rust cardigan around me protectively.

'No reason,' she flicked her long dark hair. 'I mean, if you *want* to stand in front of several million TV viewers looking Amish that's fine with me.'

I could feel myself curling up, trying to make myself invisible – this wasn't the first time this criticism had been levelled at my fashion aesthetic. I'd thought my outfit was perfect, and it was, for my world – but perhaps not for Bella's more glamorous one. 'But it's new... I bought it specially.'

'It's horrific.'

'But I've only brought a couple of things with me to wear,' I stood there, feeling naked, awkward in my new clothes.

'You need to see Miss Thing in wardrobe, she'll sort you out.'

'I thought I was okay... didn't realise I'd need sorting out,' I said, feeling quite crushed and looking down at my lovely new cardigan.

'Stop feeling sorry for yourself. All I did was tell you the truth about your sad little cardi – you've done far worse to me,' she snapped. 'You've ruined my bloody Christmas by making me schlep all the way to the Midlands to cook for a load of people on benefits.'

'They're aren't on benefits...'

'Oh no, that's a different series, but they aren't exactly the glitterati either are they? I'm not happy about being forced to hang around with a bunch of losers, up to my tits in tinsel and turkey on the twenty-fifth,' she snapped.

'I'm sorry if your perfect Christmas might be blighted by helping other people for once,' I said.

'Oh Amy, nothing is perfect – and nothing is ever quite as it seems...' she started, just as Fliss appeared in the doorway like the avenging Angel.

'Did somebody mention tits and tinsel? If so I'm your woman,' she giggled lifting her arms and shaking her ample chest.

Chapter Nine

From Laura Ingalls to Jessica Lange

'Now, my little nest of festive vipers... anything I need to know?' Fliss was flustered, excitable and obviously keen to stop Bella and I saying too much when she wasn't in the room.

'Yes – filming starts in twenty-five minutes.' Bella stood up, clearly I was now dismissed. Our reunion had resolved nothing at all, my mother's recipes were still in Bella's name and she still hadn't forgiven me – I wondered if she ever would.

'Fliss, make sure everyone is ready... I don't like to be kept waiting,' she said, assertively.

Fliss rolled her eyes. 'How many times do I have to tell you, I'm your agent – not your assistant, I don't recall "rolling over and sucking up to Bella" written on the contract. And as much as I hate to break up this cosy little chat about your idyllic childhood spent skipping through suburbia hand in hand,' Fliss grimaced, 'YOU need to get dressed,' she pointed at Bella, then she looked me up and down. 'And YOU need to... oh God... are you really wearing that?'

Bella sniggered.

'Why does everyone keep asking me if I'm wearing this?'

'Because you look like something from "Little House on the Prairie".'

'I see it as more "Amish chic"...?' Bella offered with a giggle.

'Yes that too,' Fliss said in all seriousness. 'Well, whatever you've come as, I think we need to get you to make-up and wardrobe – with some urgency.'

Fliss then rushed me through the house like it was a medical emergency, pushing open a door and dragging me into a messy home office.

'Come on, chop chop, it's not bedtime yet,' Fliss said, clapping her hands.

A woman was lying across a sofa and a youngish man was rummaging through the clothes on a freestanding rail in the middle of the room.

'For god's sake, Billy, that isn't your colour,' Fliss said as we walked in.

He pursed his lips, put down the pale pink dress he'd been clutching and turned dramatically away from the clothes.

'Now, Ruth, get off the sofa and dress Laura Ingalls here, I'm thinking more Desperate Housewife and less Breaking Amish... sex her up, but not too much,' she added. 'And Billy, get out your magic tool box, you are going to need every ounce of make-up artistry you have to get this one off the ground.'

'I'll want overtime,' he sniggered, looking me up and down.

Was I completely invisible to these people or were they really that rude? Billy was in no hurry, took out a nail file and began filing his nails. Then Ruth (who seemed to be the wardrobe department) sat up, hair on end. She was wearing jeans and a jumper – which wasn't very inspiring considering she was about to 'dress' me for television.

'You're asking me to turn one of the Waltons into Sarah Jessica Parker?' she said, looking me up and down. 'Mmmm unless we can get a Christmas miracle from somewhere, this ain't gonna happen. *Next* Christmas? Maybe.'

Billy roared at this and gave Ruth a high five, but Fliss wasn't laughing. 'There won't be a *next* Christmas for any of us if you don't get a grip of this,' she was pointing directly at me, 'and turn water into wine.'

I was incredulous. All this time I was standing in the middle of the room feeling completely exposed and they were just taking me to pieces, bit by bit.

'I'm *here* you know,' I said, in an attempt to stop any more insults, but no one was listening.

'I will be back in fifteen minutes and if she isn't looking like a vodka-drinking gardener-shagging housewife, then heads will roll,' Fliss barked. She went to leave then turned dramatically, 'Oh and when I say that – I don't mean make her look more fabulous than the original desperate housewife out there... remember, no one puts Bella in a corner.'

'God forbid,' Ruth muttered while producing a red trouser suit from the rack. I was a little surprised at their comments – I thought everyone loved Bella Bradley.

'Try this on,' Ruth said, pushing it at me.

'I'm not really a red kind of girl,' I murmured, as she virtually pulled my clothes off and forced me into a pair of trousers that were a size smaller than I was. When we eventually zipped them up, I felt quite uncomfortable but I didn't have time to think about it because Billy was now coming at me with a big sponge full of foundation.

'I don't wear much make-up,' I said, cringing from the wielded sponge.

'You do now, love. You'd disappear under those lights...so mousey.' Then he stood back and 'surveyed' me. 'Have you considered going blonder?'

'Not in the next ten minutes,' I said, worried he'd start hurling bleach at me before Fliss's threatened return. He shrugged, dabbed my whole face with concealer and threw a tonne of face powder over me, which made me cough. He followed this with several layers of bright lipstick and was just spraying a whole can of 'Bigger Blonder' on my hair when the door opened and Fliss waltzed back in.

'Dahling, it's fabulous – very Jessica Lange circa 1998,' she gasped. 'Red suits you, little Amy.'

They were all smiling at each other and I realised that as scary as all their earlier arguing and stroppiness seemed – it was just a pose. These people may not be the on-screen stars but everything they did was for the camera – even when it wasn't there. And it was clear that Billy and Ruth had timed the makeover for 'the reveal moment' as Fliss stepped back into the room. Everything was a performance and they wheeled out a full-length mirror (just like on

TV, where the woman gasps at what the experts have done to her house/hair/life) then waited for my reaction. I knew the script as well as they did and it was expected I'd be pleased – but even I was surprised and delighted and didn't need to pretend. I looked amazing and not at all like the 'mousey' Amy who Fliss had brought in. 'I can't believe it's me,' I said, looking at a red lipped blonde in a beautiful and flatteringly tight designer trouser suit in scarlet.

Gone was 'little Amy' the maths teacher in her best floral blouse and big rust cardi – here was a woman who looked taller, younger, blonder. I hated to admit it, but Bella and Fliss had been right, that cardi and long skirt weren't doing me any favours. I just had to see this – the lady in red – to realise what I could be.

'How did you do it?' I asked, looking from Ruth to Billy.

'We get a lot of practice,' Billy smiled. 'You should see that old hag Bella first thing in the morning,' and they all laughed. Meanwhile I primped and preened in the mirror like a wannabe supermodel, pursing my lips and wondering what Year Ten would say if they could see me now. My real life suddenly felt a million miles away.

❄ ❄ ❄

Walking back through the house at a more leisurely pace, I was able to enjoy the old-fashioned Christmas Bella had created at Dovecote. Beautiful trinkets and baubles of Dickensian 'Victoriana' were everywhere. Vintage, Victorian-style glass and white lace baubles decked the tree, along with hand-crafted, beaded ornaments, white candelabra and gold angels. She'd thought of everything, well, someone had - from tasteful floral arrangements to a huge swag of holly and fairy lights over the sitting room mantelpiece and the air was scented with the most exquisite smell of warm cloves laced with the freshness of pine.

'Chop chop,' Fliss shouted, guiding me into the kitchen and seating me on a stool in the corner so I could observe while she bossed everyone around.

Bella was holding a beautiful garland made from holly and Christmas roses entwined with fairy lights. 'I made this earlier,' she was saying to Tim, which I doubted because apparently she'd only just got out of bed when I arrived. Looking around me, I found it hard to imagine glamorous Bella with her perfect nails creating the huge garlanded fireplace, and attaching all the glittering lights along the high-ceilinged hallway.

'My baubles are designer – and I will only allow hand-made decorations into my home,' she was saying. 'Can you even begin to *imagine* shop-bought baubles at Dovecote?'

'Perish the thought,' Crimson muttered as she passed through with a pile of papers and her permanent frown.

❋ ❋ ❋

I watched as Billy transformed Bella with lipstick and powder and thought how this year would be very different, for Bella, not just for me. There would be no celebrity-peppered glittering luncheon for madam this year, as her programme would reflect a real Christmas with real people. My only worry was whether or not this grown-up Bella did real people anymore and how she would relate to them. Yes I know she'd said she supposedly spent time on Christmas Day at homeless hostels but I couldn't help feel that this was yet another PR masterstroke. At best I reckoned Fliss had Bella turned up and show her face just long enough to count before being whisked straight back to the glamour of Dovecote. I watched Billy carefully apply foundation then smoky eyes and as he finished off with powder, a drink was handed to Bella with a straw so her lipstick wouldn't be spoiled. She was treated like royalty, and did nothing for herself, which further worried me – what were the chances of the Queen of Christmas rolling up her sleeves, mucking in and bringing a happy Christmas to the homeless? It might just be a wish too far.

Bella had left the make-up chair and was now talking through her moves with Tim. I stayed on my stool just watching everyone preparing, still unable to believe I was actually here at Dovecote, the place of Christmas fantasy. From watching the programme over the years, I knew the kitchen inside out – which cupboard was where and where everything was kept. I knew if you turned right in the kitchen it would lead into the lovely dining room with its ladder-backed chairs and long oak table, and I knew if you turned left and through the hall you would find the duck-egg blue sitting room.

I gazed through into the conservatory, which was on the back of the house, where last year's Christmas Eve show 'Twas the Night Before Christmas' had been filmed. I'd watched in awe that night as Bella had prepared a cosy family supper – she'd dressed the conservatory in fairy lights and silver and white baubles. She'd been holding a dry sherry in one hand while giving a turkey internal with the other... without flinching and I'd gasped in admiration – Bella Bradley always had Christmas nailed. Later that night as I stuffed my turkey, she was, as usual, ten steps ahead and onto the final gift wrapping. 'Now take the contrasting bow and twist carefully around the paper,' she'd said as she placed the last present under the tree. Hundreds of other gifts in every shape and size sat under the huge bedecked pine branches in her hallway. The table in the conservatory was set, a luxury fish pie was in the oven and the family were on their way. It had all looked so beautiful, it took my breath away when I saw her standing there amid the glitter.

As the credits had rolled we were treated to a montage of lovely soft-focus shots of Bella and Peter playing in the snow. Bella all in white with fur trim; the Silver Fox sporting an expensive blue parka and designer wellies, love glittering in their eyes. I remember thinking they looked like something from a French fashion magazine, and how I'd love just a taste of what she had.

Now, sitting in her fabulous state of the art kitchen a year later listening to her eulogising about the 'crisp and plump' savoury pastries she was making for 'Boxing Day Buffet', I had to smile to myself. Somewhere in the early nineties there'd been quite a transformation from cigarette smoking, wild living party girl to kitchen goddess, and the only person I could credit with that was the divine Peter Bradley. As if by some amazing, magical coincidence there was suddenly a rush of cold air, a door slamming shut and someone 'landing' in the hall – the Silver Fox was in the building. Everyone was immediately on high alert and judging by the way

Bella abandoned her 'crisp but plump pastry pillows' and ran from the room, she was very pleased to see him. There was a kerfuffle in the hall and within seconds he was brought into the kitchen, Bella hanging on his arm. She was looking up into his eyes, his handsome rugged face smiling into hers.

If it hadn't been so crass, I'd have loved to take a picture and send it to Sylvia, because the Silver Fox was even more delicious in the flesh. Hidden behind cameras and lights, and tucked away in the corner I was able to stare openly without him even being aware of Bella's 'prize winning fan.' He was tall, with a weather-beaten tan and a whiter than white smile – and the fairy lights seemed to dim in his presence. Now I knew for certain – Bella Bradley had everything.

She fussed around him, preening and touching him in such an intimate way you just knew they were in for one hell of a reunion in the 'Bella Bradley' room that night.

After a few minutes of Bella purring and pawing, Tim suggested Peter might like to join in the filming, but Peter shook his head, he clearly wasn't up for it.

'Just a few words, a little moment?' Bella said, making big eyes at him. 'Oh go on... baby, I *need* you,' she breathed.

Eventually Peter nodded reluctantly and threw his big, muscular arm around Bella, who positively swooned (along with every other female in the room).

The Silver Fox seemed charming, and though he clearly wasn't as comfortable in the kitchen as he was in Syria, he did his bit. He made complimentary remarks about Bella's pastries while gently rubbing her back, while Mike the cameraman closed in and Tim screamed 'go baby' for no apparent reason.

Peter had a rugged easiness about him that was charismatic and completely drew you in. You wanted him to notice you, even though you just knew it was futile – he only had eyes for one woman. I was rapt watching him lean on the counter drinking in his beautiful wife as she made love to the camera. 'You have to be firm but gentle,' she was saying, never taking her eyes from his while massaging maple syrup and brown sugar into a huge ham. It might have been a Christmas cookery programme but the two of them together were almost pornographic – and if you ask me she was being far too suggestive for daytime TV.

'Ooh sweet and sticky Christmas yumminess,' she said, and I wasn't sure if she meant Peter or the ham, but she was soon going back in for more meat manipulation. She rubbed and oozed marinade with a running commentary that wouldn't have been out of place in the Playboy Mansion. 'It makes my hands really soft too,' she added, gently caressing Peter's face with syrupy fingers, leaving his neck all sticky. I just knew she was going to lick that off later... hell she might just do it now, I thought, the kitchen was positively sizzling with sexual tension.

When she eventually finished the 'ham scene', someone off camera offered her 'a post-coital cigarette', which made the Silver Fox and Fliss roar with laughter.

But Bella didn't laugh, she was still engrossed in her performance, holding the huge ham in a tray against her bosom and promising faithfully it would be 'moist... very...*very* moist.'

Suddenly, with the ham barely in the oven, the Silver Fox announced abruptly that he was 'exhausted' and off to bed.

I wondered if it had all been too much for him. Bella was a beautiful woman and men get lonely in war zones, he was probably very aroused and needed to get out of there before his lust got the better of him.

'Oh sweetie, stay a little longer?' Bella asked, eyes wide, pelvis against his.

But he kissed her on the forehead. 'Too tired, baby,' he smiled and we all watched as he slowly wandered out through the kitchen. Like a bloody rock star.

'Dahling, get a room,' Fliss said when he'd left and the cameras were off.

Tim tutted at Fliss.

'My husband likes me to be seductive,' Bella breathed, 'and so does Tim... on screen anyway, don't you, Timmy?'

'Yes, and that last scene was so orgiastic I wonder if either of you listen to anything I say,' Fliss sighed. 'Tim, Bella, we've talked about this my dahlings...we need to calm it down a little... with the sex,' Fliss said. 'I mean all the innuendo, the hedonism. It's family Christmas dinner on daytime TV not a bacchanalian feast,' Fliss barked. 'We need to think about your branding, dahling,' she said in a more soothing voice.

Bella looked from Felicity to Tim, surprised. 'But it's my trademark, sex *is* my branding, you said.'

'Yes, but that was in 1998, nowadays people are bored of sex and serious shopping. The damned economic crisis ruined things for everyone and the plebs now want more substance with their cookery shows...it's less "Bella's Breasts" and more "Bella's Benefits".'

'Damn the economic crisis!' Tim suddenly shouted, banging his fist against the nearest wall and making everyone jump.

'Calm down, Tim, you're not in panto yet!' Fliss called over her shoulder. 'Now, Amy's suggestion has been a wake-up call and has got me thinking – times are tough out there.'

Finally, someone was agreeing with me, my voice was being heard.

'Homeless hostels, poor little children starving on the streets and food banks popping up like brothels in Amsterdam. It's time to think of the bigger picture, the world has changed, Bella, and you shouldn't be doing... that... with a big *moist* ham.'

'Rubbish, people love to see glamour, sex, and moist hams in the kitchen at Christmas.' Bella was angry.

'I disagree. You don't see lovely Mary Berry massaging syrup into meat like it's a man's buttock, do you? The evidence is in front of you... look at poor little Amy starving, dressed like one of the Waltons while her husband's trawling the streets looking for loose women...'

'He's not...' I tried. 'He left me for a bedroom pole dancer...' I started.

'Thank you, Amy, this isn't about you,' Bella snapped.

Crimson cackled from her corner, her face lit only by the iPad in front of her, lighting her white make up and giving her black and green hair an eerie glow.

Then Fliss started again, 'Bella, dahling, it was all very well doing sex and soufflés and giving it to us like a page 3 wannabe ten years ago when you were nubile and Nigella was on her throne. But now Mary Berry's back you're not competing with sensuality over the salsa any more. Mary's a grown woman who knows her spices and doesn't feel the need to share her drives and juices with the world while her dough's proving. Mary's coming for you Bella – and brace yourself because she's baying for blood, and waving her rolling pin.'

I wasn't entirely convinced by this image of lovely Mary Berry, who I was sure would never wave her rolling pin... or bay for anyone's blood.

Bella looked close to tears, which I guessed was more to do with the fact the Silver Fox had just gone to bed without her rather than anything Fliss was saying.

In that moment I actually felt quite sorry for Bella. Her wonderful husband was back from a war zone and all she wanted to do was strip off and leap all over him on the stairs leading to a three-day sex and chocolate marathon in their big bed. But while he slept like Adonis upstairs she had to stay in the kitchen and get her kicks from maple roasted ham and pastry pillows. For the first time I could see a drawback to being Bella, she couldn't even welcome her husband back because she had a houseful of people and a programme to make.

Meanwhile back on planet Bella, Fliss was now holding her by the shoulders and shaking her firmly.

'Look my love, wake up, smell the coffee, brace yourself and step up to the plate.'

So many instructions in one sentence, no wonder Bella looked baffled. Along with everyone else, I watched, mesmerised, it was yet another performance and I had a front row seat.

'Stop mooning over Peter and get your pinny on.'

'Just a few moments... with him?' Bella asked, sounding like some lovesick puppy.

'No we have no time for that, you have a programme to make – we need you down here raising those ratings, not upstairs raising Peter's. On screen we need you to be strong and asexual, you're up against the Queen of cake, the doyenne of doughnuts. Dahling, it's a case of "operation Christmas Berry"... see what I did there? Mary Berry, Christmas...?'

'Oh shut up, Fliss. Stop scaring me and telling me to step up, that's your job... if my ratings are slipping then *you* need to do something, you're my agent...THIS IS AN EMERGENCY!' she yelled. Bella had always had a temper and I could see the little girl now with her hands on Fliss's shoulders shaking them quite firmly as Fliss shook her. They wound each other up and any minute one of them was going to slap the other, claiming 'she was hysterical'. It was like some weird double act.

What the hell was going on here? Why was Bella shouting, why was her agent barking at the moon, and most importantly why was the gorgeous Silver Fox in bed at ten o'clock in the morning, completely alone?

Bella was clearly upset and cross with Fliss and if memory served me well her temper may soon reach boiling point. I recalled a similar scene in our kitchen at home when at the age of eight I'd suggested my cupcakes were prettier than hers. It hadn't ended well, when Bella snatched up my plate of cupcakes and threw them on the floor, screaming 'Whose cupcakes are prettier now?'

Meanwhile, Fliss and Bella were still screaming at each other and only when Fliss told her the truth did she seem to hear her.

'Bella... when I said the ratings aren't good, I meant, bad... like dropping... no, dahling, I lied, they are plummeting.'

At this, Bella whipped off her scarlet pinafore, hurled it to the ground and stomped off through the kitchen, and from the thumping noise, I guessed she'd gone upstairs. This was confirmed when a door above us was slammed so hard it nearly took the paint off the ceiling.

Good luck getting any sleep in there now, Peter, I thought, imagining that poor beleaguered war hero in a tangle of sheets desperate for some peace while she banged on about her precious ratings.

I looked around, but everyone seemed to be taking Bella's dramatic exit in their stride, obviously used to it. Billy, who it seemed was rarely vertical, now lay on the sofa in the living room, while the camera and sound men wandered off for a bacon sandwich, unperturbed. Fliss was muttering to Crimson that 'we are a man down' and she was looking vacantly back at her, which seemed to be her default look.

'What happens now?' I asked Fliss, walking towards her and Crimson, who was now sitting on the kitchen worktops painting her nails – black.

'Hi, Crimson.' I smiled, she was obviously as crazy as the rest of them, but I was desperate to bond with somebody on this shoot.

'Hi Amy,' she monotoned without even looking up from her shiny dark talons. And just to give an indication of how lonely I felt, I was actually pleased to hear those disinterested tones laced with sinister sarcasm.

She finished panting her nails, looked up and seemed genuinely surprised, though it was hard to work out her emotions under the white make-up and eye-shadow. 'Jeez, what happened to you?' she said. 'You looked like a weirdo when you came in this morning, but you look okay now,' she said this without a smile, but I guessed coming from Crimson this was a compliment, I couldn't possibly expect a smile too. 'That red is sick on you...' she said, looking me up and down.

'Thank you,' I smiled, hoping she meant 'sick' in the way Year Ten said their favourite bands were 'sick' and not in any way a reference to me looking like vomit – it seemed with Crimson one could never be sure.

'When you walked in before, you looked like you'd just stepped out of ...'

'Yes I know. I look quite different now,' I said quickly in an effort to stop any more allusions to the Amish community. I'd arrived with little self-esteem as it was and after the battering I'd taken earlier from Fliss, Bella, Ruth and Billy the last thing I needed was Crimson the Goth researcher/maid giving me her unplugged opinion on my wardrobe.

'What happens now?' I asked.

'What always happens. We wait, the cameramen eat, the world turns...' Crimson sighed.

'Yes and the budget goes through the sodding roof,' Fliss added tightly. 'At this rate we won't be finished until midnight.'

'Do any of the recipes need preparing?' I asked. 'Can we save time before she comes back down?' I was worried hours would be taken up with waiting and there'd be no time left for me to actually talk to Bella properly after filming, which was one of the main reasons for coming here.

'What we need is Bella to actually be down here doing her job for once, I'd take a bloody Bella lookalike right now, someone to stand in for a few shots and... hang on, give me your hands,' Fliss said, nearly pulling my arms out of my sockets in her sudden desperation to get to my hands then screeching 'Billy... Billy dahling... emergency treatment needed at the bunker.'

Billy appeared at my side with his bag of tools.

'Billy, my angel, would you please brandish your magic wand and turn Amy's fingernails into Bella's so we can use her hands in a close-up. If we don't get something in the can the budget won't take all these people hanging around doing nothing... and I don't want to be the one to tell them we can't leave the trenches until midnight.'

'Erm, shouldn't we see if Bella's happy about this?' I said, worried about the fallout of me filming in her kitchen without her.

When I'd offered to help I simply meant by getting the ingredients together, maybe breaking a few eggs, not being the star's hand twin.

Before I knew what was happening, Billy was working on my nails, filing and buffing and polishing and then covering them in the glossiest reddest varnish I'd ever seen.

'Wow it's lovely,' I said waggling my new scarlet talons as Fliss gathered the crew together for what she called 'a war cabinet debrief', but what looked to me like a chat over coffee and fags on the freezing back lawn.

Eventually they all came back in and I still couldn't quite get over how beautiful my hands were. I kept staring at them. It was as though Bella's hands had been photo-shopped onto mine. Billy had done a wonderful job, and I was feeling 'very Bella' in the scarlet suit and red lipstick.

'Now,' Fliss barked and everyone jumped, including me. 'I want you all in your places we're going to do a run through with little Amy here.'

With that she stepped back, and a confused Crimson appeared at my elbow and gently pushed me behind the worktop, under the lights, in front of the camera.

'Oh Amy, you look amazing,' Fliss was shouting. 'I can't believe you have never been in front of a camera before – and so photogenic, the camera LOVES your hands.'

Fliss wasn't facing me, she was shouting these compliments from the kitchen doorway and up the stairs.

The cameraman was finding his position and the lighting woman was moving around me checking the skin tone on my hands which she said was close to Bella's so wouldn't be a problem. I felt like I was slowly morphing into Bella – I could see how easy it might be to slip into this life. Another day at Dovecote and I'd be calling everyone darling, referring to 'filthy homeless' and drinking vintage champagne.

Fliss handed me Bella's discarded scarlet apron and I tied it on over the trouser suit as the cameraman started setting up his camera and zooming in on my hands. Meanwhile Tim was chatting to Ruth the wardrobe mistress. 'I was offered Dame Judi Dench's latest stage play,' he was saying; 'she said, Tim darling, I need you to direct – I'm no one without you. But I said Jude, I have a commitment... so before you ask, yes I gave up Dame Judi to do this.' He threw up his hands in horror.

Within seconds, there was a noise from upstairs, a creaking door followed by footsteps on the landing.

'Bella... is that you, dahling?' Fliss called in a pantomime voice, her hand to her ear, smiling conspiratorially at everyone in the kitchen. There was no answer, but Fliss winked at us and continued to bustle and boss and shuffle papers while making loud comments in the direction of the hall about how 'bloody fabulous Amy is'.

Crimson handed me a large bowl filled with cake batter and manoeuvred me along the oasis as the cameraman and Tim were instructing.

'A little to the left... no more right...' and so on.

'What shall I do?' I asked.

'Make like Bella and put your hands in it,' Crimson answered, rolling her eyes at me like I should know this.

Tim nodded. 'Yes, plunge your hands deep into that world of sweet confection, my darling...'

I did and the camera filmed but bloody Tim didn't shut up; 'As you cream that butter and sugar just feel the joy of a million Christmases shudder through you...' he was saying, dramatically sweeping around behind the camera and distracting everyone.

I tried not to listen, it was quite off-putting, so I concentrated on what I was doing, praying that Bella would come back soon – this wasn't as easy as it looked on TV.

For a few minutes I kneaded the doughy batter as Tim gave me my 'direction'. 'Feel it, my love, give it your everything and baby just go with that dough...' who thought kneading a lump of dough could be so theatrical? As the camera whirred, focusing only on my hands, Tim built himself into a frenzy, 'Go on... go on...' he was saying. 'Rub it... rub it hard into your fingertips, feel the love and life in that bloody dough, darling.'

Unfortunately I wasn't feeling any love or life in the dough, just grit and vague embarrassment, but Tim was positively orgasmic at my digits, urging me on and making me even more uncomfortable. Then when he was almost spent and things were grinding to a halt everything stopped abruptly as a dark silhouette landed in the middle of the set. Bella was standing in the doorway. She had one arm leaning on the door jamb, a fag in her mouth and an evil look on her face. Tim leaped away from me and my dough like a husband caught in bed with another woman.

'Oh, now little Amy's all dressed up, I suppose you don't need me anymore?' she said, sashaying into the kitchen like a forties film star.

'No, we were doing fine without you,' Crimson sighed, barely looking up from her iPod. But Bella ignored her and was looking straight at me. I knew this look from the past and felt that old twinge of guilt as she stared me down. She'd always been the pretty one who got what she wanted, and if she didn't – like now – she could be quite a handful. Now I was older, I wasn't fooled or in awe of my old friend. I worked with teenagers and Bella was a walk in the park compared to the hormonal psychopaths of Year Ten and Eleven.

Mike the cameraman had put down his camera and was now just waiting. He rolled his eyes at me and I smiled back, it was reassuring to think I wasn't the only person in this kitchen who wasn't certifiable.

Bella slowly moved out of the doorway without taking her eyes off me and sashayed into the kitchen, *her* kitchen. She gestured for Billy to replenish her make-up, which I presumed must be a sign she was about to start filming again. Everyone stayed silent, watching sideways, like one would a naughty child who had to be ignored or they might blow again. Once her make-up was refreshed, her lips red and glossy, she came over and stood next to me in, it has to be said, a rather threatening manner. I wasn't sure whether this was my cue to leave. I glanced over at Fliss for confirmation, but I couldn't see her for Crimson's plume of black backcombed hair.

'Get on with it, Bella,' Crimson said, completely unfazed by the whole drama, she seemed to be the only person here who didn't pander to Bella and said what she thought.

I felt my basic teacher/child psychology was fitting for this situation and waded in. 'You okay now, Bella?' I said, slowly looking up at her, meeting her eyes which still held the flickering fire of her anger. 'You always had a temper when we were younger, remember when I dropped ink on your homework?' I rolled my eyes. 'You went mad and threw the rest of the bottle over me,' I laughed at the memory of her outrageous reaction to what was only an accident.

But she didn't laugh, she just stared straight ahead and without looking at me like a queen who wouldn't look at anyone she deemed beneath her. 'Have you finished reminiscing, Amy?'

I shrugged, wiping my hands on a holly-embroidered tea towel, she was tougher than some of my Year Tens, but I wasn't giving up just yet.

'My mum used to say your temper was like a force of nature,' I smiled, waiting for a glimmer of a reaction, for a moment of shared memory to bond us and calm her down. 'Like a tempest tossing sailors around the sea,' I added. Crimson sniggered at the word tossing and I heard Fliss telling her to shush.

'Mum was the only one who could calm you when you were like that and she always said "think about cool water, lapping on sand," do you remember?'

I looked at her, but she didn't return my look, she was still avoiding my eyes. It was clear that I was wasting my time and couldn't get through to her. Over the years, Bella had become harder, less accessible, and any thoughts I'd had about us ever being friends again were a lot further away than I'd ever imagined.

Wordlessly, I took off the scarlet apron and handed it to her. She took it, thanked me then turned, opened the oven door, and took out the huge ham still in its oven tray.

'Are cameras rolling?' she asked. Mike the cameraman immediately turned on the camera and a sound guy moved into position.

Everyone was watching silently. I felt at a complete loss and wondered if I should just go home. This was pointless, but I had to stay and put up with all this, because while I stuck by my agreement to go along with her programme and not say anything, Bella had to stand by hers. I wasn't letting St Swithin's down – and neither was she.

Perhaps that stuff about my mum and her temper was probably too personal to share in front of the others? Had I just completely closed the door on any kind of communication with her by talking of the past? She was now carrying the heavy glistening ham carefully, unsmiling, Stepford-like in her scarlet apron. Earlier she'd basted the ham for the camera, she'd massaged and ooed and aahed about its sweet plumpness for too long, but what happened next was quite a surprise.

Chapter Ten

Sex, Chocolate and a War-torn Husband

'I'm bored, bored, bored,' she suddenly announced, walking precariously across the kitchen on high heels carrying the huge ham. 'I'm bored of you all, but most of all I'm bored of being told what to say, how to act and who to tell what to. I can't bloody breathe in my own home!' she was yelling at anyone and everyone. 'And will you stop smirking?' she waved her arm in Crimson's direction – but Crimson stuck her tongue out.

Billy was on standby with a holdall full of brushes and make-up so he could go back in after Bella's storm had subsided and put more lipstick on. Tim was looking at Bella and telling her she was wonderful, the lighting woman was re-adjusting the lights and Fliss was taking a swig from a diamante hip flask.

'Dahling, we don't want to get all excited now do we, sweet-cakes?' she said between swigs.

'We do... oh yes we bloody do!' Bella screamed, taking a swig from the proffered flask. 'I want to get very excited,' and with that she lifted the huge ham from its tray. She was now holding it against her, and the warm fat and syrup and sugar was drenching her lovely blouse but she didn't seem to care. She stood defiantly in the middle of the beautiful kitchen and raised that wonderful ham high in the air, and it was then I realised, to my horror, that she was about to hurl it across the kitchen.

'NO,' I screamed, which of course egged her on, and she launched it through the air like a shot-putter. In a split second I leaped up to try and catch it. This was food, it might not have meant much to bloody Bella, with her fabulous cars and glittery diamonds and twenty foot tree, but throwing a beautiful Christmas ham was pure waste in my book, and besides it was dangerous. She could have knocked someone out with that huge ham, so screaming 'BELLA NO,' I lunged forward, throwing my whole body at it arms out like I was trying to catch a large ball. But as it landed in my arms I was amazed to feel how light it was, like a ball – just like a rubber ball. A rubber ball that I couldn't hold on to. I looked down in horror as it fell from my arms and slowly bounced along the kitchen floor. Everyone was staring, open-mouthed, Bella's tantrum was clearly nothing out of the ordinary, but me rugby-tackling a syrupy ham apparently was. In the silence I finally said what everyone else already knew. 'It's fake.'

'That's not the only fake thing in this kitchen,' Crimson said, rolling her eyes.

This was followed by peals of laughter from Fliss who seemed to enjoy the whole spectacle and Bella whose temper had suddenly disappeared.

'Oh Ames, your face is a picture... you didn't think that ham was real did you?' Bella asked, laughing at me, looking around at her audience, her courtiers, who laughed along politely.

'Yes... I did. I thought... silly me, it looked like a real ham, I thought as it was a food show, you might just use... real food?' I said sarcastically. Someone handed me a towel and I tried to mop the syrupy juices from my blouse.

'Is this what all TV cookery programmes do?' I asked.

Bella nodded but everyone else shook their heads.

'Well, Bella's food is sometimes..."styled", because as much as she loves to bake, the poor love just doesn't have the time. And sometimes... we need to improvise... come into the sitting room, dahling, while Bella has a touch-up,' Fliss was covering for her – again.

She bustled me out of the kitchen where Bella was now being tended to by Tim and Billy. Crimson was skulking in a corner, her mouth downwards, her eyes shifting from side to side, she was sniggering at Bella.

Fliss sat me down on the blue armchair and positioned herself on the pouffe, pulling it closer so her chin was almost on my knees. It was quite disconcerting.

'This is mad,' I started. 'I honestly don't believe this. It's all just one big lie, the food is fake, other people dress the tree and, don't tell me, someone else makes all of the other decorations?'

'Crimson does the decorations, she's been doing them for years now. She did A level art – never took it any further but she has talent.'

'So why won't Bella mention her on the programme? Why doesn't she have her on screen showing how she makes the stuff?'

'Dahling, you've seen Crimson...she looks like something from Lord of the Rings!' Fliss laughed, slapping her thighs and criss-crossing those beleaguered kitten heels that had been carrying her not inconsiderable weight all morning.

Then she turned serious, 'Bella is what people want, rich, glamourous, sexy – the perfect woman in the perfect life – and she knows how to sell it. And make no mistake, she can bake. That woman bakes a mean batch of brownies, so don't get any ideas about going to the gutter press, saying she can't. Sometimes we fake the food and we employ a little help off screen... that's all.'

'On screen she comes over as quite passionate about food and baking so why doesn't she bake her own...'

'On screen I come over as quite passionate about a lot of things, because I'm the perfect actress, I've had to be...' it was Bella, now hanging in the doorway being handed a flute of champagne by Billy.

'Bella, that's enough, Amy doesn't need to know everything,' Fliss warned.

What the hell was she talking about? I knew everything about Bella, even the stuff from our teens that she hid from the world, there was nothing else to know... was there?

'Oh chill... have a glass of champagne. I've had three this morning and it's not twelve yet,' Bella giggled, holding up a wobbly hand before almost collapsing into Tim's arms. Thank goodness he'd been standing behind her.

'No... er dahling, she's teasing, aren't you, dear?' Fliss turned back to me, wafting Bella away and clearly giving her a meaningful look, but Bella was laughing.

'Have some bloody Champagne, Ames...' she was very tipsy. She'd been sipping champagne all morning, when she wasn't throwing hams and having tantrums – I reckon the champagne had a lot to answer for.

'No... thank you, it's a little early for me,' I said.

'It's a little early for me,' she mimicked my voice while wandering into the room on wobbly legs and stood in front of me, looking directly at me, her head to one side like a puzzled robin.

'Amy, loosen up, why are you being so boring?'

I stiffened, recalling this phrase from when we were teenagers and I refused to go late night clubbing or said I'd had enough to drink.

'I'm not being boring, Bella,' I started, like I was talking to a ten-year-old. 'I'm just a bit disappointed that's all. I'll be honest, for years I've watched your programme along with the rest of the country. I've tried to reach your standards, take your advice, aspire to your life, *your* Christmas – even though I never had the time or the money you have. Watching you bake and dress the house was pure nostalgia for me because we'd done those things together. And now I discover that Bella Bradley, the brilliant cook, the woman who can dress a room in minutes and make it look fabulous doesn't exist. Someone else does it for her – and what's more, they don't even get credit. Poor Crimson over there does all the decorations, but not once have you ever given her credit. It seems that everyone else is busy making you look good and all you seem to do is put on a red apron every Christmas and have a big tantrum, while selling us all a dream we can't buy.' I'd always wanted to meet the new Bella, the fabulous cook, the creative genius, but none of it was real – it was all one big fat lie and I couldn't even enjoy the fantasy anymore.

'Oh stop it, Amy, you're not stupid, you know it's all smoke and mirrors, that's what TV is,' she said, flopping on the blue velvet sofa and wrapping herself in a throw.

'You don't get it, do you?' I went on. She was closing her eyes and pretending to be asleep but I knew what she was doing, she was still so childlike. 'I believed in you, but now I feel cheated, betrayed, like every other viewer out there who spent a fortune on the "right" bird, soaked their raisins in expensive gin for a fortnight and did extra shifts to buy bloody gold leaf for a trifle.'

'Oh Ames...' she said, giving me a jolt from my melancholy. 'The viewers aren't interested in what I do, or even if I do it. They love me, they want to be me and they want my wonderful bloody life. You're right – I'm selling them a dream and if part of that dream is a little cloudy then who cares? They don't want to see me sweating over a hot stove in my joggers and stained T-shirt because that's what *they* do. My viewers want to escape from Coronation Street and visit Bond Street every now and then – and that's what I do for them.'

And she was right. I'd been one of those viewers who was seeking an escape from the boredom of my marriage, the routine of my day-to-day life, and I'd found it in Bella's programmes. I couldn't even enjoy my own Christmas, because it always had to be 'a Bella Christmas'. I'd make lists of her preferred ingredients, her tips and advice, and save hard to buy everything she recommended when I was perfectly capable of making my own choices and decisions. But she'd offered me something else... the dream of the perfect kitchen, the perfect marriage and the perfect Christmas. What's more – I'd bought it, because my own real life had been so unbearable. I started laughing.

'What? Why are you laughing?' she said.

'You've created this business, this whole celebrity persona around food and yet it seems you've forgotten what it means to love cooking, to love food.

'Ha, Bella hates food. She hasn't eaten since 1999,' Fliss roared laughing; 'which reminds me – it must be lunchtime.' With that she headed off down the hall and Bella picked up her phone, becoming engrossed very quickly – I think I was dismissed.

❄ ❄ ❄

As filming had finished for lunch and no one was allowed inside Dovecote with hot food (oh the irony), everyone trooped out into the cold to the catering truck. I watched them through the window being handed turkey sarnies with all the trimmings followed by Christmassy cupcakes from the food truck.

As soon as I could I was going out there for a big hot chocolate and a slice of what looked like very fruity Christmas cake – assuming that wasn't fake. I had only been here a few hours and already the superficiality of these people and this world was getting to me.

Looking at Bella's skinny frame earlier had made me wonder if I should diet, something I would normally never do. Since when did I tell myself to stop eating because I needed to look right? This world was so infectious, with its unreasonable demands on the appearances of presenters and the thinness of women. I gave myself a talking to; Christmas was not the season to be worrying about me, it was a time for others, and my physical appearance on TV was the least of my worries. I was locked in a house with a mean, drunken presenter, her crazy agent, a stroppy Goth and a director who thought he was working on 'The Taming of the Shrew'.

'Darling, come over here, I need you to make some notes,' Bella was saying to Crimson who was reluctantly dragging herself across the floor like a dark-eyed sloth.

'Now we need to do my Twitter feed,' she said, patting the stool next to her. Crimson's face was crumpled as she lumbered up onto the stool; she was clearly furious at being asked to do her job. A part of me didn't blame her, she seemed to have to do everything for Bella off screen.

'Write this down,' Bella directed, composing herself while waiting for Crimson to do the same, but anyone watching knew this may take some time. Eventually Crimson found a pen from about her person, it had a fluffy top and fangs and it waggled ludicrously as she began to write.

'Now I'm going to say fabulous things and I want you to twitter it out please.'

'Tweet.'

'Yes, darling, that's right.'

'No... I mean you don't "twitter" it, you tweet it... OMG who gave old people the internet?'

I waited for a few seconds to see Bella's reaction, assuming Crimson's sacking or beheading would be on the menu.

'That will do, darling,' Bella smiled sweetly and patted Crimson's pad indicating she needed to write stuff down. Perhaps Crimson knew where the bodies were buried?

'Ate the most divine Prosciutto ai Frutti di Stagione at Como Lario last night... the winter fruits were bellissimo. A taste of summer sunshine on a snowy Chelsea night...'

How wonderful, I thought – she has such a great life and she visits all these wonderful restaurants, places I've only ever read about in Sunday supplements but doubt I'll ever eat at.

'That sounds nice,' I tried.

'Yes... my viewers love to know everything about me, and my restaurant tweets always cause a buzz in the twitterati.'

'Twittersphere,' monotoned Crimson.

'Whatever... it doesn't matter what you call it, I still cause a stir.'

'Yeah...you could say that. @cheesetits retweeted you twice,' Crimson said, without missing a beat.

'Really? Can't you do something about that, darling? I hate when lowlifes get hold of my tweetings.'

'How do you know @cheesetits is a low life?' Crimson said, looking up from her phone.

'Well, let me put it this way – I doubt it's the Duchess of Cambridge with a tweeter name like that.'

'Handle.'

'What?'

'The Twitter name is called a handle,' Crimson repeated, rolling her eyes.

'I'm sure it is, darling, and I want you to keep a handle on it, if you don't mind. Stop cheese tits and their ilk from following me and tweeting me up.'

'Retweeting.'

'Will you please stop correcting me?'

'Yeah, when you stop getting it wrong and being a judgemental old witch,' Crimson said this like she was reading a shopping list, not insulting TV's Kitchen Goddess.

Bella rolled her eyes affectionately. Yes, affectionately.

I was in shock. Grown men – well, Tim – were crumbling in Bella's wake yet this stroppy teen was walking all over her.

'I can't help being a judgemental old witch, Crimson, I take after my mother. Oh how I hate online social media and the bottom-feeding sock puppets.'

'Trolls.'

'Yes you are – now come on little troll and start hashtagging something trendy on the end of my last brilliant twittering,' Bella sang.

'I can't,' came Crimson's sulky voice from under black hair and make-up.

'No such thing as can't – do it.'

'Err, I can't add any more – a tweet can only be 140 characters and all the crap about snow in the sunshine is too long even before the hashtag.'

'Do the tweeting people know it's me?'

Crimson rolled her eyes; 'No they don't, but even if you were Lady Gaga it wouldn't make any difference – it's Twitter, one of life's great levellers. Everyone's the same; it's not like one of your elitist restaurants that only serve snail porridge with pig foam to famous people with an income over £10m a year.' She sighed, exasperated, and picked up her phone again to tweet something. I glanced over to see her brow furrowed, her fingers so fast they were a blur. If I'd been Bella I'd have checked my Twitter feed because the mood Crimson was in God only knows what could be tweeted in Bella's name. I knew only too well the horrors of that situation – when Year 10 boys hacked into my Twitter I was suddenly following porn stars and tweeting pictures of extravagant genitalia to all my followers. The pictures were profane, the details were unnecessary and the hashtags were probably illegal. Then one of the little darlings showed Mr Jones my 'online activities' and he invited me into his office, brandished his phone, showing a close-up of a diamante-studded vagina, and demanded to know if it was mine. Completely unaware I'd been hacked, I called him a disgusting pervert and threatened to report him to the teacher's union. It took several days in mediation and the upping of Mr Jones' medication to untangle that Twitter trauma. And looking at Crimson now, poised to send out her boss's tweet, one could only imagine the darkness she could unleash online in the name of Bella Bradley.

'Mon chéri, did I hear you say you dined at Como Lario last night? Love, love, love the osso buco with saffron risotto,' Tim piped up in an affected Italian accent.

'No darling... never been, hate bloody Italian... it's for my twittering,' Bella frowned.

'Ohhh.' Tim was crushed, he'd obviously hoped this would mean an orgasmic bonding with Bella to the exclusion of everyone else over the bloody osso buco, whatever that was.

'Amy, come and talk to me,' Bella was now saying as Crimson was dismissed so wandered over to the fridge to help herself to a snack, she certainly made herself at home. I watched as Billy applied eyeliner and fake lashes to Bella's lids. It had never occurred to me her lashes were fake, mind you it never occurred to me that her Christmas ham was fake either.

'We do need to talk, Amy,' she said as I wandered over to where she was sitting.

'Yes we do. I can't believe all this time you were receiving my Christmas cards and not even bothering to send one back... or at least an acknowledgement that you'd received mine.'

'Yes, you're quite right, it was unforgivable of Fliss not to respond... she used to be in charge of my Christmas cards but now I have a full-time assistant,' she said gesturing to Crimson. 'Everything will be fine now.'

I wasn't convinced.

'Bella please can you stop talking – I'm trying to apply Rouge Allure to your lips and my canvas is flapping!'

I moved away so Bella wasn't tempted to talk and Billy could finish. As much as I wanted to speak with her I was glad of the chance to walk away and process what she'd become. Bella was now so removed from her own life she couldn't even take responsibility for a Christmas card and had blamed Fliss. Now Crimson had been handed the job of 'assistant' I wondered if anyone would ever see another Christmas card again. However hard I tried I couldn't see Crimson sitting down to a pile of snow scenes and scribbling 'Happy Christmas, love Bella' hundreds of times, she seemed to be permanently glued to her phone, but what did I know. I'd been here for just a few hours and was already missing my life. It might be predictable and small to some – but it was my world and being here made me appreciate it.

Watching Crimson tweeting away alone in the corner, I suddenly felt sorry for her, she seemed so down on everyone but that was probably because she was under so much pressure from Bella. I wandered over to her, 'You have a very demanding mistress,' I whispered conspiratorially.

'Oh, she's okay...'

'Well, you are very patient – I'm not sure I could handle her the way you can.'

'She's a pussycat really, and she'd never admit it but she needs me more than I need her,' she sighed. This was the most engaged I'd ever seen Crimson, her face was almost moving.

'Yes, but you mustn't throw your future away just because some TV presenter needs someone to boss around. Is this your career?' I asked.

'Being Bella's lapdog? No. I want to be an artist someday, but I've put it on hold for a while.'

'Why? I know you're young but time goes by very quickly and before you know it you'll be forty and still here.'

'Yeah, I'm working on it, but Dovecote's so big. I stick around 'cos she can't cope here on her own... she's hopeless,' Crimson rolled her eyes.

I smiled at this strange creature who looked like someone from a horror film with big hair, facial piercings and black lips. She spoke only in mutterings and eye rolling, but underneath the mask I could see that Crimson really cared about her boss. And underneath Bella's mask, I knew the old Bella was in there somewhere... she was right when she said it was all smoke and mirrors.

Meanwhile, Billy had now worked his magic with a few flicks of eyeliner, a perfect red lipstick and another cloud of powder. Along with a couple of black coffees, Bella had been rebooted and was almost sober and ready for her public.

'We need to introduce the divine Amy in this next scene,' announced Tim as everyone took their places. I felt sick, I hadn't managed to make it to the food truck for lunch but I could manage until later, I could see how Bella stayed so slim, there wasn't time to eat in this world... make-up and tweeting took priority over Bella's lunch. I moved tentatively to the spot in the kitchen where the cameraman was pointing and someone waved a piece of paper in my face to check a light reading or something. I was hoping Bella would do a bit more cooking before I came on screen, but once we'd done the first recipe I was sure I'd be fine. Bella looked like thunder, I heard her say to Billy that she was tired and cold and just wanted 'to get this crap over with,' which didn't help my confidence. 'It's just like teaching a class,' I told myself – but under those lights with people counting and everyone's nerves jangling it was quite overwhelming. Not for the first time I wondered what the hell I was doing there, but as soon as the camera began whirring and the lights were set for Bella's face, she changed.

'Today I have a very special Christmas guest in my kitchen,' she started, the thunderous face gone, smiley red lips everywhere. 'It's Amy Lane! Welcome to Dovecote, little Amy, and season's greetings to everyone in their kitchens rustling up those sweet Christmassy treats. But first – this year's old bird... ha no, not Amy,' she pantomimed, rolling her eyes and flapping her hand. 'My Christmas bird... and this year it's going to be... drum roll please – an organic turkey!' All this was delivered confidently, with little 'humorous' asides and bucketfuls of Bella's dubious charm. Her ability to perform was amazing, just over an hour ago she was storming around the kitchen shot-putting hams and drinking champagne by the bucketload. And only seconds before she was complaining about tiredness and the 'crap' she had to get through. But here she was, the gorgeous Kitchen Goddess, gleaming from head to toe, her smile lighting up the room. The viewers would lap this up – they couldn't see what I could, that she was dead behind the eyes, her breath reeked of alcohol and she hadn't even touched the turkey until the camera came on.

'Ooh, meant to say, don't hate me if you heard the rumours on naughty Twitter that I was gagging for a goose, or dreaming of a duck,' she said, her bottom lip down like a mischievous girl. 'I'm going old-school this year. Yes, I love a good old-fashioned traditional Christmas and that's what I'm giving you... and if you know what's what and you care about your loved ones, this is the bird you'll be giving your family this year. TURKEY! So all you budding chefs and wonderful homemakers out there... let's get stuffing!'

Standing by her like a bridesmaid, I was pretty impressed how she'd turned it on as soon as the camera light was on. She was confident, articulate and... then I noticed... she was reading her words straight from the autocue! It had never occurred to me that she was scripted, she'd always made it sound so real, but as the minutes went on I could see every word as she said it – her passion for the food, her 'off the cuff' comments were all written down by somebody else and she just read them! I didn't think there was anything left for her to fake... then just when I thought it was safe, there she went again. She went on to describe the prize and how 'lovely Amy' had won because of her 'tragic story', which made me feel slightly guilty because it wasn't as dramatic as the script was suggesting. So, my husband had left me for a younger woman. That was a cliché, not a tragedy... TV people over-dramatised everything; and it was so different from my world of school and teaching.

'No crackers at Amy's table this year,' Bella was saying. Then she leaned into the camera and said in a low voice like she was imparting some dark secret, 'In fact she'll be lucky if she has a crust of bread to share with her poor, poor little children. And Father Christmas...' she paused and wiped a tear, as instructed on the autocue. Scripted tears? I couldn't believe it, was there anything about Bella's life that wasn't a performance? I smiled to myself thinking she probably needed a script for sex with the Silver Fox.

'Father Christmas,' she pretended to compose herself, 'is a distant memory for Amy's little ones.'

I stood there open-mouthed; not once did she mention the fact that I was a teacher in a big comprehensive school in Birmingham or that my kids were both at university. I was hurt that Bella knew all this and hadn't even bothered to get the script altered to give some grains of truth to the account of my life. Mind you, I had to admit she was good, I couldn't fault the delivery as she swept from tragedy to triumph in a moment. Peering into the camera she said, 'I am going to turn this poor woman's horrible, drab, tragic Christmas into a sparkly, all-singing, all-eating affair.'

Tim called 'cut' and waltzed onto the set speaking in loud Shakespearean tones about how 'bloody moved' he was.

I ignored him, I was still contemplating the fact that Bella was giving the impression that thanks to her, 'little Amy' and her family would not be 'tragic' this Christmas. And all because we'd be eating her overstuffed bird and pulling her designer crackers round the bloody Christmas tree!

'Just say thank you Bella you've saved Christmas, you're amazing... or something like that,' Bella said, impatiently.

I nodded, 'Okay.' I wanted to tell her where to stuff her turkey, but I had to think of St Swithin's.

'Gorgeous, gorgeous, gorgeous, and close-up on Amy's sad face – perfect, little Amy you look utterly tragic. I'll add sad violin music over you in the edit natch,' Tim said, holding out his arms expectantly, conductor-like directing the end of my 'performance'.

'Thank you so much, Bella,' I said through gritted teeth. 'You are amazing, but I want my prize to go to the homeless hostel near where I live...'

'Stop. Stop,' Bella snapped, pursed red lips, eyes glaring at Tim, one hand on her waist, 'that's not in the script...she has to thank me first, then we get to the hostel bit.'

Tim shifted from one foot to another; 'Darling Amy, we don't want to get to the homeless thingy yet. We want the full and frank scene over Bella's raw bird... I need you to thank Bella from the bottom of your tragic little heart.'

'No.'

'Oh sweetie, but you must. It's all about the drama, darling, you are so bloody, bloody grateful,' he was saying loudly, then in an aside, 'tears would be good here... and channelling Barbara Hershey in Beaches?'

'I'm sorry, Tim, I don't "channel" film stars or cry for nothing. I'm a maths teacher and to my knowledge I'm not dying of a terminal disease, nor am I asking Bella to look after my children when I've gone like the woman in the film,' I added. 'So let's just get on with it – no Babs, no Beaches, no tears, just cooking,' I snapped. I could feel Bella's eyes bore into me from the side, but she couldn't intimidate me.

'Amy, do as Tim says and once you've thanked me profusely, preferably with tears, you have to be quiet while I come up with the idea,' she said.

'What idea?'

'The one here... scroll down the autocue,' she called and within seconds I read how Bella was going to spontaneously suggest that 'Amy donates her Christmas to her local homeless hostel and we'll give them lunch instead...'

'Look, here it is, the homeless... thingy,' she said, sighing in exasperation at my apparent stupidity.

'But it wasn't your idea.'

'Yes it was.'

'No Bella – you can't pretend you thought of it, I'm donating my prize.'

'For God's sake will you both grow up,' Fliss stepped in. 'Bella's quite right, your suggestion was cut, Amy, but not because we won't do it – we just need to make it look like it was Bella's idea.'

'Does anyone ever tell the truth around here?' I suddenly raised my voice. No one answered, except Crimson of course.

'Truth? What's that?' she sniggered.

'The homeless thing... it's my idea according to this here,' Bella said, pointing to the autocue. 'You might be holding us all to ransom with your stupid demands but don't start trying to write the script, Ames.'

'I'm not trying to write anything. I just want to own my suggestion in the same way I want my Mum to own her recipes... you can't just take anything you want, Bella.'

Bella nodded and quickly took me to one side as the others repositioned lights and cameras in preparation for filming again. 'Look, Ames I told you I haven't taken from you – you gave me those recipes.'

'I gave them to you, but they weren't yours to take and sell on. Even as a little girl you had everything and now you think it's your right to have what you want, don't you?' I said.

'No. You're the one who had everything.'

'That's simply not true Bella, you had the best toys, the best clothes... you even had a brand new car with a bow on it for your 17th birthday – and you couldn't even drive.'

'I'm not talking about toys and cars - when we were young I envied you – your mum always home after school, watching TV with your Dad in his chair every evening, your sisters always laughing. When I wasn't at yours I'd go home to a dark, empty house, where my parents were either at work or screaming at each other.'

I looked at her, I'd never really considered myself someone to be envied, but then I'd never really considered my life from Bella's perspective.

'Ames, when you wrote to me offering the recipes and reminding me of all the good times I had with your family, I honestly thought you were giving them to me.'

'I was. I was giving them to *you* not your publisher or your accountant, not for the world to pay for and pore over. They were private memories, Bella...'

'I didn't think of it like that. Nothing in my world is private, everything I do or have done is open to interpretation, and if it's not the press it's social media. When I had something as lovely and innocent as the perfect recipe for Chocolate brownies and Christmas gingerbread along with those memories, I just wanted to share them with the world. I suppose I also wanted to pretend I was you and had the kind of childhood you had. I never really thought about your mum or what it would mean to you – and... I'm sorry.'

'I can kind of see why you might feel like that,' I heard myself say.

Bella and Fliss seemed to be paranoid about 'secrets and lies' and I knew what it would mean if Bella's past was suddenly 'out there'. She'd sold herself as this perfect woman we all aspired to and her whole life depended on that image being maintained. She was as flawed as the rest of us, unable to bake in her own kitchen, unable to even say the words she wanted to, relying on autocue for her thoughts and opinions. Everything (almost everything) was laid bare, and as much as she was feted by her fans she was open to criticism from every corner and even her happy times must have been tainted. Like me she'd found the cosiness of our childhood a comfort and just wanted to relive the memories through baking.

'I'm sorry too, Bella,' I sighed. 'I can see it's not all mistletoe and fairy lights, but you might think of how other people are affected by what you do.'

She gave me a look. 'Seriously? You're lecturing me on how my actions might affect others?'

We seemed to take two steps forward and one step back. I had just apologised, acknowledged her life was hard - yet the only thing she took from my words was the criticism.

'Look, I only told your secret because I thought it might help you.'

'Yeah and I only put your mum's recipes in my book because I thought they were wonderful... and yes, I also implied your mother was my mother, because I wished she was!'

I suddenly felt deeply sorry for her, the little girl I'd always envied, the one with the beautiful clothes and toys had, all the time, been envying me. I reached out to her and touched her shoulder, but she pulled away and I glimpsed two faint track marks down her face, a single tear perched on her chin, ready to fall.

'My mascara,' she said, as she went off to find Billy. Even her emotions have to be covered up with make-up, I thought, looking round the beautiful gadget-filled kitchen that suddenly seemed so empty.

Chapter Eleven

Amy Lane v Vintage Champagne and Lobster from Maine

'Hate to say it, but Amy has a point,' Fliss said as we reconvened for the afternoon's filming. 'It doesn't make sense if Bella suggests Amy donates her prize to a homeless hostel – it has to come from Amy.'

'But it's in the script, so I have to say it,' Bella huffed.

'I'll change it quickly now,' Fliss sighed. 'Tim's script reads like something from Charles Dickens anyway... it's a cookery show, not "A Christmas Carol",' she said, glancing at Tim.

'I'm wasted in telly. My Dickens wouldn't play well to a working-class audience - too sophisticated,' he snapped back.

Bella wasn't happy, the tears she'd shed only minutes before were now gone and the bitch was back. 'It's my programme and we're going to pay for everything, so why not just give in, Ames. I can't believe you would risk the chance of those poor, smelly homeless people not being fed, just so you get the credit.'

'I won't be railroaded by you, Bella' I sighed. 'I came here so the hostel would get the dinner... but I also wanted to see my old friend.'

I swear she softened ever so slightly at this. And Tim wiped an eye, 'If only I had caught that moment on camera,' he gasped. 'Could we go for it again?'

'You can't, no one knows they're friends... she won the prize remember, Tim?' Fliss was rolling her eyes and finishing off the few lines of script. 'Right – okay the script is loaded in the autocue and we can go now.'

Bella and I took our positions behind the huge pink turkey and judging by the mottling on her neck, I think she was surprised at how I'd fought back. As a child I gave in to most of her demands. In fact the more time I spent with her, I was beginning to think I had probably remembered our friendship as far better than it really was.

'You've got more feisty in your old age,' she whispered.

'Yeah and you've got more mean,' I replied.

We then filmed a scene where she patronised me so much over the simple cooking of a turkey, I couldn't play nice any longer.

'The turkey has to be organic, bronze... sweet, succulent meat, delicious...' she tore at the turkey – yes this one was real, apparently the home economist had been up all night cooking in her own home sixty miles away and had driven it down that morning.

'Does it really have to be organic...?' I started.

'Taste the turkey, Amy,' she demanded, pushing a lump of white meat into my face. 'Taste it!'

The hot meat was at my lips, she was grimacing and thrusting and I had no choice but to taste her bloody turkey. I smiled and chewed as she waited for a response.

'Mmmm it is delicious, but you know, Bella, so many of us watch your programme and listen to your advice about buying the best ingredients, but for those of us who can't afford a turkey costing upwards of £60 might I suggest a small frozen turkey? When cooked properly, with love and the right seasoning, it can taste just as good – and it's a fraction of the cost of this one.'

'Don't be silly, Amy, it's Christmas, you have to have the best at Christmas!' She was winking at the camera, and fondling her organic bird, confident, beautiful and spoiled – and that was just the turkey.

'You really don't get it, do you Bella? It doesn't matter what time of year it is – if you can't afford it, you can't afford it!' I snapped.

'Cut! That won't be going in,' she shouted to Tim. 'Don't want Ames banging on about the bloody poor again – BORING!' she was pouring herself another a glass of champagne.

'It's not boring, you selfish, self-obsessed Prima Donna,' I snapped. 'You'll see just how far Christmas dinner on a budget can go, and how grateful people are.'

'Yes I'm sure my viewers can't wait to take a break from vintage champagne and the best Maine lobster this year,' she snapped.

'It's not about what it costs or where it's from – my simple Christmas food tastes better than your expensive, overrated shop-bought rubbish!'

'Oh rubbish is it? You come into my kitchen and call my cooking rubbish now – go back to your little hostel, Amy,' she slurped on champagne. 'Oh no, you're filming this?' she suddenly said, glass halfway to her lips.

The camera lights were on. Tim and the rest of the crew were engrossed – they were filming it.

'Keep going, they'll sort it out in the edit, dahling,' Fliss was saying.

'Sweetie, I'm loving this salty chemistry – it's amateur hour but it's real,' Tim enthused.

So we continued to 'work together' for the rest of the afternoon. Bella contradicting me, patronising me and telling me how I should cook my sprouts, roast my potatoes and clean my bloody crystal, and me informing her that like most of her viewers, 'I have no crystal' and 'everyone knows how to cook a damn sprout.'

I wasn't allowing Bella to boss me about anymore – it might be her show and her kitchen but I refused to be patronised. I wasn't her assistant or a token 'poor person' that she could humiliate – I was Amy Lane, I was a great cook, a brilliant baker and I wasn't some fake TV chef playing at it – like Bella was.

❊ ❊ ❊

By early evening we were both exhausted and extremely prickly. And though I knew much of what I said would end up on the cutting room floor, I had to have my say. Poor Tim would get to the edit and have to cut three hours of Bella and I at each other's throats – he'd probably need post-trauma therapy.

'That's a wrap until tomorrow,' Tim announced.

'Jeez it's like watching Fanny Craddock and Jonny,' I heard Fliss remark to Tim when she thought she was out of earshot.

'More like Fanny Craddock and Fanny Craddock,' Crimson added, and they all laughed and headed for the food truck... where a decent meal awaited them, which was as well, because they wouldn't be getting anything from Bella's oven.

As there were just the two of us left in the kitchen, I didn't want to walk away leaving her alone so asked Bella if she was coming to supper.

'I don't eat supper,' she snapped, banging dishes into the dishwasher, something she would normally leave for the home economist to do, surely. She was obviously annoyed with the way I'd behaved on set and now the cameras were off I have to admit I felt a little awkward.

'Bella, I was just being myself. I love your programme, but if you want my opinion, you've been out of touch for the past couple of years...'

'Out of touch? You came here looking like one of the bloody Waltons – John Boy to be precise – and you tell me I'm out of touch. You want to take a look at yourself in the mirror, love.'

'Yes and you need to walk a mile in someone else's shoes, Bella. You think it's okay to spend hundreds of pounds on one bottle of champagne, you throw gold leaf around like it's sprinkles and, Christ Bella, you eat beef that was *massaged* daily when it was a cow. It probably had a pedicure and a day at the spa before it was chauffer driven to the abattoir. Your food is treated better than some people!'

'Oh do shut up with your sanctimonious comments. Yes, I eat good beef and that's because I can.'

'No, it's because you're selfish and spoilt, always have been,' I heard myself say. I waited for a snappy response, but instead I was greeted with silence and wondered if perhaps I'd gone too far.

She closed the dishwasher and stood leaning on the worktops, looking straight at me.

'I have never had the family I wanted, never loved like you, never been able to – I've never enjoyed a gaggle of my own children like you have. The only time I have ever had a big, loving family Christmas was when I was at your house, with you and your family as a child. So yes, perhaps I am spoiled and selfish and buy the best beef and drink myself into financial oblivion. I earned it, and I need it – but what I don't need is you waltzing back into my life reminding me of what I never had and lecturing me on what I shouldn't have now.' With that she turned away from me and walked slowly into the conservatory, just watching the snow fall.

I was shocked. Bella's feelings ran deep, it seemed she wasn't as happy and fulfilled as I'd imagined. I'd always been concerned that she couldn't have children... and now I felt sick just thinking about the agony she must have gone through. I couldn't imagine a life without Jamie and Fiona – they were everything to me. On the surface Bella had it all, but she kept buying more, wanting more – and I realised now it was to fill up the hole of sadness in her life. Perhaps she wasn't the only one who had to mind other people's feelings – and walk a mile in their shoes?

Chapter Twelve

Foie Gras and Faux Pas

The Christmas Bella and I made the shoebox dolls' house, she received a real one from her parents on Christmas Day. When I saw it I was transfixed and I have to admit tinged green with envy as I ran my hands along the brick facade, looked through the windows, and opened the little front door. It was decorated inside with gift wrapping which looked like real wallpaper and the front opened up to reveal life-like figures sitting around in chairs and leaning against fireplaces. Tiny cups and saucers sat on the dining room table, along with a teapot, and the smallest frying pan I'd ever seen was on the tiny oven hob. The curtains wafted and the windows opened, and on the rare occasions I visited Bella's home I always asked if we could play with it. Sometimes Bella would allow it, other times she refused, like little girls do – enjoying the power their toys have over others.

I was thinking about this now as she stood in the conservatory, the snow falling thicker and instead of heading out into the dark for supper I walked into the conservatory. I didn't realise, but Crimson was in there, they were talking quietly, none of the

TV speak Bella usually adopted when talking to her staff. I was intrigued, but as soon as she realised I was there Bella immediately changed the tone of her voice and 'performed,' for me. 'Crimson, I need you to twatter – ready?' Before Crimson could answer she was off. 'Okay...shimmery flakes of twenty-four carat gold leaves and the world's most expensive olive oil are the only things to toss on one's salad this Christmas.'

She looked at me defiantly, but for once I wasn't interested in what she was tossing or how much it cost. I was too intrigued by the scenario I'd just walked in on. What had she and Crimson been talking about in such quiet voices? They seemed conspiratorial even. But Bella was now egging the pudding and expanding on her largesse for my benefit by wandering over to the fridge – still 'twattering' – and uncorking a bottle of champagne. She wanted me to know she deserved this, that I had no right to criticise her and I was the last person who could take it from her. I understood how she felt, I'd taken something from her a long time ago and I could never replace that.

'Sounds like a delicious salad,' I smiled, still standing in the kitchen doorway. She shrugged; 'I thought it would be too expensive for your frugal tastes... all that nasty gold leaf?' She poured the champagne defiantly into a crystal flute and looking straight at me, she took a good, long drink.

I didn't want to argue any more, I was tired of the confrontation, and despite the front she was putting on, I guessed she was too.

'Can I have one of those?' I asked, climbing onto the kitchen stool next to where Bella sat.

'I thought you didn't drink before the sun was over the yard-arm, Miss Goody Two Shoes?' she hissed. Okay, perhaps I was wrong, perhaps she bloody loved the confrontation?

'Well, you're a bad influence,' I shrugged my shoulders as she grabbed another flute from the cupboard and poured me a glass.

'Bella, do you remember the lovely doll's house you had that one Christmas?' I asked, taking the proffered glass and nodding in thanks.

She put down the bottle and stood for a moment. 'I do... I loved that doll's house...'

'Me too,' I sighed, remembering the brickwork and the frying pan sitting on the hob.

'And we made it out of an old shoebox,' she smiled.

We were obviously remembering different dolls' houses, and saw the past and our own lives in different ways. I'd envied Bella the beautiful house her parents had bought her, but she'd had more fun with the shoebox we'd made, which said it all really.

It seemed like the mention of the doll's house had softened her slightly – or perhaps it was the champagne – but she touched my glass with hers.

'Cheers Ames! And happy Christmas.'

'Are you okay with me being here?' I asked, taking a sip and allowing the ice-cold fizziness to tingle down my throat.

'Yes,' she smiled. 'You are annoying and I didn't like you contradicting me on camera earlier, but if I'm honest... I've missed you. Ames, I don't really have any friends any more – I don't even think I have a life outside of the TV programmes.'

I nodded.

'It's so bad, I sometimes make a ham sandwich and talk through the process like the bloody camera's there, even when I'm all on my own.'

'That's weird,' Crimson said from under her black plumage. I'd forgotten she was there.

We both laughed.

'I have to say I wasn't keen on the initial idea of you being here, knowing about everything, but... oh you know what I mean, I can't think when I've had a couple of these,' she held up her flute and took a large gulp.

'Don't drink then,' I said, trying not to sound like a teacher.

'Yeah... well, like I say, I can't think when I've had a drink. And that's how I like it. I can forget about everything.'

I wasn't sure how to respond, but before I did she continued.

'A journalist once asked me the secret of my success and I said: "Three things; planning, planning and planning..." I should have said "Drinking, drinking, and drinking".' She laughed. I felt so guilty, I knew why she was drinking, she was trying to dull the pain from all those years ago. I had to say something, but before I could her mobile rang and she threw it over to Crimson who caught it with one hand without looking up.

'I hate answering the phone... why do people still call me? I mean, what can you say on the phone that you can't say in a quick text? I give five minutes to friends and family and the rest get a short sharp thirty seconds or I pass the phone to Crimson or Fliss,' she smiled, sipping her champagne, she was finally relaxing.

'If close family only get five minutes on the phone, no wonder you never responded to my Christmas cards,' I said, pointedly.

'Oh darling, Christmas cards are so bloody provincial – who has the time to read them, let alone write them? I'm far too busy. Fliss sends out the corporate Christmas cards and a few crates of champagne or whatever...who cares?'

'Some people care.'

'Oh... sorry Ames, I didn't realise.' So she did have a conscience in there, somewhere – however small.

'It's the same when people try and call me at Christmas,' she continued. 'It's my busiest time – I invariably have a new book to promote or am working on a Christmas Special. As the Queen of Christmas I don't have time for anyone – I just wish they'd understand.'

'It seems like you're so busy doing the TV Christmas you don't have time for the real one,' I said.

'Exactly,' she smiled, missing the irony completely at first, then looking at me and twisting her mouth. 'Oh Ames, I'll be honest I've resented you for so long for what you did, seeing it as a betrayal, that you weren't a good friend, but I wasn't a good friend to you either. I never responded to your calls or emails or cards because I wanted to forget everything, I didn't want the past crowding in. You know how unhappy I was as a kid, and then it all got so messy...'

'I know and it was my fault...'

'Not just you, I reckon Mum can take some of the blame for almost everything that's gone wrong in my life. She was a terrible mother, still is – but then I haven't been a great daughter. She moved to Sydney, you know?'

'I didn't realise...'

'Ha, neither did I until I got a bloody postcard from halfway around the world. Then she called me and after five minutes I said, 'Sorry, Jean, your time is up.' She never had any time for me when she was working – and I've no time for her now while I'm working. I'm a busy lady and don't have a spare moment to waste on friends, family or phone calls – I've got a business empire to run.'

I nodded. It was clear Bella was now living the life her parents had – workaholics, fiercely ambitious, constantly striving. Their business plans had consumed them so much they lost sight of the goalposts and never realised their lives were going by and their daughter was shrivelling up from lack of love and attention. Bella had grown up virtually alone – which is why when we were teenagers we'd bonded even more. I'd lost my mum – and in effect she'd never had one because hers had never been there for her. But the one time her mum could have helped her she'd simply thrown her out.

❅ ❅ ❅

Later that evening, when the first day's filming was over I tried again to talk to Bella. She was explaining to me what a brilliant assistant Crimson was, which I found hard to believe, but looking at Crimson, half-smiling into her iPad, it clearly made her happy to be described as 'an online genius'.

'She's fabulous, and saved me from myself,' Bella said. 'I used to do all my own online media – I Facebooked daily, "liking", "sharing" and congratulating myself on everything from a good show to a well-made cup of coffee. But I was cheating,' she giggled, putting her hand to her mouth like a naughty girl. 'I would put someone else's photos on my tweets, bragging about a delicious dish I'd "whipped up" for supper – or a fabulous restaurant I'd been to – which of course I hadn't,' she threw her head back and laughed. 'Too busy filming and tweeting about it to actually eat in restaurants aren't we Crimson?' she laughed and Crimson rolled her eyes.

'Anyway,' she continued, after a quick slurp, 'I was having so much fun until one day I tweeted to Fliss about a couple of other celebrities without realising tweets were public, not private. It wasn't long before my less than complimentary tweets were retweeted and sent directly to the said celebrities. Only when the newspapers called Fliss for a comment from me and she phoned me to make it stop did I realise the enormity of the situation. I was physically sick. Apology emails, Jane Packer Rose Sundae Hatboxes and magnums of Dom Perignon eased the pain for those lovely, forgiving souls, but some of them have never spoken to me since. I'm hoping one day at least one of them will forgive me and accept my invitation to stay at Dovecote,' she smiled.

So it did matter to her what people thought – she still wanted to be liked, forgiven. Perhaps there was hope for her after all?

'I should have trusted my instincts and left well alone... it was like when I texted my producer, Delia. She is very posh and quite fierce and I was flattered to think I'd reached the inner sanctum when she sent me a light-hearted text about foie gras...'

'As you do,' I said, sarcastically.

'Quite,' she answered. 'So I immediately texted back saying, "Oh Delia you are such a joker," but predictive texting had turned joker into "hooker". Delia was quite understandably offended to receive a text from one of her lovely presenters saying "Oh Delia you are such a hooker," so I tried to rectify this. Unfortunately I merely ended up informing everyone of Delia's "hookery" by pressing the wrong button and sending the message to everyone in my contacts list.'

'Don't tell me... the great Delia Smith was in your phone book too?' I said.

She nodded, almost unable to speak about it.

I was mortified on Bella's behalf. 'Oh dear... it's not easy being you, is it?' I smiled sympathetically, as the old, disorganised, more frantic and funnier Bella emerged from under the perfect make-up. It's like she'd suddenly remembered it was okay to laugh at herself sometimes.

'Fliss said to prevent any future online mishaps and faux pas I had to get a young person to do my social media and manage my texts... so I did. Crimson's in her early twenties and like the rest of her generation prefers the virtual world to the real one so it was a no brainer to involve her in the all aspects of text and twittery.' She poured us another drink, and though I was tempted to put my hand over my glass I thought 'If you can't beat them.'

'Meanwhile, I'm living to tweet another day... well, Crimson is,' she laughed. 'I now don't understand a word of what I'm saying online, but thank God she does,' she said, leaning over to rub Crimson's arm.

'God Bella, it's not rocket science,' she muttered from behind a Himalaya of hair.

I had to smile, Crimson was like my own kids, she'd probably grown up with an iPod in her hands. It was all so new and different for people mine and Bella's age, and like her I knew the perils of Twitter all too well; 'I've been there too Bella, you're not alone,' I laughed. ' Last year the headmaster thought it might be a good idea for us all to "get down with the kids," and for a while it was nice to be able to communicate outside school hours with the odd maths query. But the pupils soon saw the potential for public humiliation and when they weren't hacking teacher's accounts, they were abusing us under Twitter pseudonyms. It was a levelling experience to be told by a stranger that I was 'a minger' and a 'stupid old cow'.'

Bella laughed. 'Kids eh?'

I laughed too and sipped on my champagne, thinking how this was just like being with a lovely, old friend.

I finished my glass of champagne with Bella, feeling quite warm and comforted – yes it was partly due to the alcohol, but I had sensed a thawing from her and felt much happier about everything. As Crimson had now left the kitchen to go and have some food, I decided to take advantage of our time alone together.

'Bella...you and Peter haven't had children... is it because of what happened?'

Bella's eyes filled with tears. 'Don't, please don't, Amy. I'm sorry...' she stood up and touched my arm, then left the kitchen.

I watched her walk away, wishing she'd stayed and talked to me, but she was obviously too upset. I'd read every interview she'd ever done but she'd never mentioned having or wanting children and I wondered... was it my fault she now couldn't have children?

It all happened such a long time ago – twenty-two Christmases had gone by since then – but it still felt like yesterday. We were eighteen and it was mid December. I wasn't really looking forward to Christmas, it hadn't been the same since mum had died, but I planned to bake and revise (in that order!) for my mock A levels. Bella hadn't been herself for a couple of weeks and I wondered if she was having problems with her boyfriend, Chris. At nineteen, he was older than her and they'd been together a few months and she was crazy about him but constantly worried he was cheating on her. She kept saying how boys only liked slim girls and had gone on a crash diet, so when I'd caught her being sick in the toilets I waited outside the cubicle to confront her. Girls were squealing and chatting, toilet doors were banging and we stood among the wet confetti of paper towels and teenage hormones.

'You're anorexic, aren't you?' I said as she emerged, face wet with tears.

She grabbed me by the elbow and pulled me out of the toilets, away from the chatter and the paper towels.

She led me to our lockers where she opened the door, took out a packet of polo mints and offered me one, but I was so anxious I couldn't eat anything. She popped one in her mouth and nodded her head for me to hide behind the locker door so we could talk. 'I missed my period Ames... I'm pregnant,' she whispered, her minty breath filled my face and my heart lurched. I hadn't seen this coming at all.

'What am I going to do?' Tears filled her eyes – we were both so young and I don't know who was more scared.

I just stood there clutching my bag, all thoughts of revision and set texts drained from my head and I couldn't speak as we looked at each other. She was, as usual, waiting for me to give her an answer, to rescue her, but for once I was lost.

'Will you keep it?' was all I could say.

'Ames, of course, how could you even ask that? You know how I feel about babies...'

'Yes, but this isn't a baby yet... like you said it's a missed period, are you even sure?'

She nodded. Life had changed in a moment – Bella's exams and university hopes, our plans to go travelling round Europe, her pregnancy would change my plans too. I was still dealing with life after Mum and with no one to talk to except each other we were both lost.

Over the next few weeks Bella was a mess, she cried in lessons, never went home and the only person she wanted to talk to was me. So I would sit up all night listening and at school I'd leave my lessons to go to her and sit in the toilets holding her hand and telling her it was all going to be okay. But what did I know? Eventually I convinced her to tell Chris, who said he loved her and they'd bring up the baby and be happy ever after. She was young and in love and believed everything he told her – but he'd never had a job and I'd heard the rumours about his cheating and was worried for her future. She couldn't waste it all on this unfaithful layabout, but she wouldn't listen.

The whole situation affected both our lives and my grades began to suffer, I was unable to concentrate and wasn't revising because I was spending every spare moment with Bella. I felt like this whole problem was on top of me and I wasn't able or prepared to make the decision for her.

I remember wishing my mum had still been around, she'd have known what to do. Bella always said I took on other people's problems, I was like Mum and I wanted to help, but at the same time Bella was keen to hand me her problems, again another reason why we fit together so well, but she just kept asking me what she should do. Apart from the obvious which was to terminate the pregnancy, and just carry on like nothing had happened, I didn't know. So instead of telling Bella she must make her own choices and I'd be there for her, I'd taken matters into my own hands. One evening when I knew Bella was at Chris's I went round to her mother's and told her everything. I thought she would help, guide Bella through the decision-making and support her in whatever she decided to do as I know my mother would have. Little did I know that the fallout from my revelation would ruin Bella's life and end our friendship.

❄ ❄ ❄

I tried not to go over it all in my head, why I made that stupid decision and why her mother reacted with such anger. I hoped now, finally with some time together at Dovecote, I might be able to make amends and she might come some way to finally forgiving me.

The conversation about her childlessness had upset Bella, and given what happened to her I wasn't surprised. That might have been her only chance to ever have a baby and she'd been forced to terminate the pregnancy. I had lived with the guilt of this for years, even if my intentions were good, my actions caused this. If I'd just helped her and not gone running to her mother Bella could have had her baby and who knows, probably more. As an only child it was always her dream to have loads of kids and I'd ruined that for her. I didn't follow her when she left the kitchen in tears, I assumed she needed her space, so decided to go outside and get something to eat.

The food truck was parked a few hundred yards away from the house because apparently Bella didn't like the smell. The crew were standing in clusters in the freezing cold tent, a bare electric light dangled from the roof and snow was coming down thick now. I wondered how long they'd put up with eating their food outside? I also wondered how long they'd put up with my contradicting Bella and being stroppy during filming. I pulled my coat around me tighter, shielding me against the wind. It was late and I hadn't eaten since breakfast, and when the lady working in the truck handed me a large, warm turkey sandwich dripping in cranberry sauce, stuffing and lined with crispy bacon, I could have kissed her.

I walked into the food tent and found a small table with a plastic chair and sat down with my sandwich, there was nowhere else to go. The tables all looked very rickety but each one had a plastic floral Christmas arrangement on it and in the background was a choir recording of 'Silent Night'. Bella would have been horrified at the decorations, the dodgy tinsel hanging around the tent would have been like garlic to a vampire – but it made me feel Christmassy. I was just finishing when I felt someone standing at the table, and as I turned, I saw it was Mike the cameraman. He was holding two polystyrene cups of steaming coffee. 'Mind if I join you? Thought you might be in need of this,' he said, handing me a cup.

My heart melted. 'Oh, thank you... you've no idea. I didn't know where the drinks were.'

He smiled without looking at me, just gazing ahead, and took a sip of his drink.

'Is filming always like that?' I asked, feeling the need to say something after he'd been so kind.

'Yeah well, put someone like Bella on a high wire with someone like Fliss and add a little bit of Tim on his trapeze and you've got yourself a circus.' His eyes smiled as he took another sip. I felt comforted, I'd been right that he was someone I could relate to in the middle of this madness.

'Yes it's all so dramatic, isn't it? They can't pass each other in the kitchen without it becoming a Greek tragedy or a love story of

Shakespearean proportions. Then I enter and add my own flavour of chaos and confrontation.'

He laughed. 'Someone said you're a teacher – you sound like one.'

'Really?' I said, a little put down by this.

'Yeah, in a good way. I sometimes think it's me who's crazy and they are all quite normal.'

I laughed. 'Bella's never been what you'd call normal, even before she was on TV she behaved like a celebrity – but it was funny then.'

'So it's true? You and Bella – that's a weird thing – I heard that you knew her, years ago, but I can't imagine you being friends, you seem so different.'

'Yeah she was once a good friend of mine, but no one's supposed to know.'

'Your secret's safe with me,' he winked causing my cheeks to feel very warm.

'Yep, Bella's – a challenge – she seems to have no regard for anyone else. She insists on filming here, so she doesn't have to get up early or travel, but everyone else does. And when we get here, we are all kept outside like dogs – even in this cold.'

I nodded. 'I know, but that's because she thinks that's how she should behave – and no one's ever questioned her.'

'Until now... you did today,' he said, with a hint of mischief.

'Oh I know, and it didn't take much to light that bonfire,' I rolled my eyes. 'It wasn't a conscious thing – I didn't go on set and think – right, now I'm going to wind Bella up... she just made me angry because she can't see she's alienating her audience.'

'Yeah, but that's where you come in... that scene when you were both angry over the turkeys was priceless! Two well-dressed women smiling for the camera while battling it out over pig flesh, bleeding beef and dead bird carcasses. It was hilarious... the viewers will lap it up.'

I wasn't so sure. 'Was it really that bad?' I said.

He nodded. 'It was so bad it was great. Absolute carnage... and talking of carnage, I'd better set up for tomorrow's Christmas bloodbath,' he said, nodding to the soundwoman who was tapping her finger on her wrist to indicate lateness.

I thanked him for the coffee and meandered back towards the house in the hope of finding an overhanging roof or a porch to shelter under and finish my drink before going to bed. I doubted coffee in polystyrene cups was allowed at Dovecote and I didn't want some embarrassing incident where I was banned from the building.

I was just walking away from the catering tent, past a row of snow-covered trees when I saw a lonely figure heading down the driveway in my direction. As she came nearer, I could see it was Bella, lit by various safety lights, dressed in a long, hooded cape. She was treading carefully through the snow looking very glamorous like someone from a fairy tale.

'Hi Bella,' I said as she approached.

'Oh Amy, I thought you were having supper in the tent?'

'It wasn't exactly supper, just a sandwich, but I've finished now, I'd recommend the turkey,' I smiled, walking slowly past.

She suddenly grabbed me. 'Don't go Amy... come back in with me.'

'Okay,' I laughed, turning round and walking with her. 'You used to do this when we were teenagers, you always made me go to the toilets with you.'

'Yeah I did, didn't I? Do people ever really change, Amy? Despite everything, I still sometimes feel like a frightened little girl.'

I was surprised at her sudden honesty, her vulnerability, and felt the need to reassure her.

'We are all frightened little girls at times. My students would be amazed to know that every time I walk in that classroom I have to gather myself together, do a Lady Macbeth and screw my courage to the sticking place,' I smiled as we walked out of the freezing darkness into the slightly warmer, brightly lit tent.

'I feel like that little girl now,' she whispered, looking down at her feet as we walked through to the other side of the tent where the food truck was situated.

'But it's only the crew and your friends,' I said. 'Tim's over there telling them all about his "salty Shakespeare" and there's Billy...'

She seemed really nervous, but I could see why she felt like this because everyone was looking. People were nudging each other and staring as we passed them. Even I was beginning to feel quite self-conscious, and they weren't looking at me.

'I don't usually come to the tent... well, I've never been in before. It's only 'cos I knew you'd be here I thought I'd brave it, but I think I'll go back now,' she said in a whisper.

'No you won't,' I said, linking her and drawing her towards the little van and ordering her a turkey bap with all the trimmings and two coffees. It seemed like it was quite a big deal for Bella to turn up here and I wasn't going to let her go back and sit inside Dovecote alone.

As we walked away to find a rickety table, I waited for her shriek of horror at the sight of the wobbly Christmas table arrangements that had seen better days. But she sat down, began eating her turkey bap with gusto and said, 'It feels quite Christmassy, doesn't it?'

I nodded, surprised at her positive reaction, perhaps it was dawning on Bella that you didn't have to have the very best designer decorations to make Christmas sparkle.

'I'm sorry if I upset you before... talking about you and Peter not having children,' I started. 'I've often wondered why you didn't... if it had something to do with the abortion...'

Bella nodded. 'It was a terrible time, Ames, once you told her, Mum made me an appointment at the clinic the next day, I cried for weeks. But it wasn't all your fault. My mother played her part.'

'Still, if I'd just kept the secret and never told her, things would be different now.'

'Who knows... perhaps it just made me stronger?'

I nodded.

'But you really don't need to take any guilt on about me and Peter not having any children. I'm fine, Peter's fine – we could probably have kids, we just don't want kids together because we have our careers. Okay?'

I was relieved the reason for her childlessness was choice, but wondered if she really believed that her career was enough, especially as she'd lived through her parents' work-driven lives and always vowed to be different. I didn't pursue it, Bella was making it clear she'd had enough for now, and as things seemed slightly easier between us I didn't want to push my luck. So while she ate her bap I tried to lighten the mood and gave her a running commentary about one or two of the others in the tent. 'Tim is DEVASTATED,' I said. 'Dame Judy is waiting at The Royal Court for him but he just has to do another bloody shot with *bloody* Bella and her stuffing first,' I said in Tim's voice. Bella giggled, it was something we did as kids, saying funny stuff under our breath about whoever was in our vicinity.

'But dahling, I remember a time when breasts were in and food porn was the only thing we got off on,' Bella added in Fliss's voice. 'Yes dahling, those were the days... when you were giving it to them like a page 3 wannabe.' We both giggled, watching Fliss, who had now moved outside the tent for a fag and all that could be seen of her was a curl of grey smoke. Every now and then a car headlight would light her up in her furry pink jacket, matching kitten heels deep in the snow – leaning against the tree and breathing in huge lungfuls of smoke.

'You okay now?' I asked Bella when we'd finished laughing and she'd finished eating.

'Yes... I am... thanks.'

'Good, it's great that you came in here and... mixed with everyone.'

She looked at me over her polystyrene coffee cup. 'I wouldn't exactly call it mixing...'

I'd worried that I wasn't really fitting in, but here was Bella who had known these people for years, and she couldn't even share a cup of coffee with them.

'Why have you never mixed with the people you work with?' I asked, reverting to my role as a teacher. 'It makes life so much easier when you share stuff with your colleagues, Bella. I do it all the time at school, we complain to each other about the kids and the lack of equipment and it doesn't change anything but it does make you feel better.'

'Oh, you've always been happier around people than I have, Ames... I've never been comfortable sharing, and now it's even worse because I have to be so careful what I say in case it gets back to the tabloids. They are relentless, they even did a story on Pussy Galore last week – did you see it? They said she'd been shagging the local Tom Cat "in the walled garden of Bella's £3m Cotswold mansion" – they didn't even get that right, Dovecote is worth far more than that.'

'Poor Pussy Galore having her honour besmirched by the press,' I giggled. Bella's white Persian cat was almost as famous as her owner, often joining her on the sofa during filming, adding to the glamour. She'd even done some cat fashion shoots, modelling cat dresses and collars. And in the previous year's Christmas special she'd worn a designer gown and a handmade tiara... both costing more than my monthly pay cheque.

'Where is Pussy anyway? I haven't seen her about the house?'

'Oh he died... two weeks ago. Terrible timing given that we had this big Christmas Special.'

'Oh no, you loved that cat...'

'No I didn't... he made me sneeze. It wasn't even mine. Pussy Galore was an animal actor called Bert, we hired him for the show. I was bloody furious when he dropped dead like that... Fliss tried to stop the cheque, but it was too late.'

'So you read everything on autocue, you rarely bake, and now you're telling me that Pussy Galore... is a boy...?' I said, feeling like I was suddenly in a Christmas mystery – 'The Secrets of Dovecote Hall.'

'Yeah. But not a word, about any of it. Fliss ordered another Pussy Galore, he was delivered this afternoon but he scampered off and Fliss is distraught, she's been chain smoking since it happened – didn't you hear her shouting "where's my pussy" all afternoon?' I nodded – I'd been only too aware of Fliss making like a chimney and shouting about her pussy, but quite honestly this wasn't anything unusual where Fliss was concerned.

'Anyway, the new Pussy Galore – the one who escaped – is called Keith,' she giggled and rolled her eyes at the madness of it all. 'I told you, Amy, there's no place to hide. As if my life's not hard enough, I now have pussy problems,' she spluttered into her coffee.

'How funny. TV is a strange and magical world, isn't it?' I said, feeling a bit like Alice in Wonderland after she's taken the potion – nothing was what it seemed. 'Are you really Bella?' I laughed. 'Or... are you an actor called Fred wearing a wig and dentures?'

She smiled at this, but in an ironic sort of way. 'I don't think there's an actress anywhere who could play me, I play the part too well...but yes, you guessed it – I wear a wig, my hair's not as thick and lustrous as it was, whose is?' I didn't say anything, it was yet another confirmation of how tough it was to be at the top – and how many lies she had to tell to stay there.

'I couldn't live like you, Bella, in a world where everyone wakes up for the camera and then falls back to sleep as soon as it's turned off,' I said as we got up from our chairs and headed out into the darkness. I linked her arm in mine like we used to as girls as we walked back up the long gravel drive to the house. 'I'd feel like I was losing myself.'

'Bella lost herself a long time ago, love. And don't get me started on the Silver Fox...'

'What do you mean?' I swallowed, I could take a wig and a fake ham and even a Pussy Galore called Bert... but Peter, the husband who couldn't get enough of Bella's delicious titbits? Was he not everything he seemed either? 'You and Peter are happy... aren't you?'

'Oh I can't really talk about it. If anything got out I'd be ruined... mind you, like I said to Fliss, I could write one hell of an autobiography. The stuff I'd tell would stun the world.'

'About your marriage, you mean?'

'My marriage is some of it, yes – my marriage isn't about love, it's about money,' she sighed. 'Then there's the other thing...'

Suddenly Tim appeared at my elbow and I wanted to swat him away because Bella was just beginning to open up to me, but Bella seemed almost relieved that Tim's arrival had stopped her from saying too much.

'I love your hat, Tim,' she said, referring to his headwear – bunny ears and a sprig of holly.

'Yes, darling, Kevin Spacey bought it for me when we did Shakespeare together in London... "Tim," he said, "you are literally *the* best director I have ever had the privilege to work with".'

'Well, I think you're the best director I've worked with too – compared to Kevin, I'm nothing, but it's not all about the biggest and the best, you know, Tim,' Bella teased.

I had to smile at this.

'Thank you, my love. Can I walk you ladies back to the big house for bedtime?' he said, grabbing my arm with one hand and Bella's with the other and guiding us both back to the house. My heart sank – what on earth had Bella been about to tell me?

Chapter Thirteen

Christmassy Cocktails and Bubbly Baths

Back inside Dovecote it was clear Bella didn't want to talk any more, and she rushed upstairs two at a time, presumably to see Peter. Meanwhile, my head was fizzing with our last conversation and what she could possibly mean about her marriage. She hinted at other stuff too – it would 'stun the world', she'd said. I tried to put it from my head, there was nothing I could do and would have to wait and see if, at some point in the next day or two, she would tell me. I'd seen a glimpse of the old Bella that evening, I'd seen her vulnerability which she rarely revealed to anyone. Who knew what might happen in the future with our friendship, but just spending time with her and laughing like we used to lifted some of the heavy weight of guilt I'd been carrying around all these years. Her mother had forced her into that abortion and I'd always wondered if it had affected her fertility. Hearing that it had been her and Peter's choice not to have children was a huge relief.

Back in my room I closed the door and breathed deeply. It smelt of vanilla and Christmas, the sting of pine fragrance from the huge Christmassy flower arrangement creating a delicious Christmassy cocktail of scent. The whole conversation with Bella about being childless had made me think how lucky I was. I longed to hug my kids and couldn't wait to see them after Christmas, but for now a text would have to do. I sent them both the same one, asking if they were ok, and that I was having an amazing time and loved them very much.

Jamie's was typical, with just an 'All good, see u Boxing Day. x' but Fiona's was more 'Fiona', asking me about Bella 'what's she really like Mum? Have you two made friends now? I can't wait to hear all about it. Love you. X'

I held my phone to my chest, both my children were happy and well and nothing else really mattered in the great scheme of things. I gazed around the lovely room, feeling very lucky - the beautiful bedspread had been turned down by Bella's housekeeper and those soft pillows and high count cotton were inviting. But first – a steaming hot bath in the lovely tiled bathroom. My fingers ran along the Molten Brown bath products lining the shelf above the bath, all in the same shade of gold and chocolate. I chose Black Peppercorn body wash, which exuded a warming aromatic spiciness as I poured it under the running tap. As I undressed and sunk into the deep, hot bath, I knew I was tasting a little flake of Bella's life and I lay there for a while, the bubbles melting as I wondered some more about her secrets. Perhaps it wasn't a physical inability to have children... but an emotional one after what happened? And I wondered again if she regretted not having children and if it was more Peter's idea than hers. Climbing out of the bath, I wrapped the fluffy robe around me, thinking how money must make Bella feel cosseted and cared for. It was easy for Bella to mistake material luxuries for love, because she'd never known real love from her parents, just beautiful things instead.

I imagined now that the soft robes, silky bubbles and deep luxurious cream carpets offered a kind of loving for Bella. Her feet were hugged in the carpets, her body caressed in designer fabrics by day and cashmere and silk by night. Being Bella must be like living in a luxury hotel permanently, I thought – all her needs catered to and every sensory pleasure at her fingertips.

The hot bath and the peppercorn bubbles had re-awakened me and instead of flopping straight into bed I did some exploring. I padded around the bedroom casually opening draws and squirting 'Christmas Heaven' room scent everywhere and imagining this was my home, my life – it felt good. The bedroom even had a bowl of jelly beans and a one-touch lighting/sound system, which I decided I'd steer clear of. I wasn't sure about sound systems and it was a little late to be experimenting with noise when everyone else was probably asleep. My trouser suit was hanging on the door frame – the steam from the bathroom had softened the creases slightly by now, so I popped it in the wardrobe.

As I did, I spotted a lovely hatbox in the corner of the wardrobe floor and moved the few coats in there so I could see it better. The box was Tiffany blue with a scrawled figure of a woman in a hat – very fifties, very designer, very Bella. I imagined the hat inside was probably quite beautiful and expensive and she'd probably worn it only once, knowing her.

Reaching in to pull it out, the box was slightly heavier than I'd anticipated and it suddenly occurred to me that it might not actually contain a hat at all. I reminded myself it wasn't mine to open and I was being very nosy and intruding on someone else's stuff – but still, I pulled it out of the wardrobe, sat on the floor and slowly lifted that beautiful lid.

Inside the box were notes and cards. On top were postcards from various glamorous locations and underneath were Christmas and Birthday cards. There was no semblance of order, they'd all just been put in randomly. But delving deep and looking at some of the dates, the further down I went, the older the notes and cards were. Among the cards were old photos of Bella as a little girl with her parents, on Father Christmas's knee and one of the two of us in the kitchen at home. We must have been about seven, both smiling widely, big gaps in our teeth, icing on our faces, so happy. Mum must have taken the picture with Bella's camera – I couldn't help but be pleased she'd kept it all these years.

I delved deeper and deeper, postcards, receipts, more photos, and then I came across them, my Christmas cards to Bella. She'd kept each one and not just the ones with recipes inside. I was touched to find them in this box full of mementoes she'd obviously kept for years. Then I saw the postcard she'd mentioned, the one from her mother saying, 'I've moved to Sydney.' As Bella had said, it was short and sweet, no kisses or declarations of maternal love and longing saying how she was missing her – how very Jean, I thought. I rummaged a little deeper but was beginning to feel uncomfortable – I was in Bella's home rifling through her personal stuff. It might feel like I was staying in a hotel room, but that didn't make it right, so I stopped myself from looking any further and carefully put everything back in the box. As I gathered everything together, a card slipped out from inside another one, and I couldn't resist picking it up. The pale pink of the card was pretty and on the front of the card was a message in pink that said, 'On the Birth of your Baby Girl.' I was intrigued, I knew I shouldn't, but I opened the card and read it... 'Congratulations Bella, and welcome to the world baby Cressida, from all at the Hostel.'

❊ ❊ ❊

I sat on the floor for a while reading and re-reading the card, trying to work out if there was a different interpretation to the obvious one – that perhaps Bella hadn't had an abortion after all? Turning the card round there was a date written in ink on the back – 25th August 1992. That would tie in with Bella's pregnancy. My head was everywhere – and kept coming back to the same question: if Bella had the baby, where was she now?

I lay in bed, knowing that despite the lovely soft sheets and sumptuous pillows I wasn't going to get any sleep that night. My head was full of so many questions. What had happened to Bella all those years ago? Her mother had told me when I'd called that she'd made 'the appointment' for the termination, but had Bella refused to go? Is that why her mother had thrown her out onto the streets?

It must have been about an hour later when I heard the sound of raised voices in the hallway. One sounded like Bella, the other voice sounded deeper – like a man's... the Silver Fox perhaps?

I wondered if he knew about Bella's past, about the pregnancy? That explained why Bella was so worried I'd go to the press, a few stolen recipes was one thing, but a child out there somewhere was something else entirely. Here was a woman who presented a perfect picture of female happiness and accomplishment, the perfect life, the perfect wife. A teenage birth wouldn't quite fit into the story Fliss and Bella had created over the years, and as for Peter, who knew where he fit in? I was intrigued by their relationship, and had always wanted a taste of that wave-crashing love that they clearly had... but what challenges they must have faced. I pressed my head against my own bedroom door to catch snippets of conversation. I couldn't help it, I felt like I was in the middle of a reality show, wanting a peek into their private lives, longing to know their secrets and what would happen next. I knew the master bedroom where they slept was round the corner, so I could open my own door without being spotted, and I couldn't resist. I slowly, carefully, turned the handle and leaned out into the hallway, which made the door creak and a floorboard complain. These lovely old houses had their disadvantages, especially if you fancied yourself as a bit of a Miss Marple. I needn't have worried, any creaking noises I made were soon drowned out by the increasingly loud argument now coming from the master bedroom.

'Bella, I've told you. I won't go through the charade again, we've been telling lies for too long, it's got to stop...'

'But Peter give it another year... please darling. You know how much it will hurt me, think of the show...'

'I'm sorry, Bella, it's not just about you and me, it's not fair... there's another person to consider here too.'

Lies? Hurt? Three people? This wasn't what their love story was all about – where were the white lace and promises? And more importantly who was the third person Peter was referring to? Did he mean Bella's child... or, God forbid, another woman? Oh dear, I suddenly felt as I had with the hatbox, like I shouldn't be doing this... like a child who'd come upon unsavoury adult stuff she didn't understand. Yet... I couldn't tear myself away. Bella had been trying to open up to me and each time we were interrupted – perhaps her marriage wasn't so happy after all, and if I listened I might get some clue as to what the problem was. I looked at the whimsical drawings of a Dickensian Christmas on the landing wall by the huge festive flower arrangement as I listened to the urgent bickering coming from the master bedroom. Bella's perfect Christmas, her wonderful life, was turning out to be quite different from the one I'd imagined. God only knows what was going on, but the conversation between her and Peter was clearly private and serious and I really shouldn't be eavesdropping. But I crept out onto the landing, causing the bloody door to squeak loud and long and they must have heard it because they stopped talking. After a brief interlude, I heard more angry mutterings and the sound of someone storming from the master bedroom, and slamming another bedroom door. From my hallway vantage point I could hear Bella continuing to shout at Peter something about 'tramp camp,' which

I assumed meant our war hero was now in the Nigella room. I had to smile, imagining the rugged Silver Fox lounging sulkily in a black silk fringed boudoir after a silly row with his wife. I waited a few minutes and as I moved slowly backwards against the wall I felt something move behind me and the hairs stood up on the back of my neck. I tried not to scream and slowly turned round to see Pussy Galore II had returned from wherever he'd escaped to earlier. I wondered if he answered to his stage name or was merely Keith out of hours but whatever it was he was rubbing himself up against my legs and purring loudly. I looked down and a big white fluffy face looked up and meowed so loudly I was worried someone might hear him... and find me loitering outside other people's bedrooms like a weirdo. So I picked Keith up, wrapping him gently in my dressing gown to turn his volume down and slowly backed along the hall in the direction of my room. I was bent down, moving backwards at some speed when I suddenly became aware of someone watching me. Fliss was standing in the hall, spiky hair on end, in a black silk dressing gown decked in black and white marabou trim and frou-frou slippers. One had to wonder how many muppets had died to make that gown.

'Amy dahling, are you in pain?'

She was bending down to my level, probably trying to check my pupils to see if I was on medication – and who could blame her? I doubt many other houseguests at Dovecote had been found stalking the hallways backwards in the middle of the night with a cat in their cleavage.

'Pussy! It's Pussy... you've found her?'

'Well, he ... it's Keith.'

'Ssshhh dahling, it's Pussy Galore, not a word to anyone regarding his real identity or we'll all be ruined,' she said theatrically placing her finger on her own lips.

'Yes, yes of course. It's just that he was rubbing himself against me and next thing is he's snuggling into my chest.'

'That's what they all say, dear,' she guffawed, reaching into my cleavage to ruffle Keith's fur, which was disturbing for both me and the cat. 'Pussy only arrived this afternoon, didn't you gorgeous,' she was nose to nose with Keith... and my breasts. 'One minute he was a fluffy bundle of love the next a pinwheeling ball of hate and kitty claws before disappearing into thin air,' she giggled.

I just prayed Keith wasn't about to repeat the afternoon's 'pinwheel' performance up against my breasts - my décolletage would never be the same again.

'Yes, Bella did say he'd escaped,' I said, trying to extricate him from my chest, but even as I bent down to put Keith on the floor he clung for dear life and I felt it safer to let him have his own way.

'Ha, I assume Pussy's with you tonight?' she said, smiling at his stubbornness. 'Do keep an eye on him, dear, we don't want him running off again, I don't think my heart could take the stress.'

I nodded, I'd conceded to his demands and he was back purring in my arms, his head rubbing up against my chin and I was cat-sitting for the rest of the night.

'Now you and Pussy Galore had better get some sleep,' she said, gathering up her gown. 'You're both required for filming in the morning – and one of you is wearing a Santa's Little Helper ra-ra skirt,' she teetered off, back to the Martha Stewart room on her fluffy mules, giggling to herself.

I watched her go, silently stroking Keith and hoping to God the ra-ra skirt planned for tomorrow was his and not mine. Once she'd disappeared round the corner I returned briskly to the Mary Berry room, putting on the bedside lamp and lying back on the plaid quilt, where Keith happily joined me. My heart was pounding... it was all too much, what with Bella and Peter screeching at each other, and Fliss stalking the hallways in the middle of the night. What the hell was going on at Dovecote? You couldn't make it up – and Bella was right, the tabloids would love a snapshot of her life – marital rows, mad agents and errant pussies.

I gazed at Mary's huge portrait on the wall. I doubt her life was quite such a circus.

I imagined Peter had, by now, crept back to the master bedroom, declared undying love and they were now having rampant make-up sex, while I sat on the bed with a Mary Berry Cookbook and a gender-confused cat.

❄ ❄ ❄

Despite being desperately tired I lay awake for ages intrigued by everything I'd overheard. None of it made sense. Had Bella put the show first and Peter was now feeling neglected? That would be terrible for her – he was such a handsome, successful guy, the first hint of a crack in their marriage and women would be forming a queue for a shot at the Silver Fox.

It must have been about two a.m. when I heard it... the hissed conversation, the raised voices again.

It seemed Bella and the Silver Fox were resuming their earlier argument, so I carefully got out of bed and opened my door slightly. I loitered in the doorway a while praying Fliss wasn't on the prowl, but things seemed to have quietened down. I was just about to close the door when I saw the Silver Fox sweeping down the stairs, past the huge Christmas tree and outside, slamming the front door as he went.

Where the hell was he off to? I hung around trying to listen, and after about a minute I heard Bella sobbing. It looked like they'd had a real humdinger this time – especially as he'd rejected the silky seduction of Nigella and walked out. It made me think about my own marriage and the terrible rows that gave me hangovers the next morning. Neil and I hadn't been happy for a long time, and it was only since he'd gone I realised how peaceful life could be at home.

Knowing just how she felt and falling into my old mode of best friend I had to comfort Bella, so I knocked on her bedroom door and asked if she was okay. After a little while she appeared in the doorway, wig askew, her face wet with tears.

'I heard you crying,' I started.

'Amy, I'm so sorry, did we wake you?'

'No, no, I was just passing... I was just going to the toilet...' I lied.

'But you have an ensuite...is that not something you're used to? Would you like a bucket?' she said and started to laugh.

I rolled my eyes. 'Okay, I heard noises coming from your room and heard you crying – I was worried about you.'

'Ahhh thank you,' she seemed touched at my concern. 'Yes well, the old Silver Fox can be a little... vigorous in the bedroom,' she laughed and looked at me, standing there a crumpled mess, none of the designer clothes and grooming that made her what she was – or what she seemed.

'You're not okay are you, Bella?' I asked gently.

She shook her head like a little girl about to burst into tears and I reached out my arms to hug her while she sobbed on my shoulder. After a while she composed herself and, pulling her dressing gown around her, I saw that old twinkle in her eye.

'Sod them all,' she smiled. 'I need a drink – fancy one?' She was beginning to walk down the stairs regardless of whether or not I was going, so I followed her down and into the kitchen where Crimson was perched on a stool.

'It's the middle of the night, shouldn't you be in bed, my darling?' Bella smiled.

'Shouldn't you?'

Bella ignored this and opened up her huge fridge, which seemed bigger than my car. It contained only a couple of bottles of wine and champagne and what looked like a platter of cheese - it was a beautiful showpiece, just like Bella. She opened a bottle of cold white wine and poured it into two Christmassy glasses decorated with hand-painted holly.

'Drink?' she asked Crimson.

'No thanks, one of us has to be sober in the morning.'

Bella smiled and pulled a face like we were the teenagers and Crimson our mother.

'Fancy a bit of Stinking Bishop, Amy?' Bella asked.

'Oh God is that some kind of middle-aged sex thing?' Crimson piped up from under her hair before I could speak.

'No, it's a washed rind cheese,' Bella said, like Crimson had made a genuine enquiry.

'I'm going to bed,' Crimson huffed, picking up her iPhone and leaving the room. Bella called goodnight and turned to face me; 'I will do it,' she sighed, 'the homeless thingy. I don't want to and I worry my viewers will want glitz and glamour instead of filth and Fair Isle jumpers – but I'll do it. Tim recced the place last week and says it's 'tragic,' but then – he would.'

'It is pretty tragic really,' I said, 'even Tim isn't over-dramatising when he says that.'

Bella pushed a domed lidded cheese plate towards me and I lifted the lid.

'I wouldn't normally dream of eating cheese in the middle of the night,' I said, 'but this looks beautiful.' There were several wedges of fabulous cheese, vine-leaf covered, rich blue-veined and soft, salty goat's, with little glass pots of chutney and a scattering of figs and nuts. It was Christmas on a plate for me and I pulled up a stool, took the glass of wine from Bella and tucked in.

'Yes, this time of year I always have a winterscape of cheeses made up for Peter when he gets home from a war zone,' she smiled.

'How lovely for him. No wonder Neil left me, he was lucky if I left a lump of stale cheddar in the fridge when he came home from work,' I laughed.

I thought I saw a hint of sadness in her eyes as she looked at me; 'what happened... with you and Neil? I remember you writing to me just after you were married, you both seemed so happy.'

'Aren't most people happy just after they get married?' I smiled. 'It's all new and wonderful and everything they say is magical and amazing, but wind on a few years and the stuff you thought was magical is boring and ridiculous and they make loud chewing noises over romantic dinner a deux and say crass things in front of your friends. And then they run off with a pole-dancing legal assistant, leaving you high and dry at Christmas. Well, she's welcome to him.'

'Oh, how I envy you,' she sighed.

'You envy me? I just told you about my unhappy marriage and how he is now wrapped round a pole with another woman... there's nothing to envy, Bella.'

'Even after what you just told me, it sounds like you had more of a marriage than I ever have.'

We both sipped our wine in silence.

'I can see you and Peter are going through a rough patch,' I said, wondering if the baby mentioned in the birth card was anything to do with their current disharmony. Did Peter refuse to accept the child into their lives? Had Bella had the child adopted? Had I got it completely wrong and the 'congratulations on your baby' card was something quite different, Bella had gone ahead with the termination and there was no baby? I was desperately trying to think of a way of bringing this up, but how could I without alerting Bella to the fact that I'd been snooping in her stuff?

'I used to think, just give me a long weekend with Peter, and everything will be fine,' she was saying. 'But I know now I was fooling myself. I'll never change him.' She suddenly seemed very serious and near to tears.

Looking at the sadness in her eyes, I decided it was time to stop eating my way through the winter landscape of cheese – Bella was trying to tell me something.

'What do you mean?'

'Oh, Fliss says I shouldn't tell anyone, no one can be trusted, she says...' she broke off and looked at me as if she'd been caught, as if Fliss were there keeping her in check.

I didn't want to push her, but at the same time I could tell she wanted to talk, she just needed reassurance. 'Bella, you can trust me, I know at first I virtually threatened to go to the papers about Mum's recipes, but I wouldn't have. Let's face it, I've carried your biggest secret around for years, I'm your oldest friend...'

'Yes, I know and I do trust you. I'd almost forgotten what friendship was like until you came here, the past twenty-four hours have reminded me what it's like to have a real friend. I know we argue, we always did – but I always knew you were there, objective, sometimes annoying – but always on my side. I need that girl now Ames... that confidante, someone I can trust and who can give me advice, I've got people like Fliss and Tim, but I need someone who isn't on the bloody payroll.'

'I'm here – talk to me. I feel like I let you down all those years ago, let me make it up to you.'

'We've kept it all quiet for so long and Fliss has worked so hard to keep everything out of the papers, I shouldn't talk about it...'

'But it's not healthy to live like this. I know as a celebrity you have to be discreet and you might not want to share all your personal business with the world, but it seems to me you've created your own world and it's not real. Dovecote is like the Bella theme park, it seems so magical but in reality it's fake and full of secrets... perhaps talking about stuff to someone you can trust will help? I don't want you to tell me anything you're not comfortable with, but like I said, I'm here and I want to help.'

She nodded but didn't say anything and I presumed she'd clammed up again, she was so used to keeping everything locked up inside it must have been hard to let it all go. I couldn't imagine having to cope with all of my problems alone, no one to talk to or confide in, and all the while pretending that everything was perfect. I finished my wine and was about to change the subject when she suddenly started talking.

'When I first met Peter I fell completely in love. I thought if I loved him enough he'd love me back.'

'But he's so attentive, so adoring, surely he still does?'

She shook her head. 'He left me years ago – he lives with his lover, Sacha.'

'Oh Bella, I'm sorry, I had no idea, I thought you were happy... had the perfect marriage. I thought he lived with you here.'

'That's what everyone's supposed to think, we've kept it a secret all these years because it could ruin both of us if it got out.'

'That must be hard, sharing your husband with another woman,' I started.

'Sacha isn't a woman,' Bella said, gulping a large glug of wine without taking her eyes off me.

'What? I don't understand...'

'Sacha's a man. And the reason we're arguing so much is that he's fed up of waiting in the wings... he wants Peter to marry him.'

'Oh...oh...' I didn't know what to say. I was shocked to the core. 'You're telling me Peter – the Silver Fox – is gay?' I had to have it spelt out to me I was so amazed I wanted to make sure I hadn't misunderstood what she was saying.

'Yes.'

'But he was here, he looked into your eyes in the kitchen and I watched him nuzzle your neck. Only last week he said on TV you were the sexiest woman in the world...'

'Yes, he's a good actor. He tries, God bless him he even tried in the bedroom when we were younger. He closed his eyes, lay back and thought of war zones and there was the odd uprising when I felt we might be able to find some common ground. But then he went to Iraq to cover the insurgency and found Sacha. They spend their time between their place in London and Sacha's home in Paris – which is difficult, but what can I do?'

'Divorce him?'

'It isn't as simple as that. I always knew the score, it was a "showbiz marriage". Peter was young, handsome, up-and-coming, but in 1990 being gay wouldn't help his image, especially as there was frenzied talk of him having his own current affairs programme. Coming out would just shift the emphasis from intellectual hunk to intellectual gay man and twenty years ago that wasn't to everyone's taste.'

Peter and I were both clients of hers so in Fliss's inimitable words she "killed two birds with one stone" – and booked a wedding. Gay men weren't the stuff of TV as they are now. Hell, these days it's all about the dysfunctional family reality shows where Dad is expected to have a sex change while Mum takes a toy-boy. It was all so different back then, wasn't it? So we set off for the registry office to hide the gay macho correspondent and his new kitchen goddess under a veil of white tulle and a five-foot croquembouche.'

'Wow... I remember the beautiful wedding photos. Peter was such a big name back then, no-one had a clue. When you married him I remember thinking how well you'd done... not that you didn't deserve...'

'It's okay Ames,' she smiled; 'You're right, Peter was quite the high-profile celeb and in marrying him my own star rose dramatically, our marriage opened doors for me. And in the years since we've become the quintessential English couple with our Sunday supplement lifestyle and spreads in celebrity magazines. You have to hand it to Fliss, she engineered the whole thing brilliantly.'

'So Peter has his... lover. What about you?'

'Nada. I have been set up as the perfect woman married to a very physical man and even if another guy was interested in me he'd either be too scared of me or even more scared of my big butch husband. Besides, I can't get close to anyone because if the press got hold of anything...'

'But you share a bedroom... don't you?'

She shook her head. 'No, sometimes I'd beg him to come to my bed and keep me warm, and once or twice he obliged, but nothing really happened. The tragedy is that despite it being a relationship for show I couldn't help falling for him, just a little bit - Peter is my perfect man – so handsome, fun, charming and caring. I used to hear him on the telephone to Sacha in the other room, the soft tone of his voice, the way his eyes would soften when he spoke about him and I would cry myself to sleep.'

'I can't believe it... you two are just so good together. Peter seems like the perfect husband.'

'Yes he is – for Sacha, and for the cameras, but there's only so much you can fake when you're married to the wrong gender.'

It hit me again just how much she'd suffered just to keep her secrets safe. To live a lie like that for so many years must have been horrific and not worth the fame, adoration, or any of the wonderful things she owned, even Dovecote.

'I know I live in a different world, but I can't believe you went through with a fake marriage.'

'It seems stupid and superficial now, but if I'm honest I believed we could live that life and everything would fall into place. I stupidly thought I might be able to change him, of course I didn't... I couldn't love enough for both of us.'

'Have you ever been in love with anyone else?'

She shrugged. 'No, there's only ever been Peter... and as it was never reciprocated it doesn't really count.'

I felt so sorry for her but realised in that moment that perhaps I'd never been in love either. My own marriage was almost a parallel with Bella's. I'd found out I was pregnant just a year after Bella, I was nineteen, I wanted to live my own life – Mum wasn't around anymore and I wasn't part of my father's new home with his new partner.

So in the same way Bella had used her marriage to embrace a bigger, better life, I'd used my marriage to escape my life. I'd been pregnant when I married Neil and spent the next twenty years trying to escape my marriage. I would take on causes, work long hours, help others with their problems – and all because my own life was so unhappy. I'd thought by marrying and having a baby I could create a family, get my mum back – but all I did was become disillusioned. I hadn't married Neil for the right reason – love. This was the first time I'd realised this fully and faced up to it. Looking at Bella's marriage was helping me see my own – and it hadn't been that different to her 'arranged' one.

'The sad truth is,' Bella was saying, 'my career has always come first and I've never had time for friends and love, I can never get close to anyone because I can't tell them the truth.'

'But Bella, think about it – everything is secret because none of you want to lose money or status... but what's the worst that could happen? You say goodbye to Peter and get yourself back.'

'Yes, and I've thought about it so many times, but it's just so risky, I've sacrificed so much to get where I am – I could lose everything.'

'Or gain everything?' I said.

She nodded. 'Oh Ames, I've missed you. You always made sense. I've had no-one to turn to since.'

I smiled. 'I was lucky, I'd always had my mum to turn to – she was incredibly wise, as you know. After she died, if ever I was worried or upset about something I would say to myself "what would Mum tell me to do?" I just wish I'd listened to that voice on my wedding day – I think mum would have sat me down and told me I was making a big mistake,' I said, finally facing up to the truth after all this time.

'I know it was him who left, but it sounds like you took your own advice there, Ames. From what you say, you didn't put up much of a fight when he left – you let him go to get yourself back.'

'Yes, you're absolutely right,' I nodded. It was like Mum had just spoken to me through the years and given me the answer and the strength I needed to finally make the break.

Bella poured us another drink and we sat in silence, both pondering our own lives and marriages by the glow of the kitchen fairy lights.

'Where's Peter gone?' I asked in the dimness.

'Now, you mean? Oh he's probably gone to a friend's nearby. He'll tell them I've locked all the doors and gone to bed and he's forgotten his key, people are used to him turning up out of the blue from somewhere terribly war-like. You see, we even have to lie to our friends. Peter only stays over for filming – just a few months a year – and if there are others staying over he pretends to go to bed in my room. But he's more comfortable in Nigella.'

I looked at her.

'The Nigella room – he likes the decor... it's more him,' she said with a twinkle in her eye.

'So you've got a system, you've managed to keep a lid on things for all these years, and now Sacha wants to get married?'

'Yes, Peter's fifty this year and Sacha wants him to marry him, and come out. His timing couldn't be worse...Christmas, I ask you?'

'Yeah but if it's right for Peter perhaps he should come out now, shouldn't he?'

'Mmmm it might be the right time for him, but what about me? How will it make me look? The sizzling sex siren of TV has been married to a gay man for twenty years and didn't even notice?' she laughed and took another gulp of wine. 'Or even worse, that being married to me was enough to turn him gay! Can you imagine, the tabloids will have a field day, it'll all be how I failed to satisfy him and he found real passion and fulfilment in the arms of another man.'

'You could say you knew?'

'And I've been lying to my fans?'

'Mmm, I can see it's a conundrum.'

Bella's world had made her super sensitive about how things looked and what people thought, but I could see just from spending this short time with her how exposed her life was.

'Sounds like you're both ready for him to come out,' I tried, offering a sane voice in the celebrity wilderness.

She sighed. 'Perhaps. He says he wants to live his own life, not half of mine, but I need him in my life. He's lived a double life, a public, family life of cosy Christmases and family holidays with me for his career and a private, loving relationship with Sacha. Meanwhile I've put my life on hold.'

I nodded. 'It might surprise you to know I can relate to everything you've told me,' I sighed. I too had put my life on hold since I married Neil, just drifting along, knowing it wasn't right or good for me, but hoping for a miracle.

'Funny, isn't it?' she said, 'you and me have both given up our lives to the wrong men, to relationships that weren't going anywhere and would never make us happy.'

'Yes and now we're both standing on the precipice, scared to step out on our own,' I added.

'But Ames, however bad you think it's been for you, it's been so much worse for me...'

'God Bella, you're even competitive about whose marriage failed the most,' I laughed, and she laughed along with me while pouring us both another large glass of chilled white.

'I live in a cut-throat world,' she sighed, taking a sip and settling onto her stool. 'Even my agent wants to sell me off as a sex slave to some African royalty... so I do have it so much harder.'

'Really?'

'Yes, recently with the ratings dropping, she had this "brilliant idea" of selling me to the king of Cameroon who was apparently looking for 'another' wife. As she pointed out, "Dahling you'd want for nothing".'

'She's outrageous,' I laughed.

'Oh, you can laugh but you'd be surprised what depths that woman will go to. A Saudi oil baron once offered her £1m for me to jump out of a cake naked and she was all for it – "Dahling, you're washed up in blighty," she said. "Let's go for the big bucks in the Middle East – you're a tasty European tit-bit and they are simply gagging for a nibble of you".'

She said this in Fliss's posh husky voice which made me laugh a lot.

'There's me envying your lavish Christmases and imagining your wonderful life being offered TV specials all over the world - when in reality your agent's telling you you're a has-been and flogging you to the highest bidder!'

'Ha ha, yes and I've resisted her offers so far. As for my TV specials and "lavish" Christmases you've probably gathered by now they are totally faked up. At Christmas we usually film the 'live' Christmas lunch the day before, then everyone buggers off to their real families – including my husband.'

❄ ❄ ❄

Bella made some coffee and we drank and chatted and the more time we spent together the more I realised, especially when it was just the two of us, I'd found my old friend again.

'I appreciate you sharing... everything,' I said. 'And I can see why you might find it hard to trust anyone.'

'Mmmm, I've had some pretty bad experiences with so-called friends since becoming famous. I get taken in easily – I'm lonely and vulnerable I suppose? A few years ago I met this woman at a fashion show, and she seemed lovely all "let's go for girlie drinks, let's do lunch..." and I was flattered.'

I nodded.

'Anyway Julie – as she called herself – takes me out for a few Christmas cocktails and I had one too many.' She sipped at her black coffee, 'And next thing you know I'm pissed, Julie's got her camera out and a male stripper's sitting on my face. Before you could say "Jingle Bells" the whole sordid thing was emblazoned across the front pages of the newspapers – with a link to the four minute video online. I can laugh about it now, but at the time I was so hurt.'

'I can imagine,' I said. 'Someone who you thought was a friend betrayed you.' I sighed, thinking about my own actions all those years ago.

'Bloody journalist... I really liked her. I don't have many – okay any – female friends, this whole persona that has been built around me has kept the outside world out,' she sighed. 'So when Julie came along, I just bought it all. I was drunk and Julie was egging me on – Ames, I was wearing a Santa hat!'

'From what you just told me I think the Santa hat was the least of your problems,' I laughed.

'You're right... his groin was here,' she gestured to her chin. 'He *was* gorgeous though - and only wearing a red velvet thong and a sprig of holly.'

'He had a Christmas theme going on then?' I laughed. She joined in, and we both sat there drinking coffee in our dressing gowns and I was back somewhere in the 80s, sitting in our kitchen at home, the two of us in pyjamas chatting about boys.

Chapter Fourteen

Bowels of Hell with a Festive Frisson

The following morning I woke up wondering where I was and in my exhausted and slightly hung-over state thought I was at home in my own bed until I saw the regal features of Mary Berry peering down at me from her portrait. I'd been dreaming about Neil kissing me under a Christmas tree – and as I opened my eyes was surprised how disgusted I felt. I climbed out of the huge bed and padded over to the window, to reassure myself I'd not dreamt that I was back at Dovecote with my old friend. I opened the thick gold curtains and looked up into a greying white sky, snow was hurtling to the ground in huge white spirals, adding yet another layer of white to the enormous garden which was already completely covered with snow. Keith the cat meandered around my legs and I gazed for a long time at the falling snow, thinking about Christmas and the previous night's revelations about Bella and the Silver Fox.

Downstairs I delivered Keith to his trainer Milly, who had arrived at Dovecote to chaperone him, having been informed of his nocturnal wanderings by Fliss. She took him gratefully telling him he was 'a naughty puss puss,' and off they went for his ra-ra skirt fitting. I headed for the dining room where I sat in the rather stately surroundings and ate the most delicious scrambled eggs cooked by Bella's personal chef while the rest of the crew froze outside at the truck. Bella's 'no hot food from outside,' rule in Dovecote while filming had meant she hadn't eaten much and even though she'd enjoyed the turkey bap she had for supper, said she couldn't face going out there first thing. So it was decided that me, Fliss and Tim (as long as he promised not to be annoying – which was a big ask) were allowed to join her at her varnished oak table for breakfast.

Fliss was in winter white, enjoying a large plate of waffles and reading the newspapers. I quite liked Fliss, for all her bluster and hair-brained schemes I reckoned she had Bella's back.

'I was talking to Bella last night – she was telling me about that journalist she met once, Julie, and the male stripper,' I said, nodding towards the paper.

'It was scandalous,' Fliss said, slamming down the newspaper. 'She got Bella incredibly drunk, buying her Rudolph the Red Nose cocktails...vodka, cranberry juice and a big cherry.'

'That's disgusting,' I sighed.

'I know... what kind of animal puts a cherry in vodka cranberry?'

'No... I didn't mean that, I meant how disgusting to get someone drunk and put them in a compromising position.'

'Well yes, but we've all been there,' she sighed.

I nodded. I hadn't been there but I could see from her twitch as she returned to her paper that Fliss had – and was now recalling every tortuous second. She lifted her head up and gazed in front of her. 'I said, Bella dahling you must never let it happen again and if anyone buys you drinks or tries to sit on your face call me immediately,' she looked at me, 'and she always has.'

I smiled politely, wondering just what part of the TV chef's world would involve regular offers of free drinks and face-sitting.

'I've lived through it, Amy,' she continued, peering at me over her bifocals. 'As an agent I've seen it happen with other celebrities... you can't let anyone in.'

I didn't express my horror at Fliss's apparent 'isolation technique', but finished my breakfast wondering if Fliss's 'mothering' of Bella was even more dysfunctional than Jean's hands-off, 'I've moved to Sydney' approach.

Just as we were finishing, Tim appeared and asked if he could join Fliss and I at the table, presumably he wasn't planning on being 'annoying' as Bella had stipulated this would lose him his pass to indoor breakfast. However, as he was drinking only a vegetable smoothie and making every mouthful a moment of high drama, I wondered how long his breakfast 'privileges' would last once Bella arrived.

'The eggs are good,' I said, like I was on a two-week package holiday and he was a fellow guest at the table.

'I'm sure they are but my body is a contradiction, it would love and loathe them... in fact my body hates me right now. It is torn between being soothed by this emollient fluid and preparing to explode all over this dining room.'

'Oh dear, that is a contradiction,' I said, wanting to run for cover.

'He suffers with his digestion,' Fliss said, rolling her eyes and twisting her lips in a 'believe that one if you will' gesture.

'Suffer... suffer? That doesn't even begin to cover it – I am a slave to my digestive system, it is a sheer and profound agony that I live with 24/7,' he snapped, before slurping the last of the pungent green liquid. Fliss and I watched him in sync and if my face was anything like hers we both looked like we had a vile smell under our noses.

'Is Madame still in bed?' he asked, putting down his glass.

Fliss nodded solemnly. 'Yes and the clock's ticking. The crew are here, they are being paid an extortionate amount to work over this Christmas period, but, hey, I have my beta blockers, my hip flask and a catering pack of St John's Wort so what do I care?' With that, she shovelled a handful of pills in her mouth and swallowed them down with what was left of the dregs of Tim's green gloop.

'Jesus, that's bad,' she said, pulling a face.

'It's spicy spinach,' he said. 'Bella's chef makes it for me – she's added a little ginger and cinnamon to make it seasonal... it still tastes like the bowels of hell but with a festive frisson.'

'I reckon she's added some of her own bile too,' Fliss was now wiping her tongue with a tissue. 'Anyway... Tim and I wanted to talk to you about the dynamics between you and Bella,' Fliss had leaned forward and was now looking into my face, the bifocals now on her head.

'Oh yes, I know – I'm sorry about that. I'm sorry, I know there's been an atmosphere...'

'Atmosphere? Ha. Icicles are forming *inside* the house.' She poured herself more coffee from the Emma Bridgewater coffee jug.

'I understand – you want it all Christmassy and exciting with jingle bells in the background and Bella and I working together, smiling all the way.'

'Mmmm, not necessarily,' said Tim.

'Shush Tim, let me explain,' Fliss said wafting her hand in his face and turning back to me; 'Bringing on one of the working class to work with our star was an act of genius on my part,' she started. 'Bella takes herself and her life so seriously that she's virtually becoming a figure of fun... or worse, hate. You should read the comments on Gossip Bitch! – I have to cover my eyes. Here she is a woman who has everything when lots of her viewers have nothing.'

'Yes, that's what I've been trying to tell her, too,' Tim added, nodding. 'The internet is awash with these down and outs making dishes on a shoestring... scandalous!'

'Yep, the dreaded "benefit bloggers",' Fliss sighed, shaking her head like they were a scourge. 'These weirdos make supper for six with a home-grown leek and a bin-dipping session at the back of Sainsbury's. And middle-aged TV Execs think they've found their elixir of youth and haul them off YouTube and onto our screens.

Trust me they are taking over, like allotment-hogging, carrot-crunching zombies – before long Bella will be yesterday's breakfast.'

'Yes, I read those food blogs, they're brilliant...' I said.

Tim was shaking his head and clearly feeling energised after his smoothie. 'Oh but Amy, it's worse at Christmas when poor desperate souls like you are destitute, on the streets... eking out every last penny. It must be damned near impossible to hear Bella recommending profanely priced turkeys and truffles flown in from Florence. Though I do actually have mine flown in the day before Christmas Eve,' he smiled. 'I mean, hell, it's not Christmas without a few pig-snuffled truffles.'

'I agree,' Fliss added, 'I'd walk to the bloody Dordogne barefoot and sniff them out myself before I'd do without my Christmas truffles,' she nodded, before turning back to me. I pretended to listen while trying to get the image of the very rounded Fliss on all fours in her kitten heels sniffing for truffles under an old French Oak. 'Thing is Amy,' she was saying, 'I've also got the damn TV channel breathing down my neck telling me Bella has to change, "no-one's got any money she must be more low rent," they yell, banging their desks and issuing profanities.' She turned to me, 'I'll be honest, I've been so desperate of late I've been looking towards Cameroon and all it has to offer. The king of Cameroon is offering in excess of £3m to make Bella his concubine... I told her, I'd bloody go at the drop of a hat if he asked me... and I don't care what I'd have to do in the bedroom!'

'Yes... I heard about the Cameroon option,' I said, diplomatically, as another unwelcome image replacing the truffle-sniffing one pushed at my brain. 'But I'm not sure Cameroon is the answer.'

'It would make a fabulous reality series,' she said, her head to one side; 'But when I offered it to ITV they said "Cameroon's a republic, and doesn't even have a king." As I said to the Head of Documentaries, "who cares what he is as long as he's got money in the bank and a crown on his head?" She raised her eyebrows like she'd just said something profound, before diving into a plate of waffles covered in lashings of severely whipped cream.

❄ ❄ ❄

After breakfast, Fliss and Tim rushed off to pack up for filming. Today was our last day at Dovecote, tomorrow would be Christmas Eve, and Fliss had informed us between bites of waffles and cream that St Swithin's had been confirmed and everything was set. The plan was for us all to go to the shelter tomorrow to start preparing and pre-filming for the live Christmas lunch. I poured myself another coffee and watched the snow, thinking how quickly the season moved, and like the snow it would all soon melt to nothing. It wasn't in my nature to stand around and do nothing – but for the first time in a long time I gave myself some space to think. I leaned my head on my hands and contemplated my life, my future – and what I would do when all this was over. Would I go back to my old life and continue with the monotony of sleeping, eating and working, carrying an underlying resentment for pole-dancing lawyers? Or was there another fork in the road for me?

My thoughts were interrupted when Bella waltzed in to breakfast in one of her Christmas red robes and sunglasses.

'Bella, you are such a diva,' I laughed affectionately.

I poured coffee from an elegant pot into one of the lovely pottery mugs – today's was snowstorm, pale blue snowflakes and frolicking deer. It made me feel Christmassy just to look at it and for the first time I felt a frisson of excitement tingling through me – accepting the end of my marriage had, weirdly, allowed me to let a little Christmas in.

Bella was clearly not feeling Christmassy at all and as someone handed her a cup of herbal tea she curled her lip at me.

'What?' I asked.

'Stop being so bloody happy, you're far too perky considering you drank as much as me and stayed up as late,' she smiled as she took a sip of the foul-smelling brew.

'I don't think anyone drinks as much as you,' I said, teasingly.

'Judge Judy,' she snapped.

'The scrambled eggs are lovely,' I commented, ignoring her grumpiness, this was play, it wasn't real – the resentment had gone from her eyes – and probably mine too. We were rediscovering our old selves.

'I don't know how you can eat that crap,' she sighed, making vomiting noises.

'Charming. It's smoked salmon and scrambled eggs – you make this every Christmas for your family, or that's what you tell your viewers,' I said.

'I've never made it in my life – I can't stand smoked salmon, it's revolting.'

'Oh, of course, it was for the TV, you just pretend to cook,' I said, with a smile. She didn't respond so I made like a mother, 'If you don't like salmon just have the eggs, you'll feel better.'

'No I won't, because if I eat anything I will hate myself. I'm not like you – I'm Bella Bradley, Kitchen Goddess and if I put on a pound I'll be in the newspapers and magazines as "curvy" Bella – which in magazine speak means "fat bitch".'

At this point, Fliss joined us, now in bright blue with the obligatory matching kitten heels. 'I heard the words "fat bitch", did someone call me?' she roared laughing and her tummy wobbled up and down in a rather alarming fashion.

'Ames is trying to sabotage my perfect body with disgusting eggs,' Bella monotoned.

'God forbid you should put on an ounce, Bella,' she giggled. 'I can't sell you to the TV companies if you get all chunky, can I? You don't need to worry about your weight, do you, Amy?' she said, clearly playing us off against one another so we'd be at each other's throats by the time we started filming.

Bella gave me a conspiratorial look and winked, she was aware that conflict in the kitchen might be good for ratings and knew what Fliss was doing too.

'Come on, madam, time for your make-up,' Fliss said to Bella. She was more assertive this time, like she was addressing an unruly teenager, before wobbling off in her trademark tiny shoes. I wondered how the kitten heels were holding up under Fliss's considerable weight – and if what she was doing to those heels came under 'animal cruelty'. I heard her greet Tim with a loud squeal of delight and when I looked through into the hall she was doing a little dance – and I swear I heard those kitten heels scream.

Chapter Fifteen

Silver Crackers on a Snowy Night

After pouring herself a black coffee, Bella sloped off to make-up and I was left in blissful silence once more to contemplate my future.

Had I ever really contemplated an alternative to the life I'd been given? Had I ever really looked at other possibilities until now? I hadn't, and yet somehow my conversation with Bella the previous evening (when I'd given advice about facing the truth and changing her future – advice I should have perhaps taken myself) was making me reconsider everything. In its own way, my marriage had been like Bella's – the snow had covered everything in white and sparkle, then melted to reveal the dark earth and the imperfections underneath. Once the snow had melted and we'd fallen out of love there was no going back for Neil and I – my only regret was not ending it sooner. And the only difference between mine and Bella's marriage was that she had been lying to the world – and I'd only been lying to myself.

❉ ❉ ❉

Filming started slightly later than planned that day, partly due to Bella's dress dilemma and Tim's bowels – it seemed the smoothie had 'ripped through' him 'like a tsunami.' As if that wasn't enough to contend with on set, Keith – or Pussy Galore II was being 'un co-operative,' and very 'actor-y' according to Fliss. He was eventually brought on set sporting his ra-ra skirt with matching accessories looking like a disgruntled drag queen.

'For God's sake isn't it enough I have my own fresh hell to contend with below stairs?' Tim announced, referring to his bowels. 'Now we have an unpredictable pussy on board... you don't get this with Dame Maggie Smith. Oh let's just go with it and see what it brings,' he sighed theatrically.

Meanwhile Bella was oblivious to it all, she was in character and positively smouldering over her dried fruits.

'Today my lovely new friend Amy and I are going to bake figgy pudding,' she said, moving towards the camera lens like she was about to kiss it. 'I have to tell you Amy,' she said, 'one year I pounded the streets looking for the right figs... I needed the Portuguese fig, nothing else would do. Its scarlet flesh is so Christmassy plus it's sweet and rich and so soft it melts in the mouth. I was desperate and at my wits' end when a specialist grower in Portugal contacted me to say he was flying some over. Crisis averted, and a one way ticket to fig heaven.'

'Portugal? Really?' I smiled.

She did a double-take; 'Yes, and before you say anything – they are worth every penny. Since then only the red Portuguese fig has passed through these lips – there are no other figs, people,' she said, puckering up for the camera, a ripe fig pressed to those red lips.

'And a word to the wise,' she beckoned for the camera to come closer, like she had a great secret to impart. 'If you want your cheese plate to be the best this Christmas, you must get onto that website now and have a crate flown over... worth every penny.'

She took a deep bite and Tim demanded a close-up. 'Divine,' she breathed, coming up for air.

I gave it a few seconds then said; 'They look lovely.' She nodded doubtfully, knowing there would be a caveat.

'But is there an alternative for those of us who don't have access to a plane to fly figs over for us at short notice?'

'Oh didn't I just KNOW you'd say that,' she sighed, hugging a large glass jar of brown sugar. 'I suppose you would use supermarket sugar too? Not real, sugarcane molasses?'

'Of course I'd use supermarket sugar – probably muscovado... or brown, it was good enough for my mum's figgy pudding,' I said, pointedly.

'Let's see,' she suddenly said; 'Let's both bake a Christmas figgy pudding and see whose comes out tops... we'll let the residents of St Swithin's decide. ' This was a bit of a surprise to everyone – most of all me. It was also amazing that Bella wasn't using the autocue and had come up with this idea herself.

'Okay,' I said, nodding; 'bring it on Bella – the oven gloves are OFF!'

And so we began, various helpers were dispatched by Fliss to buy 'Amy's working class' ingredients, while Bella's 'flown in' 'organic' 'high end' stuff waited in the wings for its moment.

Once we had everything we needed we set off – both using breadcrumbs, brandy, sugar, butter, dried and fresh figs – but all with quite different origins and prices. Off camera Crimson worked it out and Bella's figgy pudding cost ten times the price of mine, and that was without the first class fig flights. Throughout filming we argued and teased, but the atmosphere wasn't the same icy enmity of the day before. We carried on through our playful taunting on screen and it had gone down a storm, Fliss and Tim were delighted as I made fun of Bella's extravagance and privilege and she teased 'little Amy' about my 'boring frugality.' The best bit was – we actually did some baking – and it was just like old times in my mother's kitchen, arguing about who was the best, and fighting for the top shelf of the oven – which was fun until Bella pointed out she had two! Ultimately we both created what looked like very similar Christmas figgy puddings to be judged on Christmas Day by the residents of St Swithin's.

'I just know mine will taste better and win,' Bella trilled as we packed everything away later.

'That's funny, because I know it'll be mine,' I giggled. The truth was neither of us really minded because we'd had such a great time and both produced what looked like wonderful puddings – and I knew mine was the best – and she knew it was hers.

❄ ❄ ❄

It was late when we finished filming and as we had an early start everyone was keen to get to bed. I wanted to practise my tin foil table crackers and make sure I packed enough tinfoil and holly for decorating the hostel when we arrived. Sylvia called, very excited to tell me she'd finished all the runners, and on my text instructions had collected empty jam jars from everyone she knew. 'I am sooo excited for tomorrow,' she said, 'I don't think I've been this excited about Christmas since... ooh, my divorce.'

I laughed, Sylvia was good for me, she was a reminder that there was a real world still out there. I was beginning to enjoy being in 'Bella land' but I would be ready to go back to reality soon.

Everyone had gone to bed but I wanted to make some crackers for Christmas day at the hostel – and I wanted to stick around and enjoy my last night at Dovecote. It was a wonderful house in a beautiful village and I knew whatever happened between Bella and I in the future it would always be a place of fond memories for me. I was sitting on a kitchen stool twisting tinfoil when I was suddenly aware of someone else in the room. I looked up to see Mike standing in the doorway covered in snow. 'It's still coming down,' he said, shaking the flakes from his shoulders. 'I've just loaded the van with some of the camera stuff for tomorrow, I like to be ready – I find it all a bit frustrating the way everyone takes their time around here and are so disorganised?' He said 'disorganised' with a question mark and looked at me for confirmation, as if to say 'are you with me? Or one of them?'

I smiled. 'Oh it's bloody infuriating. I hate that we have to wait for Bella to have a bloody shower before each scene and then she's spritzed and powdered and then she has to have a drink or a lie-down – it's like working with Elizabeth Taylor in her heyday, not some daytime cook on a food channel.' I said this with affection, and Mike knew where I was coming from, as we'd shared a few smiles and nods during filming and he knew I loved Bella really.

He laughed. 'Yes, she does have an air about her,' he leaned on the worktop, 'but I have to say, you've been good for Bella.'

'Do you think? I hope so, but I wasn't sure if it was me or she was just, somehow happier.'

'No, Bella doesn't really know "happy", from what I've seen she seems to equate happiness with the new Missoni collection, or something like that.'

'I've never heard of Missoni, I don't wear designer clothes or make-up normally,' I said, gesturing towards the designer jacket that had been thrust at me earlier. 'It's all from wardrobe and Billy's tool bag.'

'Well, it looks good on you,' he smiled, making me feel quite warm and tingly. As for Missoni – I worked on a fashion programme,' he smiled, 'I didn't know my designers either until then, and to be honest it isn't knowledge that's changed my life.'

We both smiled at this and he asked what I was doing and when I explained I was making cut price crackers he offered to help.

'Thanks,' I said, handing him a half-made one and showing him how to complete it.

'Today was good...' he said, rolling pieces of card into a barrel-shape for the cracker body as I'd shown him. 'You and Bella going for it, but your flushed cheeks gave you away,' he smiled and I felt myself flush again. I think he was flirting with me, but having not been flirted with for many years I wasn't really sure.

I didn't know what to say and I was aware that if I looked at him my red cheeks would give me away, so I continued to twist the tinfoil into a cracker shape and within a few minutes we were sitting side by side on kitchen stools and had settled into a comfortable rhythm. 'It's a production line,' I said as he passed the barrel of the cracker to me and I rolled the foil around it.

'I heard you're separated, Amy?' he suddenly said, ignoring my inane waffle about a production line.

'Yes...I am,' I stammered, surprised. Had he asked someone about me?

'Not easy is it? I divorced three years ago, broke my heart, I felt like such a failure.'

'What happened?' I asked.

'We just grew apart, I suppose, but not before she'd found someone more handsome, with more money – that kind of helped the split.' He looked up from the cracker he was holding and pulled his mouth downwards. My heart went out to him, he seemed like such a genuine guy, I found it hard to understand how someone could leave him.

'I'm sorry.'

'No, I can smile about it now – and you will too, Amy, you just need a bit of time,' he said gently, and reaching out to hand me the cracker, he touched my hand. I felt electricity go through me, and I wondered if he felt it too. Was he just being kind and understanding or were the looks we'd shared over raw turkey and dripping giblets more meaningful? I didn't have to wait long to find out, because when he handed me the next cracker our eyes met and a few seconds later he leaned forward and kissed me on the lips. At first it was just soft, tentative, he wasn't sure how I would react, and neither was I, but we were soon swept up in the moment and holding onto each other precariously, sitting on kitchen stools surrounded by tinfoil crackers, kissing.

I hadn't kissed anyone other than Neil for twenty years and for me this was earth-shattering. Neil had never kissed me like this, he'd never made me feel so beautiful, so loved. Mike held my face in both hands and looked into my eyes with such intensity I almost melted. I loved the feel of his hands under my suit jacket, up and down my back, his lips now on my neck, and I didn't want it to ever stop. A little later I heard myself ask if he was staying nearby and when he said no, I invited him to my room. I'd never done anything like this before in my life but with him it just felt right, I felt like I'd known him for ever – at the same time he felt like a stranger. He smelled of sandalwood and vanilla, softer and sweeter than Neil and his face was stubbly, excitingly prickly, unlike Neil's smooth shaven skin. As we entered the Mary Berry room together, he stripped off my beautiful scarlet suit and I lay naked on that huge, beautiful bed feeling like a supermodel. He told me I was beautiful and I believed him as he kissed me from my toes upwards. Surreptitiously, I turned Mary Berry's picture to the wall – the poor woman didn't need to see me in flagrante at Christmas with a man I hardly knew – and groaned in ecstasy.

✳ ✳ ✳

The following morning I woke feeling a strange sense of happiness and peace I hadn't felt for a long, long time. It was Christmas Eve and remembering what had happened the night before reached out for Mike to tell him, but he'd gone. I wasn't sure what this meant, perhaps he just needed an early start, or perhaps I was just a one-night stand? I really hoped this was the beginning of something, my mind going over what had happened as I was in the shower, letting the hot water kiss me all over – just like Mike had. He was a wonderful lover, I had never felt such passion, such deep pleasure before – even if I was just a one-night stand, it was worth it. This was a different Amy than the one who'd arrived at Dovecote all anxious and insecure in a big rust cardigan. This Amy wore scarlet, she took chances and had a one-night stand with a man she fancied because she could – and as I gazed at myself in the mirror that morning I thought as much as Bella needed to become a bit more like me and care about people, I needed to become a bit more like her and care more about myself – and last night I did. And it had been amazing.

Chapter Sixteen

St Swithin's Sparkle and Mistletoe Madness

Driving back through the Cotswolds on Christmas Eve morning was magical. The air was refrigerating the landscape to keep the snow perfect so excited children could wake up to a white Christmas. I missed those Christmas mornings with the kids – five a.m. starts as they squealed their way into our bedroom and leaped on the bed. Neil usually managed to stay asleep – or at least pretend to – while I was as excited as the kids and all three of us would go downstairs together to see what Santa had left for them.

I couldn't wait to see the kids on Boxing Day, there were times over the last week when it was the only thing keeping me going. And what a week it had been! I felt more confident, not to mention blonder, more stylish, and I was even wearing a little make-up. But of course the biggest events that happened for me were getting back with Bella – and last night with Mike. I had no idea if Mike and I would ever even see each other again after all this – but it was a wonderful memory and the final push I needed to free myself mentally from my marriage. I didn't feel like an abandoned wife any more – I felt like a single woman – and it felt so good.

As for Bella, I hoped she and I had a future, even if it was just a Christmas card each year – and not just me sending one to her.

Arriving at the hostel I felt a sense of relief; things were coming together at last and we were going to do this. The TV crew had left earlier and as I was travelling a little later with Tim and a hundred hand-made silver foil crackers, I hadn't seen anything of Mike. But as I got out of the car and saw no sign of Bella and Fliss – who'd set off before us – my worries bubbled up to the surface. It had been chaos at Dovecote that morning when we left and as usual nothing had been organised and Bella had taken ages to get ready. Consequently we all set off later than planned and I was cross to think she was taking her time today of all days – she could be so selfish. And now she was 'fashionably late' again, and I had no idea where she'd got to. All she had to do was go from Dovecote to St Swithin's, I just hoped she hadn't done a runner.

There was one thing worse than not having this live show go out... and that was failing to get Christmas lunch on the table at St Swithin's Hostel live on air. I was no expert, but even I knew that disappointment and hunger in a homeless hostel would not play well on Christmas Day to viewers at home. Bella would be a laughing stock and the sheer embarrassment and sense of failure on mine and Bella's part would be horrific and no doubt cause another twenty year rift. On top of all this we both had a lot to lose: Bella her show and celebrity status and I could lose the faith of Sylvia and the residents – not to mention my new-found faith in myself.

Climbing out of the car I was cheered by the Christmas tree covered in fairy lights – Sylvia and Beatrice had been worried they wouldn't be able to have a tree this year, but it looked like a local garden centre had come good. As we staggered across the icy pavement, Sylvia and Beatrice appeared in the doorway, and Sylvia screamed when she saw me and ran out into the Christmas dawn, her arms open wide. I was so pleased to see her – here was someone who wanted what I wanted and was prepared to put in the time, the love and the effort – and not just for the cameras – though I noted she'd had her hair done and was wearing a new sparkly top.

'You look fabulous,' I said.

'Wow, not as fabulous as you, Amy.'

'Yeah, you look mighty fine, girl,' Beatrice said, hugging me. 'Like you been on one of them makeovers.'

'Thanks, it's been quite a time,' I rolled my eyes and Sylvia smiled.

'I look forward to hearing ALL about it,' she said. 'By the way, the camera crew have arrived,' she gave me a wink. I had managed to fill her in on some of the past couple of days' 'highlights' by text, but I couldn't wait to tell her everything.

'Sorry we're a bit later than we'd hoped,' I said, linking arms with her as we both held each other up on the ice, walking into the hostel.

'Oh, you're here now and that's what matters – we thought perhaps the TV people had changed their minds,' Sylvia said, looking behind me. 'So where's Bella Bradley?'

'I don't know, I suspect she's broken a nail and gone back home for a lie-down – or a bubble bath,' I said, trying to make light of things while genuinely worried she'd jumped on a flight to somewhere warm instead.

'Don't worry, she'll turn up eventually – it will give us time to get set up,' Sylvia squeezed my arm. 'It's so exciting!' she said, she was like a little girl.

Then Mike appeared at my side and gave me what I think was a secret smile. Sylvia couldn't contain her excitement at a real-live telly person – even if he was behind the camera - and she almost curtseyed.

'Can I help you with your... equipment?' she asked, glancing at me in a mischievous way. Honestly, it was like being back at school; she might have been a teacher but sometimes she behaved more like the pupils.

'Thank you but I can manage my equipment,' Mike smiled indulgently, taking a sideways glance at me.

I could feel my face burning up as flashes of the previous night popped into my brain so I gave him a big smile and dragged Sylvia off before she could say anything else that could be misconstrued... or he could.

'He's a bit of all right,' she was saying. 'Big strong arms, twinkly blue eyes. Oooh, he could come down my chimney any time.'

'Sylvia calm down, he's a cameraman not Father Christmas, he's not coming down anyone's chimney.'

'Really – from your texts I thought he might be coming down yours.'

'Okay, okay there was a bit of ... oh I'll tell you all about it later... and you're right, he has the twinkliest, bluest eyes,' I giggled. I breathed in as we entered the dining hall, no fancy air fresheners of a Dickensian Christmas here – just the earthy warmth of porridge and burnt toast – and it was delicious.

There were no Christmas flower arrangements, no fancy furniture, no drama queens... just hugs and a genuine welcome.

'We're on air just after the Queen's Speech at 3.30, so we don't have a lot of time. They're going through the running order then doing a technical rehearsal first while we just have to cook around them,' I said to Sylvia like I was a TV veteran.

'I just can't wait,' Sylvia squealed and we headed for the kitchen, where I would try not to be too distracted by gorgeous Mike and throw myself into making Christmas Dinner for one hundred people.

I knew the kitchen at St Swithin's was relatively small and ill-equipped, but after Bella's high-tech state-of-the-art kitchen it looked even worse. I was quite depressed at what we had to work with. There was no Aga, no American-style fridge containing only wine and champagne, no high-end artisan mixers or liquidisers. It's funny how quickly you get used to things, and if I felt like this after just a few days at Dovecote, I dreaded Bella's reaction.

'Bella's used to having stuff done for her and even if she does have to actually pretend to cook something she has all the best ingredients weighed out ready and the kitchen utensils to work with,' I sighed to Sylvia.

Sylvia raised an eyebrow as she hauled a huge bag of spuds along the floor; 'Well, she's going to have quite a shock,' she sighed. Sylvia and Beatrice began to wash the breakfast crockery along with the other volunteers, and I went into the dining hall to see if I could at least try and make it look Christmassy with the holly I had picked from Dovecote.

Wearing my thick gloves, I dragged the holly along the floor so I didn't have to carry it and ruin my outfit. Ruth had suggested I wear a midnight blue sparkly dress for filming, so I'd put it on before we left and covered it now with a large apron. I tried not to move too vigorously as the dress was very fitted and I didn't want to split it or spoil the line of it. I had to laugh at myself, I'd arrived at Dovecote wearing something Bella described as 'Amish', and here I was less than a week later in a glitzy bodycon dress worrying about 'the line'.

My biggest concern was transforming the shabby hall into a dining room fit for Christmas with what little time and decorations we had. I'd brought bunches of holly, the silver foil crackers and some dreaded 'shop bought' baubles that Bella had rejected for Dovecote - but it wouldn't be nearly enough. I walked into the dining hall backwards, using my bum to open the double doors, dragging the holly through. When I turned round, the room was in semi-darkness and it took me a while to work out where the light switch was, tutting and swearing under my breath as I groped in the dark, eventually finding it and turning it on.

'Let there be light,' shouted one of the older men who was sitting on one of the benches at a table finishing off his porridge in the dim morning. And when I looked round, all the tables were set with tea lights in Sylvia's jam jars and fairy lights strung around the hall. There was also cutlery and glasses on the tables, and Sylvia's beautiful table runners in silver added the finishing festive touch. I stood for a while speechless, delighted – and relieved. Not only did it look lovely, the fact that it was already decorated gave us more time to cook.

Then suddenly someone came up behind me and grabbed me round the waist, I thought (hoped) it might be Mike, and my heart leaped. I turned around expectantly only to be faced with a smiling Neil. My face must have dropped, especially when I saw he was holding a great bush of mistletoe over us.

'You don't have to look so pleased to see me,' he said, in a forced jokey way.

I wanted to cry.

Chapter Seventeen

A Christmas Celebration, an Amazing Revelation

'I've been waiting for ages...' Neil was saying. 'I came here because I know this filming thing means such a lot to you.'

'Yes, it does, but why are you here?'

'I wanted to see you. I thought we could talk.'

'Talk? You want to talk now when I'm about to embark on a bloody TV programme and a Christmas dinner for over a hundred people?'

'Oh you think you're too good for me now you're on the telly do you?'

'It's nothing to do with who I think I am and why I don't want to be near you. We aren't together anymore, Neil. You left me, remember? And it was the best thing you ever did for me because I don't have to put up with your idiocy anymore, so just go. I'm sure Jayne will be wondering where you are.' I felt angry at this intrusion, but as always Neil had completely misread the situation. He presumed – wrongly – my reference to his girlfriend and my tight-lipped arm-folded body language was jealousy and taking it as encouragement, lunged at me and clumsily kissed me on the lips, just as Mike walked through the double doors and straight into us. I was shocked and angry at Neil's behaviour and when I saw the look on Mike's face I felt even worse.

Mike and I had only just met, we weren't an item, we hadn't even been out together – but I liked him, and I didn't want Neil ruining everything for me. I'd told Mike my marriage was over and here I was snogging – or more accurately being snogged by – my husband in semi-darkness. Talk about killing something before it's even begun.

'Hi, er... Mike... this is Neil,' I offered, like that would help.

Mike nodded tersely, Neil nodded back, and I was reminded of the reindeer on Bella's Christmas jumper, though it was less frolicking does, more rutting stags. I watched helplessly as Mike wandered into the hall without making eye contact and began to make notes about camera angles. Meanwhile, Neil and I just looked at each other. All I could think was 'what did I ever see in you? Why did I give up so much of my life to this man?' If I hadn't been adamant before that my marriage was well and truly dead I was now... and that kiss had sealed the deal.

'Neil, what the hell was that?' I hissed, wiping my mouth. 'Apart from the fact I've moved on - you're with someone else now, you can't just fall back into my life and expect a bloody kiss – mistletoe or no,' I spat.

I wanted to bat him away like a fly. I was desperate to run to Mike and tell him it was all fine and there were no grey areas, no vestiges of anything left with my estranged husband and I was extremely free to take things a whole lot further. Having slept with him the previous night, then finding me under the mistletoe with my estranged husband, he could already be forgiven for thinking I was a man-eating Christmas nympho. So as desperate as I was to chase him through the homeless hostel in a sparkly blue designer dress shouting, 'Come back, Mike, I want you,' I decided to choose my moment.

'I'll stick around with you and drive you home when it's over... I was thinking we might perhaps... talk about me coming home?' Neil was saying. 'Look... I'm sorry love.' I just looked at him with incredulity, which, knowing Neil he probably mistook for unbridled passion.

The woman who'd left this town had been hurt by Neil but might just have fallen for his mistletoe on Christmas Eve. Had I never been to Dovecote or met Bella again I may even have kissed him willingly and been persuaded by his apologies to fall back into my old life. But it would have been out of nostalgia for the past, with him and the children – not a desire to be with him.

'You're telling me you're sorry, Neil?' I said, astounded. 'No, I'm sorry, because I have no intentions of letting you anywhere near me or my home. You were the one who'd "fallen in love", Neil, you were the one who left – and I realise now you did me quite a favour. I'm happier now than I've been for twenty years.'

'Oh, so you've been filming in a fancy house for a few days and suddenly you think you don't need me, that you're something special?'

'Yeah... I do think I'm something special actually. It's just a pity that you never thought I was.'

'Oh Amy, calm down,' he said dismissively which made my blood pressure shoot up through my body, and I wanted to strangle my husband. I was so angry I couldn't speak, we just stared at each other.

'She's dumped you, hasn't she?' I said. 'Or has the pole lost its novelty?'

'I just want you back, I want our home – it's Christmas...' he started.

'Yes, and you left me – and our home, *just before* Christmas and in the short while you've been gone I've changed, and my life is about to change, for the better.'

'So you seem to think,' he said, a smirk playing on his lips. 'Is that a new dress you're wearing?' He was trying a different tack and I could see it coming, he was going to try and knock my confidence so I'd feel vulnerable and fall into his arms. He was looking me up and down with obvious disapproval.

'It's not you is it, Amy,' he said. 'I mean, you can't carry off a dress like that.' He was pulling a face and shaking his head, attempting to kill what little confidence I'd regained over the last few days. I felt sick. Even though I'd been expecting it, this was still like a punch in the stomach, I didn't want Neil here with his jealousy and negativity, and put downs.

Seething resentment rose up through my whole body and I was shaking with rage. How dare he think he could walk all over me and that I'd just lie down and let him wander back in. Since my time at Dovecote with Bella and Mike I felt so much stronger, so much more in charge of my own life – I wasn't weighed down by my insecurities anymore.

'You know what, Neil? You're wrong – this dress is "me" actually,' I heard myself say, putting my hand on my hip and standing in front of him, glowing with new found confidence. 'And that guy you just met, Mike? The good-looking one? He's "me" too. But do you know what isn't "me"? You!'

Neil stood there clutching his mistletoe, shocked at what I'd just said. I went to walk away, but was so bloody angry I turned back round and with a left hook knocked his mistletoe right out of his hand. 'And you can shove this *right* up your arse!' I shouted, hurling it across the room... just as Mike walked back through with the soundman.

❄ ❄ ❄

I stormed off, leaving Neil in the dining hall, open-mouthed and 'wearing' his mistletoe bush, and when I told Sylvia what I'd done she clapped.

We spent the next hour cleaning the kitchen and laughing about flying mistletoe until, finally, Bella, Crimson and Fliss arrived. Crimson immediately offered to do the off-camera cleaning and preparing, but Bella had a look of barely concealed horror on her face at the sight of the decor and Fliss was taking gulps from her diamante hip flask. Sylvia and I showed them the dining hall, but Bella just nodded numbly and Fliss just swigged her drink; 'They just need to acclimatise,' I said to a worried Sylvia.

Fliss said she needed 'a fag dahling' and Bella said she needed a lie down, so I directed Fliss to the back doorway to smoke outside and suggested Bella join us in the kitchen to start prepping.

'In a minute,' she said. 'I just don't know if I can do this... here... it's awful.'

I left her alone in the dining hall and headed for the kitchen to help Crimson. We were emptying all the cupboards of what little crockery and ovenware we had and even Crimson looked surprised at the lack of equipment. 'Nothing like Bella's, is it?' I said.

'No. But I like a challenge,' she said and I wouldn't swear to this, but I think she actually smiled.

We hadn't been in there long when Fliss wandered in after finishing her fag. 'Where's Bella?' she asked.

'Well, you didn't think she was in here working, did you?' I laughed.

'She's flirting with some old guy in the dining hall,' Crimson said in her usual world-weary way, unsurprised by her boss's behaviour.

I was intrigued and when I'd finished cleaning the trays I popped my head round the doors to see Bella sitting cross-legged on a table, twirling her hair and heaving her bosom. She was talking to Neil and despite me having told him an hour ago that out marriage was definitely over he seemed to be taking it well enough to smile and flirt. He might have tried a little harder to pretend to grieve for twenty years of marriage and the fact he wasn't coming back home with me on Christmas Eve. Perhaps he was hoping there'd be room at Bella's this Christmas?

'I wouldn't worry about them,' Mike said as I turned round to walk back into the kitchen. 'Bella likes to flirt.' He was standing in the doorway setting up his camera and still avoiding eye contact.

'I'm not worried at all. She's welcome to my soon to be ex-husband,' I smiled. 'Honestly.'

I sensed a slight awkwardness so felt I should explain. 'Mike, I'm really not interested in him,' I said. 'I meant what I said – my marriage was over a long time ago. He just needs a bed for the night and he thought if he kissed me I'd just say yes and it would all be okay – but those days are behind me.'

He put down the cloth he'd been wiping his camera with and came close, I could feel his breath on my face and I wanted to grab him and kiss him right there in the doorway. I thought about how he'd made love to me the night before and was on the verge of throwing myself on the table and demanding we re-enact the sex scene from The Postman Always Rings Twice. But fortunately he spoke before I could do any of that – which was just as well really.

'Look I'll be honest, Amy, because I don't play games... I like you, I would like to see you... if you would. But I don't want to get involved in someone else's marriage.'

'I like you too, and I'm being honest – it isn't a marriage. I mean it when I say it's over... surely the low-flying mistletoe hinted at that?'

'All I heard was you screaming "arse" and the mistletoe shooting across the room, wish I'd filmed it,' he laughed.

'Oh God, you must think I'm terrible... I just slapped it out of his hands... I'm quite a calm person usually, I'm really not a bunny-boiling-rage-filled...'

He touched me on my chin and I sort of reached my mouth towards him in expectation, but he moved away and went back to his camera. I was mortified and hid my face in the fridge to cool down for the next five minutes on the pretext of getting out the turkeys. The past few days may have given me some confidence, but I still had some way to go. Eventually I took my face out of the fridge and rushed to the toilet to compose myself before returning to manhandle the giblets.

❄ ❄ ❄

When Bella finally deigned to enter the kitchen, the sight before her did nothing to take away the now permanent horror on her face. She'd opened the door, her scarlet smile painted on just in case the press or anyone important was present, but when she saw it was just me, Sylvia, Beatrice and Stanley, her mouth visibly dropped. There was Stanley in his old stained jumper singing... or rather murdering, 'I've got you under my skin', star struck Sylvia was in mid-curtsey for Bella and Beatrice was ready to show 'that missy' the Jamaican way. Bella couldn't speak, but visibly winced at the sight of the aged kitchen with shelves full of old mismatched crockery, worn out pans and a couple of old camping stoves as back-up. It was looking like Christmas had just been cancelled for Bella.

'Ames, I'm sorry – I know I said I would, but I can't possibly work here,' she started, 'in this.' She raised her arms and did a twirl to accentuate and emphasise the dreadfulness of what she was facing. 'I mean there's nothing to cook with... I am a proper cook, I need proper equipment...' her face was red, her voice was raised.

'Hang on a minute Missy. And what makes you think you're so fine?' Beatrice was waving her finger in Bella's face.

Bella looked scared and began looking around like a hi-tech chrome kitchen was about to land from above. In Bella's world, lavish kitchen sets were built within hours, from nothing, then shiny new top of the range equipment arrived from companies falling over themselves to have her caress their latest gadget on screen. She had lived in this make-believe world for so long she couldn't cope with this taste of reality, and as annoying and spoilt as she was I felt sorry for her. She was standing in the middle of the kitchen now looking upset and frustrated, on the verge of tears – but more than anything she looked like a lost little girl.

'Bella, we're getting the turkeys ready,' I said, trying to distract her as Mum might have done when she was a child. Bella was running her hand along the tired, marked old surfaces, her mouth open in disgust, shaking her head.

'No. I know this is your "thing" Ames and I don't want to disappoint you, but I can't cook here, under these conditions.'

'Bella it's not "my thing", it's everyone's "thing", we all have to take responsibility for this. I know in your lovely world no one goes cold and hungry, they just order more truffles and add another layer of cashmere – but this is real life. It's not about disappointing me – it's about the people here whose lives are damaged, lost souls with nothing and nowhere to go. They want Bella Bradley the big TV star to come into their home and make their dinner, film with them, chat with them, sprinkle a little stardust their way. Bella, don't you get it... it won't just make their Christmas, it will make their life.'

'Oh Ames stop making such a fuss. I'll get Fliss to send them all signed Christmas photos of me, they'll love that and I can go home and everyone will be happy.'

'So that's all they are worth? A few signed photos,' I sighed, disappointed in her reaction, I thought she'd turned a corner, but being at the hostel seemed to bring back the stuck-up Bella I first met at Dovecote. 'Of course, they aren't important to you or your career, are they? These people aren't worth your time and effort,' and with that I left the kitchen.

Bella might not care about these people but I did and I was determined to make this one Christmas they would cherish for the rest of their lives. There were people, cameras and food – and I would fight to get this programme made with or without Bella, who did she think she was, taking this away from people with nothing to start with? I decided that whatever happened lunch would be ready and someone had to get the show on the road; 'Now Fliss,' I said, 'I need you to assist Sylvia in dressing those tables – she'll show you the way, and while you're doing that we can do a little preparation filming in here.'

She looked surprised at my new-found assertiveness, but I was a teacher, and used to organising other people – besides we were on my territory now – not Dovecote.

'We're not used to these kind of studios... we like things to be a little more... how shall I say it... luxurious,' she sighed.

'You can say it how you like but "luxuuuurious" is not on the menu at St Swithin's,' Beatrice piped up. Beatrice was apparently pandering to no one, she wasn't being walked over by any of these TV bods – go Beatrice, I thought.

'Oh I understand that entirely, Mrs Beatrice, but I like a little more warmth and glamour for my filming,' Tim added.

'And don't you think them folk out there want a "little warmth and glamour" for their dinner?' she said.

Tim raised his eyebrow, curled his lip and clapped his hands, 'Chop chop ladies,' he shouted before leaning into me and whispering, 'that one's going to be trouble.'

He tutted and pretended to study his running order, and Bella, who'd realised that threatening to leave wasn't getting her any attention was now screaming because the water from the tap was 'lukewarm', not hot. Having remembered how she hated it when I was her 'hand double' at Dovecote I'd hoped she'd change her mind if she thought the show might go on without her. So far it looked like she was doing just that. Meanwhile I could hear Fliss's booming voice all the way down the hall complaining to someone about the lack of alcohol in the building.

'Oh but dahling, just a teensy weensy bottle of Scotch,' she was saying in her girly voice.

'Fliss, aren't you supposed to be helping Sylvia with the tables?' I boomed back. She leaped about three feet in the air and rushed off to help, which made me smile, she was a softie really for all her barking.

As for her drinking, given that some of the residents struggled with addictions there was no way we were going to bring her a 'teensy weensy' bit of anything that might cause problems. Sylvia told me that Beatrice had been forced to ban Cointreau-flavoured cream the previous year after Stanley deep-throated four cartons of it – straight. We were already skating on thin ice with this TV programme, without the potential carnage that would ensue if someone brought alcohol in. The result would probably be enough to get the channel taken off air.

Bella was now arguing with Tim, and instead of adding to the drama I simply took Bella aside and explained that there were no 'hordes of helpers' as Fliss had apparently promised her, nor would there be a delivery from various high-end kitchen equipment specialists. It was just us volunteers, a couple of ancient ovens and a lot of hard work.

'Just accept it and get on with it Bella,' I said, hoping her whingeing was a sign she'd changed her mind about quitting and would stay and present.

Bella looked like she was about to cry and I ushered her into Beatrice's office, which was the only empty space I could find. I asked her to sit down and I leaned with my bottom on the desk as I did when I was tackling a particularly difficult pupil at school and spoke directly to her.

'Look, Bella, you don't understand what it means to have nothing, to be cold with no home and no family. These people have nothing, they are homeless. HOMELESS!' I raised my voice and she looked shaken.

She lifted her hand up like it was all too painful to hear. 'Stop it Ames...'

'NO. I won't, just because you don't want to face some of the less beautiful things in the world. Not everyone's Christmas is filled with vintage champagne and Portuguese bloody figs...'

'I know... I know.'

'You don't – you haven't got a clue, you have no idea how it feels to have nothing,' I spat.

'No... I get it. I get it more than you will ever know,' she sighed, reaching her hand out to me, touching my arm. 'Ames... coming here today has been terrible for me, and I can't take the memories. I've lived in a place like this – I've walked miles all day, waiting for the shelter to open in the freezing cold. I was seven months pregnant before anyone helped me.'

'Oh Bella, I had no idea you'd been homeless... and you were pregnant?' My mind was fizzing now, so Bella hadn't gone through with the abortion but what about the baby? But before I could gently broach the subject she started crying.

'I know you think I judge people, Ames, but it's all a front – I didn't want to avoid this place because I hate these people; I just didn't want to be reminded of the past. It was the hardest time of my life, I had nothing – no future, no family....'

'Oh Bella, I had no idea, I wish you'd told me, I would have understood, this must be awful for you.'

'The memories are flooding back, the cold, the hunger – you think I've always had it easy, but you don't know everything about me like you think you do, Ames, she said sadly. '

I nodded, she was right. I'd gone to Dovecote with so many pre-conceptions about Bella and her life only to discover I'd been wrong.

'What happened to the baby, Bella?' I asked, my voice cracking, not really wanting to know the awful truth.

'I was rushed to hospital with pneumonia… they didn't know if either of us would make it,' she fought back tears. 'She was born two months early, she was so tiny but just perfect. And then they had to take her away, she'd come too soon.'

'Oh Bella,' I didn't know what to say.

'She almost died, Ames, my little girl. But she was a fighter.'

'Oh, she survived…?'

'Yeah, and she's the best thing that ever happened to me.'

She pointed through the glass and my eyes followed to where she was pointing. Crimson was hanging tinsel around the hallway and laughing with Maisie and I suddenly saw a young Bella in her smile.

'Crimson's your daughter?' I couldn't quite take it in.

Bella nodded. 'Of course… I thought you knew, I was sure you'd guessed. Fliss says she's the image of me.'

'I didn't notice, what with everything going on, but now you say it.' In truth it was hard to tell because of all the piercings and the hair, but it was the smile that gave her away – and this was the first time, here at St Swithin's, that I'd seen Crimson smile. 'Why did you never tell me? I'd have helped if I could, you know that, Bella.'

'Oh I don't know, I hadn't heard from you and it was all such a mess, Amy. Mum was furious, she drove me to the clinic but while she was parking the car I ran away. It was awful, I had no money, no friends and I couldn't stay in town because I knew Mum would call the police and I thought perhaps they could force me to get rid of the baby. So I just walked and hitch-hiked, going from hostel to hostel, and then, I was taken to hospital with pneumonia and on Christmas Day 1991, I had Cressida. She was beautiful and someone finally loved me and I vowed I would be the mother I'd never had. I always said to myself that I wanted to be like your mum, Amy...'

I nodded, tears in my eyes at her revelation.

'That was the day I met Fliss - she was with one of her celebrity clients filming a Christmas charity visit to the mum and baby ward. We got chatting and she felt sorry for me and said there was a room at hers – despite that exterior, she has a heart of... something,' she laughed. 'Anyway the rest is history as they say.'

'But I don't understand what happened with Cressida...? Why is she called Crimson?'

'Oh she's called Crimson because she said Cressida was too middle class and her boyfriend Steve called himself Ochre - they both wanted to be "avant garde". She had Ochre and Crimson tattooed on her arm and she likes the name, so why not?'

'So why is Cressy... Crimson... a secret? Surely you're not still scared of what your Mum will do?'

'No, Mum knows about Cressy, she's met her a couple of times but Jean never was one for maternal bonding on any level. Cressy was four when I married Peter and Fliss had this plan to announce her to the world saying we had her before we were married but didn't make it public until she was older because we didn't want her chased by paparazzi or affected by fame. After the wedding we thought we could just do a few big stories about our secret love child and it would all be perfect.'

'So why didn't you?'

'Well, once we were married things started to move quickly. Peter was an even bigger name and I was landed with my own prime time show. Consequently the press were all over us and it didn't take Cressida's so-called father long to realise that his ex, Bella Bradley, might be worth a few quid.'

'Of course, Chris – I'd almost forgotten about his part in all this. Where was he when it was all happening?' I said.

'He'd been in prison for drugs-related stuff – he didn't want me or Cressy but as soon as he came out and saw I was in the spotlight he called me threatening to take Cressy off me and sell his story to the press.'

'Oh Bella, how awful.'

'As Peter and I weren't exactly the perfect married couple I was frightened Chris might actually find this out and get custody. My biggest fear was always that Cressy might be taken off me, so I just closed myself off from everyone... it was a scary time. Fliss paid him off and Chris left the country, but a couple of years ago I heard he was back, so Fliss said I must never to talk to anyone from my past. She's been like a mother to me.'

I smiled, only Bella could see a mother's love in this way – paid for. 'So why didn't you just "out" Cressida then, once Chris was out of the country?'

'Chris may have been out of the country, but he owed people money and they wanted their pound of flesh, we had no way of knowing if Cressy would be safe. I was already a big star and it was too late to just leave and live in the highlands of Scotland, the press and whoever else would just follow us there. I wanted her protected from the press, and more than that I wanted to protect her from her dad and his lifestyle. Chris had been bad for me and he'd have been bad for her too.'

'I can see that, you did the right thing, Bella,' I said, understanding the maternal pride and love Bella had for her daughter.

'The other issue was that Peter didn't want to be committed forever to a child he hardly knew that wasn't even his,' Bella went on to say. 'If our marriage broke up and a child was involved, he'd have been hounded and the press would have given him a terrible time for not seeing his daughter. Our marriage was about business, and I became quite paranoid and wanted Cressy protected from anything and everything. I didn't even send her to school, she was home taught.'

As she talked, I just kept listening, growing more and more amazed that someone could live a life like hers, so full of secrets. Part of me admired Bella for what she'd been through to protect her daughter. Crimson wasn't Bella's lackey, she was with Bella because she wanted to be not because she had to be. It explained the time I heard them talking quietly together in the conservatory at Dovecote, and why Crimson was always around prepared to help Bella, from tweeting to tinsel – because she was her mum and she loved her. And watching Crimson come alive at St Swithin's, helping out in the kitchen, almost smiling and suddenly interacting with everyone in a more positive way showed that Crimson's indifference was actually just a front, to keep the world out.

'I considered so many different ways of bringing Cressy "out" as you put it – Fliss did too and was coming up with more and

more outrageous suggestions as to where the baby had come from
– one being found in a bin – I ask you!'

I had to laugh. 'That sounds like Fliss.'

She nodded. 'Oh it was awful, Ames. If ever I needed a friend
it was then, but Fliss wouldn't allow me to contact anyone because
the fewer people who knew the better, we couldn't risk the secret
getting out because we didn't know if or when Chris would come
back to the UK. We all had so much to hide and so much to
lose. Stupid really... but the press were everywhere, like ants they'd
climb the back of the house and peer in through windows. Peter
and I appeared to have the perfect life – but that doesn't make
a good story – ha, if only they'd known... what a headline that
would have been.'

'But Crimson's okay – and so are you, that's the most important thing in all this.'

'Yes. I owe Fliss everything, there's nothing that woman won't
do for her clients. Having said all that, we're victims of our own
success and now we're on a merry-go-round we can't get off. Peter
has a million swooning female fans, and his own show on Discovery network and I'm... well I'm the Kitchen Goddess... yet
we're stuck in a loveless sham of a marriage. As for Cressida – by
keeping her secret we protected her from scandal and being the
subject of a million gossip columns, but I worry she's missed out
on real life.'

'Yes, being a secret all these years might have had an effect on
her self-esteem.'

'Mmm, I worry about that too. She's a brilliant artist and I think she needs to spread her wings, go to art college and find herself, but I think she's scared to go out into the world.'

'I'm not surprised; she's spent the first twenty years holed up at Dovecote with you and she can't leave you now.'

'What do you mean?'

'Well, she told me – in her own way – as 'Crimson the star researcher' that she doesn't want to leave you on your own.'

'I need to talk to her, don't I? She has to make her own way eventually, I guess. It's just hard, you know, to let her go, especially after the start I had when I left home. 'Yes...but you survived, and look how far you've come. All those years I blamed myself for you being forced to have an abortion...'

'Oh Ames...'

'Your mother has a lot to answer for,' I sighed, 'I called so many times but she said you didn't want to speak to me.'

'And all those years I thought you'd never even bothered to call... Having children changes you. Being a mother helped me to forgive my own mother. It's only when you have a child of your own you really understand how hard it is.'

'It's so true – and you only ever begin to comprehend how much your parents love you when you love your own kids – it's huge, breathtaking.'

'I know, and whatever my mum did, I know in that cold black heart she loves me and I have to believe she was only doing what she thought best.'

'Yes, in her own way she was just saving you from what she thought was a life with no future, but you are so strong, you fought tooth and nail for what you've got. And here's me always thinking it was about luck and that your life was sprinkled with fairy dust,' I sighed.

'It is – because I have Cressy. I had to run away to keep her and it was hard, but it was worth every moment of pain and struggle. We always spend Christmas Day – her birthday – together... and if I'm honest, it's the only day of the year I'm truly happy.'

'Tell her that,' I said.

'She knows... I'm sure she does.'

'Well, tell her anyway.'

She nodded. 'I will, thank you, Amy. It's good to have you back.'

'It's good to be back,' I smiled.

Chapter Eighteen

T'was the Night Before Christmas

I was still in shock about Crimson and Bella and I still had so much to say when Fliss popped her head round the office door and asked if 'Madam' was ready to do a pre-recording. This involved making short five-minute films of Bella and I and the rest of the team that could be slotted into the live action.

'Yes, I'm ready,' Bella said. 'I'll work in the kitchen – I've told Amy why I was being such a diva about working in a hostel.'

Fliss raised her eyebrows. 'Well, equipment and decor aside it won't be easy dahling, but you're a tough Christmas cookie – so let's get going.'

We gathered ourselves together and both walked numbly into the awful kitchen. It had been decided that Bella and I record the Christmas Eve show that afternoon to go out later that night. It was a programme illustrating our two very different approaches to food and cooking and Tim told us to be 'brutal, raw and honest.' Good old Fliss did her bit to fan the flames just before recording by commenting on how 'gorgeous Amy looks', without referring to Bella at all. She wasn't trying to reignite our old feud, nor could she now we'd made up, but she was keen to set off that playful teasing between us, which was apparently TV gold.

And it wasn't long before we were both elbow-deep in raw turkeys arguing over the price of stuffing. Secret daughters, gay husbands and real lives now lost to the cameras, as we played it to the hilt.

'You do not need Tuscan truffles with turkey,' I was saying as the cameras rolled and I delved inside the turkey to remove the giblets. Tim thought it would be good to have us both side by side, with a turkey each and Bella 'coaching' me, which was hilarious as she probably hadn't cooked a turkey for years. 'It's ridiculous to pay out loads of money for expensive ingredients just to shove up a turkey's backside – and what's more you'll never taste the truffles with all the sage you put in,' I was saying as I jammed the turkey innards into a pan for gravy.

'Ew, what are you doing?' she gasped.

'Gravy...why?'

'That's not gravy, it's a cry for help! I NEVER make my gravy like that – I always use a good red wine and a good poultry stock.'

'I'm making poultry stock from the giblets,' I said, 'some of us can't afford wine to drink, let alone make gravy out of it.'

'I'm sorry, but do you live in the 60s, Amy? Hostesses today are working women who don't need to come home from the boardroom to do something vile with turkey innards. And why ruin just manicured Christmas Day nails by delving around in giblets when one can buy perfectly good stock and keep one's acrylics intact?' She smiled, flirting with the camera while caressing the bird.

'What you seem to forget, Amy, is that my way means not only does the table and the food look good – but so does the cook...' she sighed, breathlessly, then she licked her lips and pouted for the camera.

I waved the giblets at her, blood oozing from my fingers. 'This is real cooking, not buying stock cubes and doing your nails.'

'Yes Amy, but no one wants Carrie at their Christmas table.'

And so it went on. Yet in between comments and insults, we both managed to make a turkey dinner.

Tim had set up two tables in a separate room to film our Christmas Cook Off and my table was set simply using the tinfoil crackers Mike and I had made and sprigs of holly from Bella's garden. My Christmas dinner was made with a turkey from a local butcher, vegetables from a nearby allotment, with a home-made Christmas pudding for dessert. Meanwhile Bella's Christmas dinner was an elaborate, elegant affair involving organic turkey, cut glass and a table runner that cost a month's wages. Both tables had their pros and cons and Bella's whole concept cost about a hundred times more than mine, but the idea would be that the viewer could mix and match. But for us both, the real fun would be with the figgy puddings we'd made the day before that had been brought up from Dovecote. They both looked very similar sitting on their respective tables – it would be interesting to see which one of us won the ultimate figgy 'Christmas Bake Off.'

'You may want to spend more on a turkey but less on the table and vice versa,' Bella breathed, her heaving bosoms displayed in a low cut little black dress.

'Or you might want to have a go at making a Christmas figgy pudding costing a few quid, like mine,' I said, gesturing towards the rich, treacle-dark pudding. 'Or you might prefer to make Bella's identical one costing an arm and a leg,' I smiled serenely.

'Bella's like a tempest... a Christmas snowstorm, and Amy is like a calm, beautiful Angel,' Tim whispered.

'Less of the beautiful or I'll have you sacked,' Bella shouted and for a moment everyone looked round wondering if she meant it, until she gave a little snigger. She was like the old Bella again and I hoped perhaps I'd played a part in that by being honest and making her look at herself. Until now she'd been lost in this crazy sycophantic TV world where everyone told her she was right all the time. She'd also changed me too – I would never take anyone or anything at face value again – and I certainly wouldn't envy someone for having what I considered to be a 'better' life than me. You never really know what goes on in other people's lives – and you never know what people have been through – even your oldest, best friend.

Filming the Christmas Eve show together proved the old dynamic was slowly returning, our bickering was playful, funny and it provided an outlet for our real feelings about how different we were. I disapproved of her decadence and she frowned at my 'make-do-and-mend' approach to life – and that would never change. But this way we could actually say whatever we were feeling – it made us laugh – and we stayed friends. It was like being ten years old again and arguing about who had the best cupcakes, which was ridiculous – because as I pointed out, everyone knew mine were the best!

'Just try my gravy,' she said, halfway through filming, force-feeding me with a large spoon.

'I hate to say this,' I started, 'but it's quite delicious,' and it was. Bella still had a talent for taste and later – when we'd finished filming the Christmas Eve show and the cameras were off – I told her she really should start cooking and baking again.

'You used to make the most amazing lemon meringue pie,' I said.

'Mmmm I did, didn't I? I still bake at home for me and Cressy... in fact Cressy's started baking too and she's really good.'

'I feel a mother/daughter cookbook coming on,' I smiled.

'That's a fabulous idea, I'll talk to Fliss,' she said, genuinely excited. The idea seemed to light a fire in her eyes I hadn't seen since we were kids.

'Cressy loves it here,' I said. 'She's eager to help, I've never seen her more animated, happier. She isn't glued to her iPhone, she's working and chatting – I saw her laugh earlier.'

'I find that hard to believe,' she smiled.

Walking back into the kitchen, she linked arms with me. 'Hey Ames, I think I'll book a trip to Paris just for me and Cressy – a birthday and Christmas present combined... and while we're there I'll talk to her about what she wants to do with her life.'

'That's wonderful, Bella,' I smiled, opening the door of the kitchen and gesturing her through.

'Well, tomorrow's not going to be easy – it's more shabby than chic,' she said, faced once more with the prospect of the dreaded kitchen.

'There ain't no pretending, love,' Beatrice piped up, without looking up from behind a mountain of unpeeled potatoes. 'It's damn shabby and that's for sure.'

The door flew open and in came Mike with his camera, guided by Tim and a soundman. 'This is marvellous, just keep rolling,' Tim was saying to Mike. 'Let's get everyone in, we need to show all this preparation on tomorrow's show, we'll insert it in between the big lunch.'

'You want some music? Beatrice asked.

'Oh darling that would be magical... do you play?' Tim asked.

'No but my man over there sings,' she smiled, and called Stanley over to give us a song. Then Maisie talked to the camera about what it was like to be homeless at Christmas and in the corner of my eye I saw Bella put her arm around Crimson.

That night when Bella and the crew went to a hotel, I went home to my own bed. I arrived back and it was late and cold but I felt the warmth of my home as I walked in and despite it being so small and my kitchen being a quarter the size of Bella's – it felt good to be home for Christmas.

The following day – Christmas Day – I woke early and went downstairs to find a card posted through my door and when I opened it I was delighted to see a beautiful, sparkly snow scene. I opened it and tears sprung to my eyes. 'To my oldest and dearest friend, Happy Christmas, love from Bella xxx'

❄ ❄ ❄

Arriving at the shelter was pure Christmas, the turkeys were cooking, potatoes almost peeled, so I started on the carrots and found peeling them to be quite therapeutic. It reminded me of being with Mum in the kitchen at Christmas. From the moment Mum died I'd had to take all the memories, all the knowledge and advice she'd passed down to me and whenever I was unsure or worried and needed advice I'd think 'what would Mum do?' It was like having a big box of ideas, random thoughts and wise words – and thinking about her now I knew Mum would have allowed Bella to use those recipes without any mention of their provenance. I also understand now that for Bella using the recipes wasn't an insult to mum's memory or stealing her legacy. It was remembrance of the only time she'd ever been truly happy and safe – because my mum in her kitchen was the nearest thing to a mother Bella had ever had. In a way this was Bella's tribute to my mum.

'So, when are the kitchen designers arriving to sort the kitchen out for filming?' she asked. We all looked horrified until she started laughing. 'I'm only joking!' And I knew the old Bella was back for good…

Later, Tim explained the concept behind filming 'warts and all', and admitted he didn't know if it would work, but was, as always, diplomatic in his way. 'If someone with pots of cash and oodles of style tunes in they'll want Bella's Christmas,' he said, giving her a reassuring smile. 'On the other hand there are those poor wretches who live on council estates... do they still have those?' he asked as an aside. I couldn't believe he was serious but he was looking around expectantly, so I nodded. 'Oh good... so yes those poor damned souls who've never even heard of a bloody organic turkey and work their fingers to the bones in mills and down mines will LOVE Amy's sweet little ideas with jam jars and tinfoil.'

I tried not to be offended by his patronising, he didn't mean it – Tim was just trying to be nice – but the lights inside my jam jars cost nothing and they weren't sweet – they were stunning. As for the home-made crackers, not sure they would look as good as any fancy bought ones on the Christmas tables... but they'd do the same job.

Before Bella had the chance to peel the carrot in her hand, Billy appeared with his huge box of make-up tricks.

'Oh sorry, Ames,' she sighed, putting down the carrot and wiping her hands on a tea towel in disgust. 'I have to have my face done if we're going to film more preparation scenes.'

'You think you're so fine,' Beatrice huffed. 'You don't need no damn make-up girl, you need to get peelin them carrots, now jump to it.'

Bella looked shocked. 'Oh I'm sorry, I don't peel carrots... Mrs... erm.'

'The name's Beatrice and you damn well do peel carrots, Missy,' she said, thrusting the discarded carrot at her in a threatening manner.

Bella looked uncomfortable, she wasn't used to this and looked at me for help. 'Will you explain to Mrs Beatrice that I don't actually do anything in the kitchen...'

'You don't do...? What you tellin' me now, "Mrs High and Mighty I got my own telly show"... if I'd told my mammy I don't help in the kitchen she'd have cuffed my ear!'

'Come on, get your potato peeler, we've got a million potatoes to peel, then we're starting on the mince pies!' Crimson added.

Bella softened at this and I saw the pride in her eyes as she went to hug her daughter. 'Oh Cressy... you're so much better than me. I'm proud of you.'

Cressida was the antithesis of all the drama around her, she'd developed a shell of heavy make-up, tattoos and piercings to hide the soft and caring woman she really was. There would never be loud declarations of love or elaborate gestures of kindness from Cressida – but the love and kindness was all in there.

'Okay, okay there's loads to do, Mum – that's enough, let's get on,' Crimson rolled her eyes and returned to potato peeling.

Bella looked at me. 'She called me "Mum",' she mouthed, and I smiled, knowing how much that meant to Bella.

'Dahling, you're busy little fingers are already at work?' Fliss said, sweeping into the kitchen.

'No, my busy little fingers are getting ready to wring your little neck for getting me into this.'

'Now now, my little Christmas fairy – we need you cooking and frolicking around the kitchen.'

'Frolicking... pissing frolicking? I don't frolic. I'm wearing a fabulous suit from Armani's new season collection, sent from Paris in time for my Christmas special. I've got a crate of vintage Krug at Dovecote – and I'm standing in a kitchen that's like the set of a horror movie. Frolicking is NOT on my agenda.' She winked at me. This was pantomime Bella, the old one had emerged like a butterfly, but this one she saved just to wind up Fliss.

'Did Crimson tell you we're doing a road trip in the New Year – just the two of us?' Bella was addressing me, but again it was for Fliss's benefit – she looked like she was about to faint.

'But dahling – you can't just go off on a road trip. What about little things like filming schedules, appearances and book sign-ings?' she asked, alarmed.

'I can do all that – but it will have to fit round mine and my daughter's trip – we're going to rediscover food, find ourselves and spend quality time together. It's a sort of Eat, Pray, Love trip,' Bella smiled.

'Yeah – with double the eating and none of the praying,' Crim-son added, smiling over at her mum.

Bella winked at her as both their brittle exteriors visibly melted.

'I'll give you eat, pray, love - I'm just praying we get to eat to-day, so roll up them sleeves missy,' Beatrice instructed.

'Look,' Bella started, 'I can stuff turkeys, create beautiful mince pies and Christmas cakes, but I'm going to be brutally honest here – I have never really got the hang of peeling a potato.'

Beatrice took a sharp intake of breath.

'It's just that the home economists always do stuff like that so I can get on with the "prettier" aspects of cooking.'

Beatrice shook her head and got up from her seat, walked over to Bella and gently took her hand. 'Did your mammy never show you how to peel a 'tato?' she asked.

Bella shrugged. 'No... I never saw my mum peel a potato – the only thing she ever peeled was a face mask. The stuff I learned in the kitchen was from Amy's mum, and we were too young to peel potatoes,' she smiled over at me.

'Well, you come and sit over here with me, Missy, and I'll show you how – and all them people out there might just get fed by 3 p.m.,' Beatrice said, taking her hand and leading her to the potato mountain.

I glanced at Mike who opened his eyes wide, waiting for a nuclear reaction from Bella. Fliss looked up anxiously from her script and was sitting with her hand over her mouth, frozen to the spot. And we all held our breath as Bella obediently sat down on the floor between Beatrice and Crimson – all cross-legged – something childlike about the way she was allowing Beatrice to guide her.

'You have to grip, love – you've got hands like bear paws,' she was saying, as Bella struggled with the peeler. 'Hold the tato firmly like you do with your man.'

Bella and Crimson looked at each other and giggled. I don't think any of us were quite sure which part of the man Beatrice was referring to.

So for the next thirty minutes the great Bella Bradley – Kitchen Goddess – sat with Beatrice and peeled potatoes, a sight I thought I'd never see.

Later, Maisie turned up in the blue glitter jumper that Neil had bought me the Christmas before.

'I'd like to help,' she said, her frail body staggering across the floor.

'We're making mince pies now, come and join us,' Bella said, introducing herself and beckoning Maisie over to the work surface. She began making pastry and as I mixed the mincemeat with grated carrot, Maisie brought out the trays to put the pies on.

She began to tell Bella the story she'd started to tell me on the first day we'd met about how 'daddy' had stopped her from marrying the love of her life.

'I was eighteen,' she sighed, 'and I never saw him again... never loved anyone again.'

'Oh Maisie that's awful. I knew on our wedding day my husband was never going to truly love me – but who in their right mind would agree to something like that?' She sighed. 'You did it so you wouldn't get hurt,' Maisie said, dolloping mincemeat into pastry cases. She sighed, completely unperturbed by the fact that Bella Bradley had just confessed that her marriage was a business arrangement.

I looked at Bella and she raised her eyebrows at me. 'I'd never really thought about it like that,' she said.

'That's just what it was,' Maisie nodded. 'I did just the same, I stayed home, didn't want to face the world.'

'Oh, Maisie,' Bella sighed. She was now putting the pastry lids on the mince pies and Maisie's gnarled arthritic hand reached out to hers and held it.

'Don't make the same mistake I did; fall in love again, before it's too late.'

Bella took Maisie's other hand so she was holding both.

'I'll try, Maisie,' she said, and kissed her on the cheek.

I looked away, it was a private moment between two very different women who lived in very different worlds – who'd just realised their lives weren't that different after all.

As we continued to make piles of mince pies, Crimson joined in, mixing the mincemeat and laughing with me at Bella's messy apron. 'I bet you've never had potato starch and flour on that Christmas pinafore in your life,' I laughed.

Bella looked down to see the stained red silk and pulled a horrified face.

'Yeah, Mum's keepin' it real,' Crimson laughed.

'Mmm I like that... hey, I'm just keepin' it real,' she said.

'You wouldn't know "real" if it bit you on the butt, Missy,' Beatrice said with some affection as she handed Bella and me a slice of her home-made Jamaican Christmas cake. It was dense and fruity and delicious but laced with rum and I just hoped we could keep it away from Stanley– who was currently entertaining the troops in the dining hall with a rendition of Frank Sinatra-style White Christmas.

'Oh Beatrice, I MUST have this recipe,' Bella was saying. I caught her eye and gave her a look.

'With full credit of course,' she added, smiling at me.

❈ ❈ ❈

As we were tight for time and short of helping hands Tim recruited two more 'assistants', along with Maisie and Stanley, who were delighted to be included in filming.

So as we all started working in the kitchen. Bella stayed with Crimson and Beatrice, rolling out pastry and listening intently as the older woman told her stories of her childhood in Jamaica and how she'd been brought to the UK by her parents as a young girl.

'I missed the food, especially at Christmas,' she sighed, and paused for a moment to recall how as poor kids in rural Jamaica they never had – and never expected – a visit from Santa.

'Us kids used to think he didn't come to us because we didn't have a chimney... never occurred to us it was about having no money,' she laughed.

'So you didn't have any presents as a child?' Bella asked, horrified.

'Nah, but we had our mammy and daddy and lovely food. I loved helping Mammy make our Christmas cake.'

'Yes – I had lovely Christmases making brownies with Amy and her mum,' she said, putting a floury hand on my shoulder. 'We made Christmas cakes and gingerbread and all the scrummy Christmas stuff together, didn't we Ames?' she smiled fondly and I smiled back.

'...We didn't call it Christmas cake,' Beatrice continued. 'It was "Hell a bottom, hell a top and hallelujah in the middle",' she roared, laughing, and we all joined in.

'Oh I say, what on earth was that?' Tim wandered over, smiling. There was no room in this little kitchen for a chair but Tim was so intrigued he sat at Beatrice's feet, cross-legged like a little boy, and Fliss moved closer with her tea towel.

'Well we didn't have no fancy ovens like these,' she pointed at the broken-down appliances lurking in the corner. 'We had a Dutch pot we'd put on a grid over burning coals then more coals on a sheet of zinc on top of the cake, inside the pot. So the cake was in the middle... that's hallelujah, and the burning coals at the top and bottom were hell.' Everyone laughed and she smiled at the memory, her face glowing.

'Did you have turkey?' I asked, I'd moved on from the mince pies and Bella and I were now about to embark on a million sprouts.

She shook her head vigorously as she put huge trays of mince pies in the oven. 'Ooh no only them's that could afford it had the turkeys, but we ate curried goat with rice and gungo beans,' she smacked her lips at the memory.

'But surely you decorated your home for Christmas?' Bella asked.

'Yes we did... but not with tinsels like here, this is all very fancy. We used coloured papers and plastic flowers and always sparkling windows and a polished floor for Christmas to receive our guests on Christ's birthday. Christmas is a wonderful reason to all be together... something people seem to have forgot,' she waved her finger in the air as a warning.

'Yes, I can see that,' Bella said, thoughtfully. 'We need to get back to real Christmases... good food, friends and family together enjoying precious times.'

'Hallelujah,' I said. 'So you finally got it, Bella – we need good basic ingredients locally sourced... no fancy hampers and posh champagne...'

'Aah, that's not what I said, Amy Lane,' she waved her finger at me jokingly. 'Christmas is about friends and family around a table – precious time... which means the best Christmas pudding money can buy and the best champagne one can afford.'

Everyone laughed. Bella was never going to change completely and neither was I, but it was what made us work, our dynamic, both on screen and off. I'd loosened up and given myself permission to enjoy life again and Bella had started to see there was an alternative, there were options in life – different people live according to their means and their choices and she wasn't judging them.

We all continued to work hard in the kitchen, pulling together as a team. We were all from different worlds, but in St Swithin's Shelter on Christmas Day we were all the same.

❄ ❄ ❄

As she basted turkeys and boiled sprouts, Beatrice went on to tell us about early church on Christmas morning, the Christmas breeze that blew across the island, carols on the radio, and pepper lights in the trees. And Bella was transfixed, eagerly helping Beatrice with the cooking, like a child listening to a mother.

Tim had asked Mike to film all this and I was glad Beatrice would get to share her story, she told it with such love and warmth and it mingled with the recipes and baking.

'I'm tearing up for my childhood in Jamaica and I wasn't even there!' Tim screamed, laughing, and Fliss was nodding energetically, both having such a lovely time listening to Beatrice. 'Let's have a ten minute break, eat rum cake and reminisce,' Tim said, clapping his hands together, so Mike put the kettle on and we all drank tea and ate a slice of the delicious fruity confection and listened to Beatrice's lovely lilting voice – which I imagined sounded just like that Christmas breeze that blew right across Jamaica.

We had made dozens of mince pies, peeled hundreds of potatoes and even Fliss had cast off her glittery kitten heels and they were purring in a corner somewhere. She was dressed in designer glitter, cross-legged, and sitting on the floor with Bella peeling spuds and listening to Beatrice's Christmas stories – it reminded me of the way Bella and I had listened to Mum reading 'Twas the Night Before Christmas' on the Christmases she stayed with us.

'I remember the Christmas cake Amy's mum used to make,' Bella suddenly said, mid-mouthful. She looked at me. 'I remember her baking the cakes and you and I "helping",' she giggled.

'I think we ate more batter than we actually used,' I nodded, smiling at the memory.

'And the Christmas tree, Amy... your Christmas tree was always so much lovelier than ours.'

'No. Our decorations were so old,' I said. 'But yours was beautiful – you had a big tree which I loved and you always had new baubles and flashing lights.'

'But there was never anyone in to put the lights on at my house. We'd go to yours after school and your mum would be there, waiting, the house was always warm and smelled of cinnamon... it was more like home to me than my own home. I miss those days. I miss you... and I miss your mum.' Her voice cracked and I knew then that my mum's death had sent her off the rails, spending time with boys like Chris Burton who used her when all she was doing was looking for love.

I glanced around me at Stanley and Maisie, both working, but listening, Mike was filming, and Tim was sitting with his hands under his chin. The kitchen was silent except for Beatrice's lovely lilting Jamaican voice, telling of somewhere long ago and far away. And it made me think how our strange group of misfits with no-where else to go had magically found ourselves here, together on Christmas Day... and as Beatrice spoke and everyone listened I swear I heard my mother singing.

Chapter Nineteen

Turkey , Tinsel and a Televisual Feast

A little later, Bella and I were alone in the dining hall, lighting the candles and doing last minute, finishing touches before everyone arrived.

'Bella, this time together, it's been important to me,' I said. 'I feel like I've come through a snowstorm, but it was necessary, to come out the other end into the sunshine.'

'I know... and we have a lot of time to make up for – we'll see each other now, won't we?'

'I hope so,' I nodded, knowing that we both meant it now, but who knew what the future would bring. 'Bella, telling your mother...'

'Leave it, we don't have to go over it again... we both know you meant well.'

'Mmmm that's the thing. I don't know if I did and that's what kills me. Were my motives good? Yes, but not selfless, there was a part of me that thought if you had the baby, I'd lose you. We had our great travel plans, you and I, for the following summer and the pregnancy scuppered everything. All these years I've felt guilty and questioned if that's why I went to your mother... perhaps I also wanted you to have an abortion too?'

'We were both kids, Amy. Neither of us knew what to do and nor will any of us ever know why we do the things we do when we're young – it's like another life. I'm just glad I found some strength somewhere inside to fight for my baby and stop trying to please my mum. I was always seeking her attention, her approval, but having Cressy liberated me – I didn't need Jean anymore.'

'You didn't need me either.'

'Perhaps not, for a while – I had to plough my own furrow... but, Ames, I need you now.'

'Me too... I'm a bit scared about what's going to happen next, but that's good isn't it?'

She nodded. 'Yeah... and me. I've got some talking to do – to my husband, my agent and the bloody press. To think I never saw the irony of criticising my own mother for worrying what the neighbours thought, when I've spent the last twenty years worrying what the bloody nation will think.'

I smiled. 'We're more like our mothers than we think.'

I could hear carol singers outside singing 'Silent Night', my mother's favourite Christmas hymn – she'd hum it all Christmas while she floured pastry and kneaded dough. I looked across at Bella now sitting opposite me at the table, black mascara tears running down her cheeks causing cracks in her immaculately made-up face. But she wasn't calling for Billy and his bag of tricks as she would have done a few days ago. This was the real Bella, her tears were real and she was finally facing her own truth.

'Amy, you said you felt bad about not being there for me when I had Cressy, but I wasn't there for you. I left home and I left you and I started a new life – I wasn't there for your wedding, or your kids – your best friend but never there for the moments of your life a friend should be,' her voice cracked with emotion.

'Yes, I could have done with you on my wedding day asking me if I was sure I wanted to go through with it,' I smiled.

'Sorry, you didn't have your mum there either.'

'I wouldn't have listened... it was my wedding day and I only wanted good things, that's been the problem ever since. I refused to hear the voice in my head telling me we weren't right for each other...'

'That voice was probably your mum's – she knew everything, didn't she?' Bella was smiling at her memory. 'I feel terrible about the recipes... I did steal them, technically – of course I did, they aren't mine to publish. As I told you, I just didn't see it in those terms, they all represented such lovely memories for me, for us... the gingerbread houses and the Christmas brownies... Rudolph the Red Nose Brownies we called them,' she smiled wistfully.

'Yeah... Mum put dried cranberries in the brownie batter and we said they were Rudolph's noses.'

'Mmm, I loved the way the sourness of the cranberries bit into the rich sweetness of that fudgy icing.'

'Bella, you must really have loved those brownies... I've never heard you say anything quite so descriptive without an autocue,' I joked.

'You'd be surprised what I'm capable of if I feel passionate enough about it,' she smiled. 'And I was passionate about your mum's Christmas brownies... I would get the home economist to bake them every Christmas and Cressy and I would share them watching "Miracle of 34th Street"... just me and my girl and a batch of your mum's brownies... that's what Christmas is all about for me.'

❄ ❄ ❄

It was almost time to serve dinner and despite Fliss running round the kitchen barefoot demanding 'a Scotch, dahling – for my nerves', and Tim shouting, 'this will be the televisual version of "It's a Wonderful Life", the rest of us were working hard. Bella had really pulled it out of the bag and with Beatrice's guidance had produced several large trays of wonderfully light mince pies and gravy to die for.

'Bella, that's gorgeous,' I said, sampling the rich brown, meaty liquor again and again.

'Before we start filming and I forget, I'm thinking of making some changes to the programme in the New Year. I'll tell you all about it once I've spoken with Fliss and we have Tim and the TV company on board.'

'Baking is just so therapeutic,' I said as we lifted tray after tray of warm mince pies from the oven. 'Honestly, after a day of battling Year Ten I find there's nothing more calming than coming home and baking a cake.'

'Yes, I can see how that would work,' she smiled, 'and my New Year's resolution will be to bake again, and devise some of my own recipes rather than using other people's.'

At 3.30 p.m. exactly we were all ready in the kitchen, and thanks to Beatrice it was a military operation. Tim went into his van in the car park where the outside broadcast unit was now housed and the cameramen, including Mike - who'd been giving me secret smiles all morning - were all ready for the signal.

The dining hall looked amazing, fairylights lit, Sylvia's table runners shimmering and twinkling tea lights in jam jars clustered on all the tables. Mike filmed me doing a quick demo on the silver foil crackers and we flirted shamelessly. Crimson had directed Beatrice and Bella in making festive paper lanterns with remnants of coloured paper and string. 'Just like home,' Beatrice smiled as they strung the lanterns along the walls. 'You can buy paper lanterns too,' added Bella, 'if you don't have the time and you're busy, large department stores also stock paper lanterns – but you will have to put them up yourselves,' she smiled, like that might be an issue. I could see the way Crimson hung the decorations, set the tables and positioned the jam jars in little clusters that she had a genuine eye for style and Beatrice was impressed too. 'Clever daughter you got there, Missy,' she nodded, and Bella glowed with pride. Now the secret has been outed (at least in St Swithin's) it seemed to have taken a weight off both Bella and Crimson's shoulders. Bella was especially enjoying being around her daughter naturally, openly hugging her and praising her in front of everyone else.

Just before filming started and we stood and admired the finished dining hall, Beatrice looked at Bella; 'And there's me thinking you Miss High and Mighty – girl, you worked hard as me today,' she smiled. A compliment indeed coming from no-nonsense Beatrice – and Bella glowed again – she'd gained a daughter and a mother today.

A couple of researchers had appeared with mics and headphones so Tim could communicate with us, and Bella and I were fitted with talkback so Jody the live producer – or most likely Fliss – could talk to us while we were on air. As I wasn't used to talkback – which involved someone speaking to you in one ear while you talked at the same time – I was hoping there would be no need for any communication.

'You know what we have to do, don't you?' Bella said, as the titles rolled.

'Be ourselves?' I said.

'Exactly... bitch,' she said with a smile.

So for the next sixty minutes we were filmed serving lunch. This was interspersed on air with pre-recorded segments of the morning's preparations – Beatrice, Crimson and Bella making mince pies, me demonstrating a cheap alternative to Bella's usual stuffing and lots of lovely bits with Sylvia and the residents decorating the hall.

As we produced huge, plated Christmas dinners smothered in gravy, studded with roast potatoes, stuffing and sprouts – the sheer joy on the faces of the diners was a delight. Their happiness was infectious and like them I just couldn't keep the smile from my face, after everything - this was what it had all been about.

❄ ❄ ❄

Bella, Crimson, Sylvia, Beatrice and I were in a conveyor belt in the kitchen, dishing up and passing each plate along and singing Christmas songs. Mike kept stopping us as we served so he could film each perfect dish, saying he and the other cameramen had so many options of lovely close-ups of food and smiling faces they were in cameraman-heaven. Then Bella did a piece to camera about how this was her best Christmas and I really believed her. 'I'm missing the champagne and organic bird but I'm loving the taste of this frozen one,' she said. I pointed out that it was as good as any organic, corn-fed, hot-housed educated bird and an argument ensued about succulence and taste. All the time Fliss was in my ear saying 'Bella's talking absolute rubbish!' This caused me to instinctively repeat this and randomly shout 'rubbish!' at Bella. I later learned that Fliss was doing the exact same thing to Bella and shouting insults about me and ridiculing what I was saying so Bella would react. Regardless, it was all part of the fun and we both loved it. Even when Maisie and Stanley were introduced as the judges of the 'Figgy Christmas Bake Off' we didn't get too competitive. And when Maisie chose Bella's pudding and Stanley chose mine we were very sporting about it, though privately Bella said she'd won really because Maisie's palette was 'posher.'

'Ames, you never had any taste,' I won the bake off and your loser pudding lost,' she was teasing towards the end of the show.

'Go on... say something,' she said, clutching her figgy pudding in one hand and embracing Maisie with the other. But before I could have a go back, Stanley set off singing; 'I've got a crush on you...' we both started giggling.

'Happy Christmas and vive la différence,' Bella said, hugging me.

I hugged her back as the cameras whirred and she whispered in my ear, 'Love you, Ames. Happy Christmas.' It had all been so choreographed until then but Bella's warmth was genuine.

'You too, love,' I whispered.

'So thank you for joining us here at St Swithin's Hostel on this fabulous Christmas Day,' Bella was talking straight to camera now, reading the autocue for the final thirty seconds. 'I want to thank everyone here – from helpers, volunteers and, of course, the diners, who have been so appreciative of this very special lunch – and such fabulous company. But most of all I want to thank my friend Amy, who made all this possible. She won the competition to have a Christmas lunch of a lifetime made by me – and chose to donate it to St Swithin's and the poor folk who needed it far more than she does... and that's what Christmas is all about. Thank you Amy,' she smiled and started to clap me, followed by everyone else in the hall, and Sylvia started singing 'Have yourself a Merry Little Christmas', joined by the rest of the diners. My eyes were blurred with tears – I looked at Bella and she put one arm round me, the other around her daughter – and to my surprise I could see Crimson crying too... was this another Christmas miracle?

Chapter Twenty

The First Christmas of the Rest of your Life

Later, when all the residents had finished, the staff, TV people and volunteers sat down together to Christmas lunch. We pulled tinfoil crackers and Bella made a hat from her napkin and put it on, causing roars of laughter from Fliss – who'd apparently found a teensy weensy bit of Scotch, probably from Stanley. We all cleared up then and as no one wanted the day to end, I invited everyone round to my house. 'Oh yes that would be wonderful,' Bella sighed; 'Let's make this Christmas go on and on.'

'It's nothing like Dovecote, darlings,' I said in a Tim-voice, 'it's just a semi in suburbia, but everyone's welcome, I have wine in the fridge and Christmas cake, but little else.'

'No worries,' Fliss said. 'I brought champagne supplies and a couple of hampers that were sitting around at Dovecote, I was going to take them to the B and B, but let's open them up back at yours.'

Tim said he'd drive me, Fliss, Crimson, Bella and Beatrice, and as Fliss and Tim moved champagne crates around in his car to make room for passengers Bella and I gathered our coats and headed out of the kitchen. Mike was just packing all his camera gear away and walking through into the dining hall and I asked if he was coming back to mine with everyone else.

'I'd love to, thanks,' he nodded. And my heart soared.

'Amy,' Bella suddenly said, holding my elbow as Mike walked away, 'will you stop looking at his bum and come over here a minute with me.' She guided me through to a table in the now empty dining hall.

'I was going to give this to you later,' she said, 'but looks like there will be quite a few people at yours and I don't want an audience.' She awkwardly thrust a beautifully wrapped gift into my hand.

I felt terrible, I hadn't even considered buying her a gift. 'Oh Bella, I'm so sorry, I didn't expect... I haven't bought you anything,' I said.

'It's not a Christmas gift... well, perhaps it is, but not like that,' she said. 'Open it.'

I stood in the hallway struggling to open the parcel and she took my bag and coat off me to help, something the old Bella would have done.

As I undid the wrapping, I could feel it was a book and as the wrapping fell to the ground, the cover was revealed. It was Bella's Christmas cookbook. I looked up, puzzled, had she simply wrapped up her book to give to me? I wasn't sure how to take that.

'Your book, how... lovely,' I said, unconvincingly.

'It's not *just* my book, look at it properly, Ames you daft cow,' she commanded, reverting to a teenage phrase I'd heard Bella use so often.

I took the book completely from the wrapping and realised the title had been changed, it had been 'My Mother's Christmas Table' and now it was 'A Mother's Christmas Table... a book by Bella Bradley, with recipes by Eleanor Brown.' My mother's name. I felt tears pricking my eyes, Mum would have been so proud.

'Now open it,' she said, like an excited child.

Inside the jacket was a message which read

To Eleanor and Amy,

For all the times I sat at your table and the hours I spent in your kitchen tasting love and happiness,

Thank you for a lifetime of memories,

Love always,

Bella

'Do you like it?'

I was stunned, my throat was hot with tears.

Bella was beaming, holding onto my arm. 'That's why Fliss and I were late getting here yesterday morning – I made her go to the printers and get this done... they weren't happy printing it on Christmas Eve but Fliss paid extra – it was worth it. I know it's a bit late and we've sold thousands already, but Fliss has sorted it with the publishers and the next print run will be like this – with your mum's name and everything. We're also donating a big chunk of the proceeds of the book to a homeless charity, it just seems… appropriate doesn't it?'

I nodded, unable to speak.

'Hopefully the book will sell again every Christmas – and each year your mum's recipes will teach a new generation of bakers,' she said, putting her arm around me.

I didn't know what to say, this was more than I'd ever hoped for and I knew if Mum were here she would have been so delighted. It wasn't just about the recipes, it was an acknowledgement of the part she'd played in Bella's childhood, in her life. And the gift of love she had given to a little girl who wasn't even her own.

I started to cry.

'Oh stop that. Come on, let's get to yours and drink that champagne, you daft cow,' she said. 'You do have crystal flutes in your little semi don't you darling – if not I'm going home,' she linked arms with me to Tim's car where we laughed through tears all the way to my house.

When we got back, we opened Bella's posh hamper which contained lovely luxuries that were pointless on their own. But we ate the olive biscuits and the chocolate mints and the jar of cherries in kirsch as well as Christmas cake and Beatrice's Jamaican rum cake and we drank champagne.

'Here's to two kinds of Christmas cake,' I said, raising my glass when we'd all run out of drunken toasts.

'Yes, and here's to two kinds of women, both friends, both very different, with their own ideas on food. But I'm the one who's always right,' Bella laughed and we all joined in.

'That's enough, ladies,' Crimson shouted, before I could retaliate. 'I need to get my mum home – it's very late, we've got "Miracle on 34th Street" to watch, and a batch of Rudolph brownies to consume.' She gave me an awkward hug, grabbed Bella's arm and they walked together to the car waiting to take them back to Dovecote.

'I'll call you,' Bella said when we hugged goodbye.

I smiled and nodded, finally feeling good about our friendship.

I turned to go back indoors to an empty house, but when I walked back in, there was one guest remaining... Mike.

Epilogue – 12 months later

'You can NOT use cheap ham,' she yells across the kitchen.

'I would rather buy a small car than spend the same amount of money on your snobby, overhyped Iberico,' I spit back.

'Don't forget you're only a guest on my show... remember the line, viewers,' she looks straight into the camera to deliver the show's catchphrase, 'Amy is for Christmas, not for life.' This is followed by her tinkling laugh.

'Very funny,' I snap, taking out a supermarket frozen turkey and slapping it on the marble work surface.

'You're only a maths teacher, don't get above yourself,' she says, holding her organic bird in her arms like a newborn baby.

'I'm proud to be a maths teacher. I'd rather spend every day with stroppy teenagers than with the bossiest, most unbearable woman I know,' I hiss, stuffing the turkey with gusto.

This goes on until the dinner is cooked and we've argued, criticised, compromised and then argued again. Finally we end on a glistening shot of the two of us standing by candlelight, surrounded by the bakes and baubles of Christmas.

'Oh what a tear-inducing finale,' Tim sets off; '...a happy ending at last after all that delicious conflict my darlings... worthy of

Macbeth. That's a Christmas Eve wrap!' he shouts as Bella and I descend into giggles like two teenagers.

It's hard to think it's only twelve months since we rediscovered our old selves and became friends again. Such a lot has happened in that time, we're both divorced, both happier, Crimson's changed her name back to Cressida, and she's at art college now. Last summer Bella and I went to see her work at a college show and I've never seen my old friend more proud or happy. 'I can finally tell the world about my wonderful daughter,' Bella said, though sometimes I wonder who's the mother and who's the daughter, because Crimson has more of a grip on real life than Bella does. Meanwhile, my own kids Fiona and Jamie are now in their final year at uni - I can't wait to be the proud mum at graduation – and lucky me I get to do it twice!

As for our futures, Bella's was saved by 'The Christmas Special', or 'me' as I often remind her. The public loved our festive feuding the previous year, it reignited Bella's career, and the audience ratings shot through the roof. And as a result of all the publicity, and Mum and Bella's cookbook, St Swithin's has lived to see another year, and another Christmas dinner.

Bella's new idea was to involve me in her show as a co-presenter, and the TV company offered me a fortune to give up teaching and join 'Bella's Bake Off.' I surprised everyone and said 'no thanks,' because I've seen what that life can do to a girl, and I don't want to lose myself as Bella once did. So I'm still a full-time maths teacher, I just visit Bella's show on special occasions to keep her and her spending in check.

My day job is still tough, but rewarding, my Year Elevens did exceptionally well in their GCSEs this year and Mr Jones was forced to admit at prize-giving that 'Amy Lane's rather unorthodox teaching methods seem to have a plus side.' Working with the people 'on the telly' made me appreciate my teaching job – even after Josh Rawton and his pals sold his video of me to the press. I woke up last New Year's Eve to the headline 'Bella Bradley's Feuding Friend Fights Homeless Man for Booze!' Pictures and an online video of me and Stanley marauding in the street over a cheap bottle of brandy went global. Fliss put out a statement explaining I'd bought the brandy to put in my Christmas cake, 'vehemently' denying my 'alcoholism', 'attempted theft' and 'physical abuse' of a homeless person – but you know the press, they never let the facts get in the way of a good story. Anyway, seeing a 'story potential' Fliss called the magazines who, in return for my tale paid for a hedonistic week in a spa in the Indian Ocean. There by a turquoise lagoon I told the press my 'real and exclusive' story about how amazed I was to win the prize to star on 'Bella's Christmas Bake Off'. I also 'shared' with readers how Bella the TV celebrity and Amy the teacher (who came from the same town but 'surprisingly' had never met before) were now the best of friends.

I've grown to love Fliss too, she's the only person I know who could turn a video of me clambering over a homeless man into a week's stay in a five star resort with my best friend and a delicious cameraman. Oh yes - having attended my impromptu Christmas gathering the previous year, Mike never went home, and I've never been happier. And to add icing to my Christmas cake, Mike, Bella and Cressy joined me at the spa, so Bella could *'exclusively reveal her beautiful daughter Cressida, who the brilliant cookery star has kept secret all these years to protect her from the price of fame.'*

While in the hot tub, Bella was also interviewed by 'Star Life' magazine about the *'shock at discovering her wonderful husband was in love with another man and had been living a lie, torturing himself until caring Bella realised and told him to go and be free.'* Peter has since married Sacha - Crimson and Bella both attended the wedding and were pictured laughing and throwing confetti over the happy couple. Ironically, the lavish nuptials haven't put off any of Peter's adoring female fans – in an unexpected bonus he's gained a lot of new male fans!

It's a year down the line and Bella's gone from strength to strength, as her new, imperfect life endeared her to the nation. But she's still banging on about posh ingredients and telling me how 'low rent' my Christmas cake is with a twinkle in her eye. Mike catches the close-ups of her disgruntled face and captures my responses to her caustic, culinary comments. Watching it back I realise what great actresses we are on screen, because no one would ever guess how much we like each other.

After filming, Fliss smiles and teeters over on abused kitten heels to hug us both. 'Fabulous dahlings – two women arguing ferociously over Christmas truffles and Boxing Day ham, it's what Christmas is all about.'

So here we are – Bella and I back together at Dovecote on Christmas Eve, our friendship re-established and both our lives on a kind of happy parallel. Bella would disagree and say her life is far more glamorous and successful. And she still insists she's the better baker, but I'm quick to remind her, "my cupcakes were always the prettiest, darling."

We may argue on screen and sometimes off – and every so often I get a strong urge to push her smug face in a bowl of 'very naughty' trifle. But one thing we do agree on is that these days our lives are so much richer for having the other around... especially at Christmas.

A Note from Sue

Thank you so much for reading Bella's Christmas Bake Off I hope you enjoyed a little Christmas glimpse into the world of TV cookery shows. As a TV producer I've worked on several cookery programmes and trust me Bella's crazy production team and gadget-rich kitchen is nothing compared to the real thing!

Anyway, if you liked the taste of Bella's Bake Off and would like to know when my next book is released you can sign up at the link here:

www.suewatsonbooks.com/email.

I promise I won't share your email address with anyone, and I'll only send you an email when I have a new book out.

I would love for you to follow me on Facebook and please join me for a chat on Twitter.

In the meantime, thanks again for reading, and do try the Rudolph the Red Nose Brownie recipe and let me know what you think. I love them... and sadly so does my figure, which expands with joy every time one touches my lips!

Sue x

www.facebook.com/suewatsonbooks
www.twitter.com/suewatsonwriter
www.suewatsonbooks.com

Rudolph the Red Nosed Reindeer Brownie Recipe

These delicious, cranberry studded brownies always take me right back to my friend Amy's house at Christmas. It was always warm and cosy and in the vanilla and cinnamon scented kitchen we would 'help' her mum by sampling the batter and scattering the dried cranberries, which we'd pretend were Rudolph noses. Every Christmas Eve, Amy's mum would leave one of these for Father Christmas and one for Rudolph, and on Christmas Morning they were gone - which is why we kept believing in Father Christmas.

This is Amy's mother's recipe...

- 250g dark chocolate
- 100g butter, plus a little extra for greasing the tin
- 3 eggs
- 250g cooked beetroot, drained
- 250g light brown sugar
- 150g ground almonds
- 2tbsp cocoa
- 1tbsp baking powder
- 50g dried cranberries
- Teaspoon of cinnamon

Preheat the oven to 180°C and grease a 23cm square baking tin with a little butter and line with non-stick baking paper. Leave two 'tails' at either side to help you lift the cooked brownie out of the tin.

Break up the chocolate into squares, place in a heatproof bowl with the butter, and set over a pan of barely simmering water. Allow the mixture to gently melt, while stirring gently.

Tip the beetroot into a food processor and purée, (Amy's mum used to mash with a strong potato masher, but I love my gadgets!) Then add the melted chocolate, butter and eggs and whizz again until combined. Then add the sugar, ground almonds, cocoa, baking powder and cinnamon and process until you have a smooth batter. Lift the lid off - breathe in, and the sweet, spicy fragrance of chocolate and cinnamon will take you straight to Christmas heaven.

Now pour into the baking tin, sprinkle on the cranberries (Rudolph noses) and bake for about 30 minutes until the top is set and the brownie is starting to pull a little away from the sides of the tin.

Once out of the oven, ease the brownie from the tin with the paper 'tails' and cut into 16 squares. When cool, dust the surface with a little icing sugar, while singing 'I'm Dreaming of a White Christmas.'

Happy Christmas!
Love, Bella x